For Felicia Dames

1

UNFAITHFUL

"In a way, you're a lucky woman," I said.

"Lucky? How do you figure that, you asshole?"

I knew I'd made an unfortunate choice of words as soon as I spoke them. How many of you have done that, though? Your brain tells you that it's not a good idea to say what you're about to say, but your mouth just can't stop speaking for some odd reason.

I didn't immediately reply to the woman because I was so taken by her choice of words. I've been insulted many times by women of all ages. I'm sure most men have. What I found interesting, though, was her use of the word "asshole." I don't mean to imply that I keep a chart on my laptop where I regularly record the descriptive insults women call me, but the term "asshole" is by far the most common word women hurl my way when they get mad at me for one reason or another. My own mother has even called me that a couple of times, but I was a teenager when it happened, so should that count against me?

Please allow me a moment to rewind a bit and set the stage for you. My name is Edgar Allan Rutherford. Yes, my parents were huge fans of the legendary mystery writer, and no, I don't think they ever gave a second thought as to how naming a child Edgar might affect his popularity.

Both of my parents are deceased - God rest their souls - and I never got around to asking them how they could bestow such a challenging name on me. I knew they loved the name, and I was worried they would be offended if I told them I abhorred it. I tried many times to get people to call me Allan, but it never stuck, probably because my schoolmates knew I only wanted to be called that since I hated Edgar. Kids can be cruel, as we all know.

Fortunately, my best friend, Doug Foxx, started calling me Poe in our high school years. That new moniker was successful for whatever reason, probably because Foxx was such an intimidating figure. I'm in my mid-thirties now, and Poe is the name I go by. Nevertheless, I'm no longer bothered by the name Edgar, so you may call me that if you wish.

I was born and raised in Virginia, and I was a lifelong resident of that state until I relocated to the tropical paradise of Maui a couple of years ago. Foxx had been a resident of the Valley Isle for several years prior to my arrival. He'd invited me numerous times to visit him. However, I'd always said no. It took the loss of my architecture job and the ending of a long-term relationship to get me to make the long journey to Maui. The vacation did not go as planned, though. Foxx was arrested for the murder of his girlfriend, Lauren. She was a successful artist worth millions of dollars, and the bloody knife used to kill her had Foxx's fingerprints all over the handle. I was actually the one to discover her lifeless body behind the art gallery.

Foxx looked guilty as hell, and I would be lying to you if I said I had no doubts as to his innocence. Nevertheless, I decided to throw myself into my own investigation since the police were convinced they'd nabbed the guilty party.

It was during this investigation that I clashed with a local police detective named Alana Hu. The word "clashed" is perhaps not the best word to describe our interactions. There was an undeniable chemistry between us, but we both knew it would be inappropriate for us to be romantically involved during the investigation. Did that stop us? What do you think?

It was my burgeoning relationship with Alana that convinced me to relocate to Maui. I sold everything, including my house and most of my possessions, to move several thousand miles to be with the beautiful detective. Do you think I'm crazy? Perhaps, but you only live once, as people like to say. The risk actually paid off as Alana and I are now engaged to be married.

I won't ruin all of the details of that investigation into the murder of Foxx's girlfriend, but I did manage to catch the real killer and set my best friend free. That investigation led to another one, which led to my professional involvement with a local attorney named Mara Winters. She calls me from time to time whenever one of her clients needs an investigator who knows how to keep his mouth shut.

I wish I could say that my working relationship with Mara has been fruitful and has led to several criminals ending up in the slammer. Unfortunately, or fortunately, depending on your point of view, real life is not like television, and the guilty party doesn't always end up in handcuffs. Still, I don't mean to imply that my time on Maui has been consumed with murder investigations. They are a small part of my time, most of which is spent exploring the island and enjoying all of the beauty that Maui has to offer.

If you read my last tale, *Hot Sun Cold Killer*, you'll know that I recently purchased a home with Alana. It's a beautiful place in the Kaanapali area of Maui that sees sunshine and warm weather all year long. I was lounging by our backyard pool when Mara telephoned me. Apparently, she had a client who was staying at a five-star hotel in Wailea, and this client was desperate for help. I don't want to give the specific name of this property as I imagine the management would not want it affiliated with the story I'm about to tell. If you must know, however, you can Google five-star properties in Wailea and only one will come up.

I told Mara I would be there as fast as I could, so I changed out of my swimsuit and flip-flops and hopped into my BMW Z3 convertible for the long drive across the island. Mara texted me the number of the hotel room just as I pulled my car into valet parking. I admired the hotel as I made my way through the busy lobby. It was quite possibly the most beautiful property on the island.

I was pleasantly surprised to run into Ray London. For those of you who read my first book, *Aloha Means Goodbye*, you may recall that Ray is the artist who makes the fun clay creatures that range from large-lipped fish to dragons and fairies and all sorts of imaginative characters in between. Apparently, the hotel management had asked him to start selling his merchandise here. I was happy for him since I knew this was a clientele that could easily afford his work. We chatted for a few moments before I had to take off for my meeting with Mara and her anxious client.

The client in question was Mary Anne Portendorfer. I know, I'd never heard of that last name, either. I knocked on the door of Room 354. Mara Winters answered. I guessed her client was too shaken to make her way across the hotel room to greet me. I found Ms. Portendorfer standing by a balcony that overlooked a small collection of palm trees.

Mara introduced me to her. Seeing the two ladies standing side by side was a study in contrasts. Mara is just a few inches shy of my six-foot-two-inch frame, whereas Ms. Portendorfer would have been lucky to break the five-foot mark. Mara's hair is dark red, and her skin is pale, despite living on a tropical island. Her client had jet-black hair and dark eyes. Her skin was deeply tanned, as if she'd spent all of her time sunning by the hotel poolside.

The lady looked to be in her mid-forties, which would put her about the same age as Mara. We'd only been talking for about ninety seconds when she'd called me an asshole. She'd just finished telling me that her forty-thousand-dollar diamond ring was stolen, and she was pretty sure she knew the guy who had taken it. Yes, it was then that I had made the unfortunate comment that she was lucky, and yes, I'm sure you're now siding with her and you would have undoubtedly called me that name, too.

"I'm sorry for saying you're lucky, Ms. Portendorfer. What I meant to imply was that it's fortunate you know Mara, who could then call me."

She didn't nod or do anything else that signified that she'd accepted my apology. Instead, she continued to glare at me. Did I blame her? Not really.

"Why don't you start from the beginning, Mary Anne? How did this man even get into your hotel room?" Mara asked.

Portendorfer looked away from both Mara and me, and I immediately knew what was going on.

"Do you have a moment, Mara?" I asked.

Mara looked at me with surprise, which I could understand. We'd only been speaking for a couple of minutes and already I'd asked for a sidebar with the attorney. We walked outside the hotel room and stopped in the hallway several feet from Portendorfer's door.

"How do you know her?" I asked.

"We went to law school together. We've stayed in touch, and she wrote me a month ago to say that she was coming to Maui for a law conference," Mara said.

"Wow, people get to go to places like Maui for law conferences?"

Mara shrugged her shoulders.

"Maybe I should have gone to law school," I continued.

"Trust me. It's not all it's cracked up to be."

"I don't want to put you in an uncomfortable position with your friend, but I don't do these kinds of cases."

"What kinds of cases? We don't even know what's going on yet," Mara said.

"I think we do. There's a reason she called you and not the hotel security or even the police. She let the person into her room, and he's not her husband."

"How do you know that? All she's said so far is that the ring is gone."

"I'm sorry, but I can't help her. I don't do adultery cases."

Was that judgmental of me? Probably, but we all need to have standards.

"Adultery? You don't know that," Mara said.

"Maybe I'm wrong, but I think it's better if I just walk away now instead of hearing her out and then walk away."

"Listen, she's a dear friend. Do this for me, and I'll owe you one."

I hesitated a moment. I didn't consider Mara a friend. She was more of a colleague, but maybe she and I were moving more toward the friend status. If you know me by now, then it won't come as a surprise to you that I will do anything for my friends. Perhaps Mara realized that, and it's the reason she pulled the friend card. I didn't resent her for that. Rather, I found it clever. If there's one thing I find attractive, in a platonic sense, it is intelligence.

"Okay, but if it turns out it's adultery, then the next sushi lunch is on you," I said.

"And if it's not?"

"Then the next three lunches are on me."

"You're quite sure of yourself," she said.

"Not always, but this time."

We walked back inside the room and rejoined Ms. Portendorfer near the balcony.

"Do you know the name of this person?" I asked.

"His name was Burt or Bret or Bart, something like that."

"Where and when did you meet him?" Mara asked.

"In the hotel bar last night. He was here for another conference, some sort of hotel sales thing. We got to talking, and we ended up back here."

I looked at Mara as subtly as I could. She ignored my gaze. Intentional on her part? Probably. She was about to lose a sushi lunch, and she knew darn well that I can really put that stuff away.

"Tell me about this ring," I said.

"My husband gave it to me last month. We'd been separated for a while, and he got it for me when we decided to get back together."

"Is Thomas here on Maui?" Mara asked.

"Not yet. He's supposed to arrive tomorrow afternoon."

"How do you suppose this man got the ring off your finger?" I asked.

"I took it off. I put it in the nightstand drawer. When I woke up the next morning, it was gone."

It all seemed pretty clear to me. Ms. Portendorfer came to Maui for a lawyer conference. Her husband was to join her later in the week, so she took the opportunity to have a little extramarital fun before he arrived. I guessed she had too much to drink at the bar, invited this Burt, Bret, or Bart guy to her room and promptly fell asleep after wrestling with him under the sheets. He saw her put the ring away, so he took advantage of his snoozing companion and lifted the jewelry.

"Did you alert hotel security?" Mara asked.

"I can't do that. Don't you see? How do I explain to Tommy that the ring is gone? He'll be here in less than twenty-four hours. I can't have security coming up to us and asking me questions about some guy in my room."

"Either way, he'll see the ring is gone," Mara said.

"Not if you find it first."

"You could always tell him it fell off while you were swimming or snorkeling. Happens all the time," I said.

"I have to get it back. That ring means something. It took me months to convince Tommy to take me back."

Apparently, last night's romp wasn't the first time she'd stepped out on Mr. Portendorfer.

"Is there anything else you can remember about this person other than their first name?" I asked.

"No. That's it."

I wasn't sure what else I could ask her since her recollection of the previous night's events had to have been dulled by the Pina Coladas or Blue Hawaiians or whatever her flavor of drink was.

"I'll do my best," I said. "That's all I can promise."

"Do you think you can get it back?" she asked.

I thought I could, but I didn't tell her that since I found the woman's behavior deplorable. Instead, I just repeated that I would do my best and left Ms. Portendorfer to sulk in her room. Mara followed me back into the hallway.

"I owe you one," she said.

"I can already taste the shrimp tempura roll."

"What are the odds that you can get it back?"

"Pretty good, but don't tell her that."

I said goodbye to Mara and made my way down to the lobby. One of the undeniable facts about Maui is that it's a very expensive place to live. People can always use extra money, even if they already have a good job. The first thing I did after arriving in the lobby was to make my way down to the hotel security office. Yes, I realize that Ms. Cheater didn't want them involved, but I wasn't about to secure their assistance on any kind of official status.

I waited a few moments for one of the security personnel to leave the office. I then casually approached them and offered a tax-free way of helping me. I don't want to mention names or even genders since this could potentially get the person fired, but the security employee was able to locate the previous night's footage of Burt or Bret or Bart leaving Room 354 at approximately one-thirty in the morning. The security person then used the hotel's cameras to track the man's movement to his own room, which was Room 222.

I thanked the security person, tipped them even more money than I'd promised, and made my way to the concierge desk where I made a similar cash transaction. This employee discovered it was a man named Brad Collins who was in the aforementioned room on the second floor. You didn't read that wrong. His name was Brad, not Burt or Bret or Bart. At least she got the "B" and one-syllable parts correct.

Mr. Collins was supposed to check out at noon that day. However, he'd actually checked out during the middle of the night. Strange? Not if you've just stolen a ring worth tens of thousands. It all made sense since I doubted Brad wanted to risk the chance that Portendorfer would run into him by the Jacuzzi. Brad also had no way of knowing that she would be reluctant to contact hotel security or the police. A stolen ring of that worth amounted to a felony.

Come to think of it, I was perhaps being too hard on Ms.

Portendorfer for getting the guy's name wrong. Perhaps he'd given her a wrong name to begin with. Maybe he'd spotted the ring at the bar and made the decision there and then that she was his mark for the evening. Maybe this wasn't even the first time he'd pulled a caper like this.

I asked the concierge if they had his flight information. They did since he'd scheduled a ride from the hotel to the airport. He had a flight on Delta, and it was scheduled to leave Kahului that evening. He hadn't bother to cancel the car, but I assumed it was just an oversight on his part as he rushed off the hotel property before she woke and discovered the ring gone. I doubted he'd run the risk of returning to the hotel just to get a ride. I figured he was either holed up in another hotel near the airport, or he was spending his last day on Maui sightseeing far away from Wailea.

I didn't bother telling Ms. Portendorfer any of this. Instead, I left the hotel and made my way back home. There was no reason to head to the airport several hours before his flight. I killed the time by lounging by my pool as well as taking my dog, Maui, for a walk. He's a ten-pound mix between a Yorkshire Terrier and a Maltese if you're wondering.

I called Alana a couple of hours before I was due to leave for the airport and asked if she could meet me there and put her detective's badge to good use. I filled her in on that morning's activities, and she was more than willing to stop a thief.

"How do you get yourself involved in these things?" she asked.

"This one wasn't my fault. It was all Mara," I said.

"I'm sure, but she calls you for a reason. She knows you love this stuff."

"Do you think you can help me get this ring back?" I asked.

"Of course. I'll meet you in the Departures area. You said it was Delta?"

"That's right."

"Did you think to get a photo of him from the security footage?"

"I did."

"Good. I'll see you this afternoon."

I arrived at the airport about twenty minutes before Alana did, so I was already outside the Delta check-in counter when I saw her approaching. She was still dressed in her business suit since she had come from work. Her long black hair was usually in a ponytail, but now it was loose and hanging below her shoulders. God, she was a good-looking woman, and I had no idea how I'd ever convinced someone like her to agree to marry me.

"Sorry I'm late," she said.

"You're not late. There's only been a few people to check in so far."

I showed Alana the still frame from the security video. It was a bit fuzzy but more than good enough for us to make the identification.

"What's your bet? Did he try to pawn the ring on Maui or does he still have it with him?" I asked.

"Too risky to sell it here. There aren't that many places, and my guess is he's figured she's already called the police. You said the victim's name is Portendorfer?"

"Yeah."

"Interesting name. Do you want me to arrest this guy or just get the ring back?" she asked.

"That's really up to you, but my vote would be just to get the ring back."

We stood beside the entrance to the Delta check-in counter for another twenty minutes or so before our thief arrived. He was a good-looking guy, and I could see how Ms. Portendorfer would be taken with him.

"I think that's him," I said.

Alana took another quick look at the security video image and then glanced back to Brad.

"Mr. Collins," she said as he approached us.

Brad pretended to ignore her, and he started to walk past us.

"Mr. Brad Collins," she repeated louder.

Brad stopped this time and walked back over to us.

"Yes."

Alana held up her detective's badge.

"I'm Detective Hu with the Maui Police Department. I'd like to have a word with you."

"I'm actually late for my flight," Brad said.

"Your plane doesn't leave for another two hours. I think you can spare us a few minutes," she said.

"Okay. What is this about?"

"You have something that doesn't belong to you. You can either give it to me, or I'll arrest you for theft," Alana said.

"I don't know what you're talking about," Brad said.

He was a smooth character, and his face showed utter confusion as to her statement. Did I think it genuine? Of course not.

"It belongs to Mary Anne Portendorfer. She wants it back," I said.

"Portendorfer? That's her name?" Brad asked.

"The jewelry, Mr. Collins. Please hand it over," Alana said.

"I don't have a ring, and if this lady says I have it, then she's wrong."

"We never said it was a ring," I remarked.

Apparently, he wasn't as smooth as I'd just given him credit for.

"Three seconds before I arrest you, or you can hand me the ring and be on your way," Alana said.

"You'll just let me go?" Brad asked.

"One second," Alana said.

"Fine."

Brad reached into his front pocket and removed the ring in question. He handed it to Alana.

"Enjoy your flight, Mr. Collins, and please don't return to Maui. We don't like thieves on our island," Alana said.

Brad turned away and walked quickly toward the Delta counter before Alana could change her mind.

Alana took a long look at the diamond ring and then handed it to me.

"Nice, but I like mine better," she said.

"Thanks. I took a long time picking yours out," I said.

"What now?" she asked.

"I drive back to Wailea and return it. Want to tag along?"

"No, thanks. I want to get home and rest. It's been a long day."

"Understood. Sorry for having you come out here."

"It's no problem. Hopefully, Ms. Portendorfer will show genuine appreciation for what you've done."

I kissed Alana goodbye and drove back to the hotel. I called Mara along the way and informed her of my successful mission. I pulled up to the hotel entranceway again and was surprised when I saw Mara waiting outside for me.

"I thought I'd save you the trip upstairs," Mara said.

"Did you tell her I got the ring back?" I asked.

"Not yet. She's been so stressed throughout the day that she's consumed several of those little mini bottles of liquor in the hotel refrigerator. She passed out about an hour ago."

"I don't know if that's a good thing or a bad thing," I said.

"I don't know either, but she's not the person I remember her being."

"How often do you two see each other?"

"Not often. It's been over ten years since the last time."

"People change," I said.

"Maybe."

I handed Mara the ring, and she stared at the impressive diamond for a few seconds.

"She said it was a second engagement ring of sorts."

"Mr. Portendorfer is a kind and forgiving man," I said.

"Perhaps he's just naïve," Mara said. "Thank you again for doing me this favor. I'll make sure she rewards you well for this."

"I'll put the money toward the wedding fund."

"How is the wedding planning going?" Mara asked.

"Not well. Alana just fired our wedding planner."

"That's not good. What was the problem?"

"She thought she was overcharging us," I said.

"She probably was, but then again, people always add a few zeros to their prices when they know it's for a wedding."

"Isn't that the truth? Call me again if something interesting comes up," I said.

I waved goodbye to Mara as I pulled out of the hotel entranceway. I had no idea how soon she'd actually be calling. The case was much larger than Ms. Portendorfer's assignment, but it did have a few things in common. Betrayal. Greed. Crime. Some of the things that we humans find so fascinating.

2

THE MOTHER-IN-LAW

NOTHING OF MUCH INTEREST HAPPENED THAT NIGHT AFTER I RETURNED home from the hotel. When I got back, I found Alana lying on the sofa and watching a World War II documentary. Lately, she'd gotten obsessed with watching these shows that focused on Hitler. Did I find that odd? Not really, since I knew Alana was a student of human nature. It's one of the things that made her good at her job. Nevertheless, I wasn't thrilled about spending the night learning even more about the rise and fall of the Third Reich. Yeah, it was good to know about history, but there is only so much Hitler a person can take.

Probably the only thing of note that occurred that evening was Alana asking me to visit her sister, Hani, the next morning. For those of you who read the last book, you already know that Hani dropped a bombshell on us during our housewarming party. She announced that she was pregnant, and Foxx was the father. The news turned his world upside down, as I'm sure you could have imagined. Things had not gone well since then, at least as far as Hani and Foxx being on good speaking terms was concerned.

Foxx and Hani had started fooling around months before. They'd both lost loved ones, and neither of them was in a committed relationship. For Foxx, that was more the rule than the exception. I suppose you could have described their relationship as friends with benefits. That's not something that I've ever done. However, my gut instinct told me that it was a bad idea, and I advised Foxx of that.

Nevertheless, Foxx is an adult, and he was under no obligation to follow my advice, which he didn't. He continued to see Hani for fun and games until he decided one day that he no longer wanted to play. She didn't take the news well, which left Foxx surprised. I didn't know how he could be. Sex often turns into an emotional connection, and I didn't know how he couldn't see that coming. Don't get me wrong. Foxx is not a dumb guy, but he had serious blinders on for this relationship that wasn't technically supposed to be one.

Hani tried to get back together with Foxx for a few weeks. She even tried to lobby Alana and me to speak on her behalf. It wasn't something we were willing to do, especially since Alana had issued the same warning to Hani about fooling around with Foxx. Later, we'd discovered the true reason for her anxiousness, and it all should have been painfully obvious in hindsight. Although Foxx was committed to providing for his child, he still had no desire to get back together with Hani. He was never officially with her, he kept informing me, but I think there's a certain unspoken level of togetherness when you're spending several times a week in the other person's bed.

Now that you understand the delicate situation, you'll understand what was going through my mind as I made my way over to Hani's house that morning. I had no idea what I was supposed to say or do when I got there, but Alana told me that I needed to express, once again, that we would be there for her. I thought that I'd mentioned that a thousand times already, but I wasn't about to refuse Alana's request, especially the day after she helped me retrieve Ms. Portendorfer's stolen ring.

I figured I would spend thirty minutes or so catching up with Hani, and then I would make my way over to Harry's bar to grab an early lunch. Imagine my surprise when I saw Alana's mother's car in the driveway when I turned down Hani's street. For those of you who have read all of my previous stories, you will know that I have only made one small reference to Alana's mother. That was when Alana told me that her mother had worked as a model for a local photographer who had a small but pivotal part to play in my first murder investigation.

Of course, I'd met Alana's mother several times since then. You certainly don't become engaged to someone without meeting the future in-laws. Luana Hu is a beautiful woman, and it's quite obvious where Alana and Hani get their stunning good looks. However, there are a couple of reasons I haven't mentioned the lady before. The first is that my interactions with her have had no bearing on my investigations. The second, and more defining reason is because the lady hates my guts. I'm not sure what I ever did to earn this disdain. If Alana knows, which I suspect she does, she's not willing to tell me.

I almost pulled a quick U-turn when I saw her car, but that would certainly have been a cowardly move. I also didn't know how I would explain to Alana that I hadn't fulfilled her one request of me since I didn't have the stomach to spend a few minutes in her mother's presence. I decided to take the opportunity to try, yet again, to win favor with the lady. She was going to be my future mother-in-law. I needed to determine what the problem was so that I could find a possible solution. What's that sound I hear? Is that you laughing at my naivety?

It was actually Ms. Hu who answered the door, and things definitely didn't get off to a good start.

"What are you doing here?" she asked.

"Good morning, Ms. Hu. I came by to see how your daughter is doing."

"She's fine."

I stood on the porch, but she made no move to step aside and allow me to enter. I debated whether to turn around and head back to my convertible since I'd technically fulfilled Alana's request to see how Hani was doing. She was "fine" after all, but I also realized Alana would have follow-up questions, and I didn't want to admit that her mother scared the living hell out of me.

"Do you mind if I come inside?" I asked.

She didn't answer me. Instead, she turned around and headed back toward the living room. She hadn't slammed the door in my face, so I assumed it was somewhat safe to proceed indoors. I walked to the back of the house where the living room and kitchen were located. I found Hani standing in front of the kitchen counter. She was busy stuffing large pieces of fruit into one of those souped-up blenders that you often see on television infomercials.

So, how would I describe Hani for those who have never met her? On a scale of one to ten, in terms of pure physical attractiveness, I would rate Hani a twelve. Maybe you think that's weird of me to judge my future sister-in-law's attributes, but I'm not blind. It doesn't mean I'm going to act on it, though. In relation to Hani's personality, I would give her a six. Yes, that sounds harsh, but it's the truth, at least as far as my opinion goes. She has a way of keeping important facts from others. Perhaps you would call them lies of omission. There's also her self-centeredness, which I believe is the main reason Foxx never bothered to pursue a long-term relationship with her.

"How's it going, Hani?" I asked.

"I'm fine. Is Alana with you?" she asked.

Maybe now I could leave since I'd gotten the "fine" answer twice.

"She's at work, but she asked me to swing by and see how things are."

Ms. Hu cut into the conversation before Hani could respond.

"Don't you think it's your friend who should be coming by?"

"I'm sure he would love to, Ms. Hu, but he's at work right now."

"Hani hasn't seen him in at least two weeks. What's she supposed to make of that?"

I thought the answer was rather obvious, but certainly no good would come from me stating it out loud.

"Alana wanted me to ask you when your next doctor's appointment is," I said.

"Not for another week. She said she would try to make it to my next one. Does she still want to do that?" Hani asked.

"I assume so. I guess it all depends on her work schedule."

The conversation continued like this for another fifteen or twenty minutes. We went over the usual topics like the weather, how Hani was sleeping, whether or not she needed me to pick something up for her, as well as Ms. Hu's continued observations on how irresponsible my friend was being for not getting down on one knee and proposing to the woman he'd gotten pregnant. What did I think of Foxx's lack of a proposal? Not much. I certainly didn't think one should get married for the sole reason that the woman was pregnant. Divorce was such a high probability in those situations, at least that's what my instinct told me.

I wished both ladies a good day. Hani returned the farewell. Ms. Hu did not. I walked myself to the door and did my best not to break out into a mad dash for my vehicle. I thought about immediately calling Alana and letting her know how the meeting went, but I decided to pass and keep my view of the unpleasant encounter to myself. Alana knew how her mother was around me, and it wasn't like she had any power to change things. Ms. Hu was part of the package deal if I wanted to be married to her daughter. I had zero desire to be around her any more than I had to, and I assumed the best thing I could do was to smile and keep my criticisms to myself. My only realistic option was to continue to vent to the dog since he was quite good at keeping his mouth shut.

I drove directly to Harry's, which is a bar Foxx and I had recently purchased in Lahaina. We made the decision not to change the name, mainly because the bar was already doing such vibrant business. As successful as it had been under the original ownership, Foxx had doubled the earnings in the short time that we'd been owners. He has a magnetic personality, and people are just drawn to him. It wasn't like he walked up and down the street with the name of our bar on his chest, but he had a casual way of bringing up the business in everyday conversation with locals and tourists alike.

I entered Harry's and immediately saw Foxx sitting at the bar. He was talking to Kiana, an attractive Hawaiian woman who had been a bartender since the establishment opened. I walked up to them and took a seat on the stool beside Foxx.

"What can I get you, Mr. Rutherford?" Kiana asked.

I'd asked her several times to call me Poe, but it was a fruitless request. She was determined to stick with Mr. Rutherford despite the fact that I was only a few years older than her.

"I'll have a Manhattan, please."

"Whoa, a Manhattan, and it's only eleven in the morning. You must have gotten into something," Foxx said.

I gave him a brief rundown on my interaction with Hani and her mother.

"Better make that two," Foxx told Kiana.

She smiled and started to mix our drinks.

"How is dear old mom?" Foxx asked.

"She sends her regards," I said.

"I'm sure she did. How many times did she mention that I'm a deadbeat dad even though the kid isn't even born yet?"

"She did want me to deliver a few insults to you, but that wasn't one of them," I said.

"Do I want to hear them?"

"Not really."

Kiana placed our two drinks on the bar in front of us. Foxx and I both said thanks and sipped our drinks in silence for a few moments.

Then Foxx turned to me and said, "I still think Hani got pregnant on purpose."

I was tempted to chug the rest of my cocktail and immediately order something even stronger since I knew exactly where this conversation was headed. Instead, I remained calm and kept my opinions to myself.

Foxx had told me that Hani had mentioned to him that she was taking birth control pills. After doing some quick online research, I discovered that they are 99.9 percent effective, so you do the math. Had she been dishonest with him? I thought so, but I also wasn't willing to say that to Hani or Alana and have it constantly thrown back in my face for the next few decades.

Foxx was a wealthy man, and Hani had a thing for money. I didn't blame her for wanting to be secure. After all, she and Alana had grown up poor after their father abandoned them and returned to his home country of Japan. They never said why he did that. Maybe they didn't know. Maybe only their mother did, and she wasn't talking. Instead of working hard and earning her own money, though, Hani used her considerable beauty to trap men. She certainly isn't the first gorgeous person to do that. There was also the time she'd gotten pregnant by another wealthy man. Unfortunately, that pregnancy ended in a miscarriage.

Back to Foxx, though. I knew money wasn't a big deal to him, probably because he's had it for so long now. We all tend to take things for granted even when we know we shouldn't. Foxx had been a professional football player for the Washington Redskins. His career ended from injury after two seasons, but it still earned him a fair amount of money that I helped him carefully invest. That money had greatly increased when Lauren's will left him her sizeable estate, including all of her artwork and her oceanfront home just down the street from mine. There was also Foxx's fifty percent ownership of Harry's, which as I mentioned just a short while ago, was doing very well. I had no doubt Foxx had a big target on his back, and Hani hit the bullseye in their short time together. Maybe I shouldn't say bullseye since there was no chance of him marrying her, if I believed Foxx, that is. Yes, I'm being quite judgmental right now, but it's one of my many flaws. I hope you'll forgive me.

"When was the last time you two spoke?" I asked.

"A couple of days ago. I called to see if she needed anything."

"How did the conversation go?"

"It was short. She said she didn't need anything, and that was about it. I'm sure she'll be fine as long as my checks keep coming," Foxx said.

"Are you even somewhat excited about having a child?"

"I've thought about that a lot, maybe almost nonstop. It's tough because I see pluses and minuses. I just wish it had been with someone I really cared for. I can't figure out how all of this is going to work."

I wanted to strangle Foxx because he wouldn't have been in this mess if he'd just listened to Alana and me. Instead, I assured him that everything would work out fine even though I didn't believe that for one second. Yeah, the kid would probably turn out okay. I had no doubt Foxx would support him or her, but there was undoubtedly going to be friction between Foxx and Hani every time they were around each other. Alana and I had seen it coming from a mile away, but we'd been powerless to stop it.

I ordered a second Manhattan from Kiana since I was still smarting from my encounter with my future mother-in-law.

My phone pinged, and I saw Alana's text message on the screen. There had been a murder in the Wailuku section of Maui. Alana had gotten the case, and she had no idea when she'd be home. Such is the life of living with a cop, I thought.

I turned to Foxx.

"You working tonight?" I asked.

"Nah, Kiana has it covered. Want to do something?"

"Why don't I pick up some beer and a couple of pizzas," I suggested.

"Your house or mine."

"Yours. I'm sure Maui the dog would like to visit his old stomping ground."

Kiana placed two more drinks in front of us. I picked up mine and held it toward Foxx.

"A toast to your future child. May they find nothing but happiness in their life."

Foxx touched his glass against mine.

"Thanks, buddy. That would be the dream. Wouldn't it?"

3

GUTTED

MAUI THE DOG AND I SPENT A FEW HOURS AT FOXX'S HOUSE THAT night. It's where I had lived for my first two years on the island. We passed the time watching *Planet of the Apes*, the original film that starred Charlton Heston, not the god-awful remake with Mark Wahlberg. I certainly don't blame Mr. Wahlberg for that one, but some classics should never be remade.

Foxx and I consumed two large pizzas and two six-packs of beer throughout the movie. It was close to midnight by the time Maui and I stumbled back home. Truth be told, I was the one who stumbled. The dog was fine.

I still hadn't heard anything from Alana since that text in the morning when I was at Harry's. I wasn't surprised by her silence since I knew these murder cases were always all-consuming. I plopped down on the sofa and decided to try to stay awake for her eventual return. They were rerunning the first *Rocky* on television, and no matter how hard I tried, I couldn't resist it. Say what you want about the sequels, but the original film is damn good and holds up well after all of this time. I don't remember when I fell asleep, but I'm pretty sure it was before the climactic boxing match.

I woke up around two in the morning. The television was off, and

I took that as a sign that Alana was home. I walked upstairs to the master bedroom but didn't see her there. I looked in the bathroom. She wasn't there, either. I walked over to the bedroom window that overlooked the backyard and saw her sitting outside by the pool.

I looked down at my feet and saw that the dog had followed me upstairs.

"Come on, Maui. Let's go say hi to Alana."

We both walked back downstairs and joined Alana by the pool. She did her best to wipe away her tears, but it was obvious that she'd been crying.

"Do you want to talk about it?" I asked.

"Not really. I'll be okay."

I nodded and hung around for a few moments in case she changed her mind. She didn't, at least not then. It wasn't until I was walking through the open sliding glass door that she said something.

"I knew it. As soon as I heard the address come over the radio, I knew who it was."

"Who was it?" I asked.

"Her name was Nalani. She was my best friend at one point."

I walked back to Alana and sat down on one of our patio chairs.

"I've never heard you mention her name before," I said.

"We had a falling out. It was her husband."

"Had he done something to you?"

"Nothing specific. I just didn't like him. He was no good. I never asked her to choose between him and me, but I guess she thought she had to. She stopped calling me, and she was always busy when I'd invite her to lunch or some other event. I got the picture. She couldn't be my friend anymore."

"Do you know what happened to her?" I asked.

"She was murdered in her own kitchen. They used a wine opener. You know, one of those corkscrews with the wooden handle. They stabbed her in the throat and face a dozen times. There was blood everywhere. I could hardly recognize her."

"Did you catch the person?"

"No, but I know it was him."

"Her husband?"

Alana nodded.

"Why do you think that?" I asked.

"She'd left him. She didn't tell me that, but I'd heard it from Hani and another mutual friend. I almost called her when I heard, but I didn't. I should have been there for her."

"How could you have known something like this would happen?"

"Liam was the one to call the police. He said he'd found her like that, but why was he even there if they'd broken up?"

"Liam's her husband?" I asked.

"Yes."

"What was his answer when you asked him why he was there?"

"He said they'd gotten back together. Can you believe that? He actually thinks I'm going to buy it."

"Did you arrest him?"

"Not yet, but I'll get him," she said.

"How long did you know Nalani?"

"As long as I can remember. I lived across the street from her when I was growing up. After my father left us, we had to move in with them since my mother couldn't afford the mortgage anymore."

"You lost your house?"

Alana didn't answer me immediately, and I knew as soon as I'd asked that it was a dumb question.

"They opened their house to us. How many families would have done something like that? Hani and I slept in Nalani's bedroom. She was so mad that she had to share her room. I didn't blame her, but we became good friends. She was almost like a second sister to me."

"How long did you live there?" I asked.

"A year. It gave my mother enough time to save some money so we could rent a small apartment."

"Why haven't you ever told me this story before?"

"I was too embarrassed."

"Why? Did you think I would judge you for that?"

"No, but it's still not something you want to admit to anyone."

"You don't have to answer this if you don't want to, but when was the last time you saw your father?" I asked.

"The day he went back to Japan."

"You really haven't heard from him since then?"

"He's sent cards from time to time. I even spoke with him once. The conversation lasted less than a minute. He called, and I made the mistake of answering the phone without checking the caller ID first."

It all suddenly made sense. I still didn't know why he'd left his family to fend for themselves, but that didn't really matter in a way. They, especially Luana Hu, would have still felt abandoned and betrayed. She'd been left to care for two small children.

"That's why your mother hates Foxx and me."

"What do you mean?" she asked.

"I suspect it's a bit different between Foxx and myself. She thinks the lack of commitment from Foxx is the same as your father having left you guys. As for me, maybe she assumes I'm going to leave you, too, but it won't happen. I promise you that."

Alana didn't say anything in reply to my theory, which made me assume I'd gotten it right. Maybe her mother had never directly expressed those thoughts to her daughters, but I'm sure they knew her well enough to get why she disliked us. Alana had made the decision not to tell me since it wasn't like she could ease the fears and anxieties her mother had in place for years.

I couldn't relate to what Alana had been through, and I certainly couldn't relate to her mother. Both of my parents had stayed married to each other until death did them part. Our financial status was also on the opposite end of the spectrum. My mother came from old money, and my father did very well by himself. Their wise financial investments had greatly increased that money, and it was my inheritance that allowed me to lounge around Maui and play detective from time to time. I hadn't earned that money, but I never took it for granted. I also didn't think I was obnoxious about it. It's not like I go around the island bragging about anything. I tend to keep a low profile with the exception of this big house by the water, but that's just as much for Alana as it is for me. Granted, I had no idea just how poor Alana's family had been, but I was aware that she'd been through hard times. I saw this house as a reward of sorts for her. She worked hard, and I thought she deserved something this nice.

"What's next? How do you prove he did it?" I asked.

"I'm not sure. His prints are bound to be all over that wine opener, but his attorney can easily cast doubt. He lived there for years. It makes sense that his prints would already be on it."

"Maybe you can catch him in a lie about his relationship status. You can try to find some family members or close friends who can prove she wasn't about to take him back."

Alana started to cry again.

"I should have been there for her. I can't believe I let her down like that," she said.

I knew there wasn't anything I could say to convince Alana that she'd done nothing wrong. It was apparently Nalani who'd made the decision to end their friendship, but I knew logic never entered into the equation during times like this. Alana would continue to blame herself until enough time had passed, and she would finally have the clarity to realize there was only one person responsible for Nalani's death.

Our conversation by the pool had brought up an interesting revelation that had nothing to do with the victim. I realized just how much I didn't know about Alana. I knew I loved her and that I wanted to spend my life with her. Here was a pivotal part of her history, though, that I had no idea about. She'd spent a year living with another family because her father decided he no longer wanted to be with his wife and children. I couldn't imagine doing that to my family. It certainly painted her father in a terrible light, but it also made me admire Alana even more. She'd faced tremendous adversity, and she'd dug herself out of it. She had a solid job, and she was contributing to her community. How many others would have turned out like that even when fate had dealt them with a favorable hand from the beginning?

I also realized that I owed Ms. Hu my respect. Sure, I'd never actually been disrespectful to her, unless you count the times I vented

about the woman to Foxx, but I thought those occasions were understandable. I had enough self-awareness to know that I shouldn't be
too hard on myself when it came to Ms. Hu, especially since the lady
had a tendency to use me as a verbal punching bag. Nevertheless,
she'd done an amazing job in raising Alana to be the incredible
person she is today. Now Hani is another story, but no parent is
perfect, are they?

Alana said she wanted to stay outside for a while longer, so I went
back into our bedroom to give her some space. I plopped down on
the bed and rolled onto my back. I stared at the ceiling and contemplated how we are all mysteries to each other, even the ones who love
us the most. Perhaps, we are even mysteries to ourselves sometimes.

I heard a strange sound coming from the floor. I rolled onto my
side and looked off the edge of the bed. Maui was on his back. His
legs stuck up in the air, and he was snoring away. Talk about fate
smiling on you. This spoiled dog had won the lottery when I adopted
him.

I climbed off the bed, careful not to step on the sleeping pooch,
and I walked over to the window. I saw that Alana was still by the
pool. I thought about opening the window and calling for her to
come to bed, but it wouldn't do any good. She'd come upstairs when
she was ready.

I sat back down on the bed and thought about something Alana
had said. She'd mentioned that her friend had been murdered by a
wine opener. It didn't seem like the type of weapon one would use if
they'd planned the attack in advance. They'd probably have used a
gun, or they might have selected a knife if they'd assumed the gun
would be too loud and would attract the neighbors' attention. Did
that lend credence to Alana's assumption that the estranged husband
killed Nalani? Maybe they'd gotten into an argument, and he'd
grabbed the first sharp object he'd come across. That certainly made
sense. I didn't just dismiss these thoughts, but I also pushed them to
the back of my mind as I realized this was Alana's investigation and
not my own. Little did I know that was about to change.

4

LIAM HAYES

A FEW DAYS WENT BY, AND I BARELY SAW ALANA. IT WASN'T A SURPRISE since I knew she would be consumed by the murder investigation. We spoke briefly each night in bed, but she didn't have much to report. Sometimes she liked to keep things close to her chest, but I didn't think that was the case in this situation. My guess was that she didn't have the evidence she needed to arrest the estranged husband. I knew she'd pegged him for the murder, so did that mean he didn't do it? Not at all. She just needed time to prove it.

There was a second topic that I'd hoped to bring up, but I didn't in those few days since I knew it would have been nothing but a distraction. There was our wedding to plan. Our wedding date, if it held, was only five months away. We'd sent out the "save the date" cards, but we still hadn't settled on a wedding or reception venue. Did that make me nervous? A little since I wanted Alana to have the perfect wedding. She'd fired our wedding planner and had made no indication to me that she'd even thought about finding another one.

I sat down at my laptop and Googled "wedding planners on Maui" when my phone vibrated. It was Mara Winters. She said she'd found another case for me and asked if I could come to her office in the early afternoon for a meeting. I agreed without even asking for details of the assignment, mainly because I wanted something, anything, to distract me from the search for a new wedding planner. Sure, I still had a few hours before the meeting, and I could have easily spent that time making calls and sending emails.

Nevertheless, I convinced myself that I needed to spend those hours mentally preparing for my meeting. So, how did I spend that time? I took Maui the dog for a long walk, swam laps in the pool, and got in some light reading while I sunbathed. Yes, it was exhausting preparation, but you have to be in top mental condition for these meetings.

The traffic was light on the way to Mara's office. The weather was gorgeous, so I popped the top down to enjoy the breeze as I made my way down the coastline. I arrived to Mara's building on time, but her assistant informed me that the client was running late. She escorted me into the main office where I saw Mara typing on her computer.

"Two seconds, Mr. Rutherford," Mara said.

Sometimes she called me Mr. Rutherford. Sometimes it was Edgar. Never Poe. I'm not sure how and why she decided which greeting she would or would not use.

Mara finished typing and looked up at me.

"Thanks for coming by on short notice. I have something for you before the new client gets here."

Mara reached into the top drawer and pulled out a white envelope. She stood and walked over to me.

"Mary Anne was beyond elated when she woke up and saw the ring on her nightstand," she continued.

Mara handed me the envelope.

"Were you there when she saw it?" I asked, and I took a quick glance inside and saw a thin stack of cash.

"No, I went back up to her room after I got the ring from you. She was still asleep, so I left it in her room. I put the 'Do not disturb' sign on the door and drove back here. She called me a couple of hours later."

"So Mr. Portendorfer is none the wiser," I said.

"I'm actually supposed to have dinner with them tonight. They leave the island in a couple of days."

"I'm sure she won't forget this trip. Do you think she learned her lesson?" I asked.

"One would have thought she learned it the first time, although something tells me that wasn't the first time, either."

"Probably not."

"I know you don't like adultery cases, so I thank you again for helping me out."

I nodded.

"What is this new case about?" I asked.

Mara's assistant knocked once on the door before Mara could answer. I turned and saw a man in his mid-to-late thirties standing beside the assistant. He was of average height and build. He had short brown hair and a thin beard with no hint of gray yet.

"Mr. Hayes is here to see you," the assistant said.

"Yes, thank you. Please come in, Liam."

Mara's client entered the office, and the three of us sat on a leather sofa and matching chair that Mara had in the front corner of her office.

"Liam Hayes, this is Edgar Rutherford. He's the investigator I use for cases like yours."

Liam and I shook hands.

"It's a pleasure to meet you," I said.

"Thank you for helping me," he said.

His voice was deep and rich, and it instantly reminded me of one of those voices you might hear while listening to a movie trailer.

"I've worked with Edgar on a couple of investigations before. He's quite good, and he uncovered the truth each time."

As I write this chapter and look back on the conversation, I'm fairly disappointed in myself for not immediately realizing who this potential client was when Mara clued me in to the fact that this was a murder investigation. It's certainly not every day that a crime of that nature occurs on our island paradise. The only thing that I can suspect that caused my brain to not process what was going on was my anxiety over Alana's fragile state of mind as well as the wedding.

"What can you tell me about your case?" I asked.

Liam hesitated a long moment. I glanced at Mara, and she was about to take the lead when he finally spoke.

"My wife was murdered four days ago. She thinks I did it."

His statement confused me because at first I thought he was saying that his wife thought he'd killed her. Yes, that doesn't make sense, but then I realized that the "she" was clearly someone else. The third thought I had was that I knew exactly who that person was: Alana.

"Your wife's name was Nalani," I said.

I saw the surprise in Liam's eyes.

"How did you know?" he asked.

"I'm not sure if this is a conflict of interest, but I don't think I can work on your case," I said.

"What do you mean?"

"It's Alana who's investigating this?" Mara asked.

"That's right," I said.

"How do you know Alana?" Liam asked.

"She's my fiancée."

Liam turned to Mara.

"What do I do now?"

"Why don't we go ahead and finish this meeting? I'm sure Edgar will keep anything we say confidential, including from Alana," Mara said.

That was never something that I'd run into during the few investigations that I'd conducted. It was true that my first murder case, which had been the one to prove Foxx's innocence, had caused Alana and me to go head-to-head. We weren't romantically involved at that point, at least not at the beginning. I also hadn't kept anything from her. I'd told her everything that I'd discovered, mainly in an effort to convince her that Foxx hadn't killed his girlfriend, Lauren Rogers. Now, Mara was asking me - actually, she was telling me - to intentionally keep things from the person that meant the most to me. I didn't think that was something I could, or would, do.

I realized I had two options. I could either respectfully decline to continue the conversation and leave Mara's office, or I could sit there and listen to what Liam Hayes had to say about the death of his wife. I wasn't sure what to do, so I just sat there in silence. What is that saying? That doing nothing is also a decision?

"You won't say any of this to Alana?" he asked.

I decided to make a compromise with myself. I would tell Alana about the conversation in very general terms, especially if I thought the guy was lying to me. If he wasn't, or if I didn't think he was, then I would only tell her that I had the meeting and declined to take the case.

"I won't reveal your secrets to her," I said.

He hesitated a moment, and I didn't blame him one bit. Would you tell the fiancé of your number one adversary the inside scoop? I wouldn't. He must have been desperate, though, and he decided to continue the meeting.

"I didn't kill my wife. I loved her."

"I'm sure you did love her, but I was under the impression that you and your wife had separated," I said.

"How much of this have you and Alana talked about?" Mara asked.

"Very little. She told me that she knew Nalani and that she'd considered her a friend."

"That's funny. I can't tell you when the last time was that Alana saw her or even called to see how she was doing," Liam said.

I didn't bother responding to his comment since I didn't want to reveal any more information about Alana's feelings toward him or her approach to the investigation. I also knew next to nothing about their relationship beyond Alana's comments about it ending due to Nalani's marriage to Liam. Was Alana's view of the facts biased? Of course, we all see things through our own unique perspectives. I have no doubt that Nalani and Liam saw things differently.

"Let's go back to your relationship with your wife. Why did you separate?" I asked.

"There was someone else. I wasn't surprised when it happened. Nalani and I had been drifting apart for a while."

"Can I ask why?"

"There were a lot of different reasons, but mainly it was her work. She worked so many hours that I rarely saw her. I kept asking her to scale back, but she wouldn't."

"She worked with her brother, didn't she?" Mara asked.

"That's right. He and my sister-in-law own an import-export business," Liam said.

"What does he specialize in?" I asked.

"Mostly goods from Asia. Artwork, statues, stuff like that. There's a huge Asian population on the islands, and he sells to them. He also sells to galleries and businesses in southern California."

"Was your wife one of the owners of this business?" I asked.

"No, and that's one of the issues I had with it. Her brother and his wife own one hundred percent. Nalani worked her butt off there, but she never got a share of the profits beyond her salary. They wouldn't even give her the chance to buy into the company."

"How and when did you discover the affair?" I asked.

"It was about four months ago. I didn't suspect anything. Like I said before, my wife was always working late. Her brother called one night and asked for her. I told him that I thought she was with him, and he said no. That's when I started to get suspicious. It didn't take long for her to admit the affair."

"Who is this person?" Mara asked.

"I don't even like saying the guy's name. He's this photographer who does work for the import-export business. He takes pictures of the stuff they sell for their website and catalog."

"One of the few things that Alana mentioned was that you had moved out of your house. Is that correct?" I asked.

"We decided to separate, and I left. I was gone for a few months. Then one day she called me. She said that she'd made a mistake and wanted me back."

"So you two had gotten back together?" Mara asked.

"Not at first. I was still hurt. I didn't know if I could get past the affair and ever trust her again. I finally decided that we'd been through too much together to not give it another chance," he said.

"Is that how you ended up back at the house? You were moving back in?" I asked.

"I actually had my suitcase in the house. Did Alana mention that?"

I ignored his question and asked another of my own.

"That's when you found her, when you were moving your things back in?"

"I called her when I was driving to the house, but she didn't answer. I didn't think anything of it. I let myself in since I still had my key. I found her on the kitchen floor."

I could see Liam start to tear up as he remembered the vision of his murdered wife. His emotions looked genuine. Of course, he could have just been a good actor, or maybe he did kill his wife but he felt truly sorry for it.

"I called 911 as soon as I found her, but she was already gone."

"Since you didn't kill her, who do you think did?" Mara asked.

"I don't know. The only person I can think of is the guy she had the affair with. I'm sure he got angry when she told him she was going back to me."

"Let's do this: I'll talk to Mr. Rutherford and see if he's comfortable taking this case. If he's not or if you'd like to work with someone else, I can find another investigator for you," Mara said.

Liam turned to me.

"This isn't just about clearing my name. I loved my wife. I have to find out who did this to her. I know Alana's only looking at me, which means she'll never find out who really did this."

Mara escorted Liam to the door after asking me to hold back for a few minutes. I thought Liam had taken a clear shot at Alana's professionalism. I didn't respond despite wanting to tell him that he had her all wrong since I knew he wasn't in the right kind of emotional state to hear my words.

Mara came back into the office a moment later and sat down on the sofa opposite me.

"What do you think?" she asked.

"You want to know if I think he did it."

Mara nodded.

"What do you think?" I asked.

"I think he's innocent. I don't know why. Just a gut instinct," she said.

"Maybe, but my gut has been wrong before. I learned that on the last murder investigation."

"Was he right about Alana? Is she only looking at him?"

"I'm sure she isn't. If she suspects him, though, then she probably has a good reason."

"Do you want to take this one or pass?" Mara asked.

"It's not just what I want. What does Liam Hayes want, and what about you? You're his lawyer, either way. How comfortable do you feel knowing my relationship with Alana?"

"I won't speak for Mr. Hayes, but I can't see you ever doing anything to railroad an innocent person, so I'm fine with you taking the case."

"Let me speak to Alana. I'm not about to put this case between us. Are you okay if I don't give you an answer until tomorrow morning?" I asked.

"Sure. That will give Liam time to think about it, too."

I stood.

"If it wasn't Liam Hayes who murdered his wife, who do you think it was?" Mara asked.

"It's almost always someone close to the victim, isn't it?"

"So the lover?"

"Probably," I said.

I patted my back pocket where I'd placed the envelope that Mara had given me when I'd arrived.

"Please give Ms. Portendorfer my best. On the other hand, don't. I just remembered her husband isn't supposed to know she hired an investigator to get back her diamond ring."

Mara laughed.

"I'll try to remember that tonight."

"Where are you meeting them for dinner?" I asked.

"At the hotel. There's supposed to be a great steak restaurant there."

"Enjoy your dinner."

"I will, and please give Alana my best."

I thanked Mara again and headed for my car. I opened the envelope after I climbed inside and did my best to discreetly count the cash. It was five thousand dollars, way more than I thought it would possibly be. I'd assumed it would go directly to the wedding fund, but now I was worried about money from an adulterous case jinxing my union with Alana. What would I do with it then? I didn't know. Was I being overly superstitious? Undoubtedly, but you know me by now. I can be a bit weird sometimes.

I didn't see Alana until later that night. I didn't immediately tell her about my meeting with Liam Hayes since I could see that she was in a rotten mood. We had dinner by the pool while Maui ran around the yard and occasionally barked at an ocean wave that had dared to get too close to him. By the end of our quiet dinner, I wasn't even sure if the meeting was something I wanted to disclose at all. Basically, I chickened out and went inside to do the dishes and put the leftovers away in the refrigerator.

Alana joined me in the kitchen a few minutes later. She watched me for a while, and I knew it was only a matter of time before she sprung something on me. I was wrong, though. She was actually studying me, much like a detective staring at a criminal from across the table in an interrogation room. Did I think our kitchen qualified as such? It certainly felt that way on this night.

"What's bothering you?" she asked.

"Nothing."

"You sure? You seemed distracted at dinner."

"I'm fine. It's nothing."

Our roles had reversed since I was usually the one trying to drag the truth out of her, and she was usually the one responding with the two-word reply: It's nothing. I think that's a common female response to prying males. I wasn't sure if I'd subconsciously used the line against her, but I probably had.

I thought about blaming the wedding for my distraction during dinner, but I ultimately decided against that since I didn't want to get into a one-hour discussion on flowers, invitations, and whether we should go with a red velvet cake or some more predictable flavor like vanilla. I know that sounds horrible, especially when I realize I'm negatively comparing the planning of our wedding to a murder investigation. The former sounded like torture, though, while the latter was infinitely more intriguing.

"There is something that happened today. I know you're going to be upset about it, but I already said no."

"What happened?" she asked.

"Mara called me this morning and said she had another client. I met with the guy at her office and realized from the start that I couldn't take the case," I said.

"Who did you meet?" she asked.

Then she realized who it was before I had the chance to answer.

"Don't tell me, it was Liam," she continued.

"I turned him down already."

I knew that wasn't technically true since I'd ended the conversation by saying that I'd think about it. However, I had made that decision during my dinner with Alana. I just hadn't gotten around to telling Liam and Mara that.

"I can't believe that son of a bitch. He really thinks I'm going to back off if he hires you?"

"He said that he had no idea what my connection was to you."

"And you believed that?" she asked.

"I didn't just assume he was telling me the truth, but he also didn't sound like he was lying."

Alana didn't immediately respond to my comment. Instead, she leaned against the kitchen counter and stared out the window.

"Why does your dog bark at the waves like that?" she asked.

"My dog? I thought he was now our dog."

I turned and tried to see what Alana was looking at. Sure enough, Maui was back to barking at the ocean.

"He is our dog when he does something cute. He's your dog when he acts weird like that," she said.

We both watched the dog run back and forth for a few moments. Then Alana turned to me.

"It was Mara's plan. She assumed there was a good chance I'd get the case. Liam probably told her that when he called her. This was her scheme to get you involved. That really pisses me off. You can't trust these lawyers."

"I thought you liked Mara?"

"What did Liam say? Did you just leave after you heard who he was, or did you two actually talk?" Alana asked.

"We spoke for a little while. I didn't learn that much."

"Tell me what he said."

And here we were, the exact place I didn't want to be when I first learned who the potential client was. There was also the comment I'd made to Liam Hayes when I said I wouldn't disclose the contents of our meeting to anyone, including Alana - especially Alana. This was one of those little moments of truth when you keep your word and piss off the one you love, or you completely cave. Once again, I tried to please both sides and come up with a compromise, and once again, I completely failed. You can't please everyone, so why did I always seem to try? I decided to tell Alana some things that were probably public knowledge and hope it was enough to satisfy her curiosity.

"He said he thought you were out to get him."

"That's because he did it. What else did he say?"

"Not much. He said he loved his wife and that he would never hurt her."

"How did you end the conversation?" Alana asked.

"I told him it was a conflict of interest and that I couldn't work with him."

"And what did Mara say about that?"

"Not a whole lot."

"She had nothing to contribute? She didn't agree that it was a conflict?"

"Not really. I don't think it bothered her. She said she thought Liam could trust me."

"So it was her plan to get you involved."

"What do you mean?" I asked.

"She knew it was a conflict of interest, but she didn't care, mainly because she's hoping you'll try to convince me that he's innocent. It's not going to work."

"That might be her plan. I don't know."

"Here's what we do. We play her while she thinks she's playing us."

"What are you talking about?" I asked.

"You call her in the morning. Tell her you've rethought things, and you want to take his case. Then you report everything he tells you to me."

"I can't do that," I said.

"Why not?"

"Because it would be a betrayal of my word."

"You want to catch her killer, don't you?"

"Of course, but I don't know he did it, and I certainly don't want to work with someone who you're convinced murdered your friend."

"You've worked with guilty people before," she said.

"Somehow that feels like a cheap shot."

"That's not how I meant it. I know you didn't know they were guilty at the time."

"This is exactly why I didn't want to bring it up before. I'd knew you'd act like this."

"Like what? What am I doing? I just want to nail this guy."

"If he's guilty, you'll catch him. You don't need my help."

"Really? That's what you're going to say?" she asked.

"You're putting me in a no-win situation."

"Whose side are you on? His or mine?"

"I'm done talking about this. I'm not taking the case, not under any circumstances."

I walked outside to join the dog, and no, I don't mean to say that I intended to help him bark at the waves.

I fully expected Alana to eventually follow me and apologize for trying to lure me into her little devious plan. I'm sure you're laughing at me right now as you immediately realized that was never going to happen. You're right, of course. She didn't come outside, so it was just me and the dog for the next hour as we sat around the pool and stared at the ocean and the crescent moon.

I walked back into the house after I'd cooled down and found Alana lying on the sofa. She was watching that show about six-hundred-pound people who try to lose weight through surgery and completely changing every aspect of their diets. At least Alana wasn't watching another documentary on Hitler. I told her I was heading upstairs. She ignored me until I got to the bottom of the staircase.

"That's not all he said, is it?" she asked.

"Who? Liam Hayes?"

I wasn't sure why I asked the question since I clearly knew who she was talking about.

"You gave him your word that you wouldn't talk about it. Didn't you?"

I didn't know how to answer her without resuming the fight, so I said nothing.

"I'm sorry for asking you to break your word," she said.

I walked over to the sofa and sat down beside her. She'd clearly just extended an olive branch, and I wasn't about to break it in half and storm off.

"Why do you think he did it? Give me the specifics if you can."

"This wasn't the first time they broke up. Nalani cheated on him early in their relationship. Liam beat her after he found out. He sent her to the ER with a broken nose."

"Why did she take him back?" I asked.

"I begged her not to. She actually blamed herself. She said she never should have cheated on him. She asked him to take her back. Can you believe that?"

Unfortunately, I could. People often do crazy things like stay in abusive relationships. Does it make any sense? Of course not, but it happens all the time. Maybe you even know someone like that.

"I told her I couldn't be her friend anymore if she was going to be with someone like that. I didn't really mean it. I just hoped it would shock her into reconsidering what she was doing," Alana continued.

"She picked you over him," I guessed.

Alana nodded.

"We tried to save our friendship, but it just didn't work out."

"Did she tell Liam that you'd given her the ultimatum?" I asked.

"Of course, and he never forgave me. I wasn't a cop when he beat her. I figured it would happen again, though, and I promised myself that I'd be the one to arrest him when he did it."

I made a decision in that moment that I don't regret now. Yes, I went back on my word to Liam, but Alana's story about Liam breaking Nalani's nose pushed me over the edge. Maybe that had been her intention all along, but I couldn't keep a promise to a man who would put his hands on a woman.

"Was his suitcase in the house when you got there?"

"What do you mean?" Alana asked.

"He said he came to the house because he was in the process of moving back. Was his suitcase there? Maybe in the foyer or some other place between the front door and where the body was."

"I didn't see it, and I know I would have remembered that. Is that what he told you? That he'd brought his suitcase into the house?"

"What about his cell phone? Did you get access to his records?"

"I did."

"He told me he called her on his way to the house, but he never got a response."

"That's not what the records say. There's not even a record of him calling her the night before. In fact, he hadn't called her for days, at least not from his cell phone."

"That means one of two things. He either lied to me to help convince me to take the case, or he was calling her from a phone that wasn't his own. What about the lover? I'm assuming you already met with him."

"He said Nalani never mentioned to him that she was going back to Liam."

"Did you believe him?" I asked.

"I did, but I'll admit that his comments reinforced my belief that Liam was lying."

"Mara asked me who I thought it was if Liam hadn't done it. I guessed the lover."

"There was something about him. I don't know."

"What do you mean?" I asked.

"He didn't react when I'd told him that she was dead. I chalked it up to him being in shock."

"What about his phone records? When was the last time he called her?"

"The night before."

"Do you remember how long the call lasted?"

"Not sure, but I think it was pretty short."

"Like a minute or two?" I asked.

"Something like that. I remember because it was the only call she got that night."

"Usually when you make a call that short, it's just to confirm a plan or some piece of quick information, like 'Hey, I'm about to come over.' Something like that."

"He said they had dinner together at his house the night before she died."

"This is your case, and the last thing I want to do is cause you more stress."

"You're not causing me stress."

"Then there's something I want to ask you," I said.

"What is it?"

"Do you want my help? I'm not saying you need it, but two people looking at a puzzle are always better than one person."

"Are you suggesting you take Liam's case?" she asked.

"No. I'm suggesting I help you. I don't care about Liam Hayes, but I care about you. I see what this is doing to you. You can't go on like this. I'll make a deal with him. I'll help you find the killer. If he didn't do it, then I'll be helping him for free. If he did do it, then he's going to jail."

"What makes you think he'll agree to that?" she asked.

"Because he's desperate, and he's scared."

"And Mara? What will she think of this plan?"

"It doesn't matter what she thinks. I technically won't be working for her client either."

"So you're working for me? What if I can't afford your rates?" Alana asked.

"I accept payment in other ways."

"Oh, really? Do you make similar deals with all your clients?"

"Only the good-looking ones, and Liam Hayes doesn't qualify. There's one more thing I need to ask you."

"What is it?"

"Do you really think something is wrong with the dog?" I asked.

Alana turned and looked at Maui. He was on his back on the floor in front of the sofa. We were both quiet for a moment, and we could hear him snoring softly.

"No, there's nothing wrong with him, but you do spoil that dog."

I smiled. It was the first time I felt somewhat good all day.

5

THE AGREEMENT

I CALLED MARA THE NEXT MORNING AND PITCHED HER MY IDEA OF working with Liam Hayes on an unofficial basis. I told her my main goal was to help find the killer. If that wasn't Liam, then he had every reason to work with me, especially since I wouldn't be charging him for my time. I also made it clear that I would share everything I learned with Alana to aid her in her investigation.

Mara told me she'd pass the offer on to Liam and get back to me as soon as possible. She called me less than an hour later, which only confirmed my suspicion that Liam was a desperate man who was convinced it was only a matter of time before Alana showed up to slap the handcuffs on him. He agreed to my terms and also suggested that we meet that afternoon at Harry's to discuss the case. I guessed Mara had told him that I was one of the owners of the bar since it seemed like too much of a coincidence that he would name our establishment.

I got to the bar a little early so I could have a brief conversation with Foxx about the business. We went over the accounting numbers on a weekly basis which was born more out of my obsession over the business staying profitable. Foxx isn't an irresponsible guy by any means, but I assumed he'd be okay if we just went over the accounting at the end of every one or two months. The business was doing better than either of us could have imagined. Foxx had turned it into the top watering hole in Lahaina. I didn't have specific numbers to back up that claim, but it was pretty obvious judging by the nightly crowds.

Liam showed up for our little meeting on time, and I escorted him to a booth at the back of the bar. We both ordered a drink, even though it was still in the afternoon. Liam asked for a beer, while I requested my usual Manhattan.

"Mara surprised me when she called this morning. I really didn't think you were going to help me," he said.

I wanted to point out that I was technically helping my fiancée, but I decided not to get off on the wrong foot by immediately contradicting him.

"No problem. I think the first thing we should do is create a list of people for me to interview. I know you said in Mara's office that you think the photographer might have been the person responsible for your wife's death. What can you tell me about him?"

"His name's Gabriel Reed. He's done a lot of work for my brother-in-law's business, but that's about all I know about him."

"Do you know how long they worked together?" I asked.

"No idea. Nalani never mentioned him before. I only found out about his work when I looked him up online. His website has a portfolio of his work, and I recognized some of the stuff my brother-in-law sells. I asked Nalani if that's how she'd met him, and she said yes."

"Have you seen him before?"

"Just once. I followed him and Nalani one night back to his house. It's just beyond Paia. I wrote down the address. I can give it to you."

"What does he look like?" I asked.

"He's about my age, maybe a little taller. He's kind of thin. He has long blonde hair that he had pulled back in a ponytail. He looks like one of those obnoxious artist types."

"Have you seen or heard from him since Nalani's death?"

"No. He hasn't reached out to me, but I don't blame him. I don't even know what I would do if I ran into him. Do you know if Alana's looking into him or not?" Liam asked.

"I'm sure she's talked to him, but I don't know what she might have learned yet."

"Will you tell me what she says?" Liam asked.

"I'll have to get Alana's permission first. You said you moved out of the house after you discovered the affair with Gabriel. Where did you stay?"

"With a friend of mine. His name's Mason Howard. I can give you his contact information."

"How did you meet Mason?" I asked.

"We used to work at the same hotel together. I was the event planner for the hotel."

"You were the event planner, meaning you don't work there anymore?"

"No, they let me go a few months ago."

"Does Mason still work there?"

"Yes. He works nights, so the best time to reach him at home is the early afternoon."

"Are you working anywhere now?" I asked.

"No. I applied for several positions but haven't gotten anything yet," he said.

"How well did Mason know your wife?"

"He knew her well since we used to have him over all the time."

"Did you tell him that you were moving back in with your wife?"

"Absolutely. He can vouch for that."

"Were you with him the night your wife died?" I asked.

"I was at his house, but he wasn't there. He was at the hotel. I was asleep by the time he got back, but he should be able to tell you that he saw my car in front of his house."

"Did he see you pack your things and leave his place that morning?"

"No, he was still sleeping by the time I got ready to leave."

"So you didn't pack your suitcase the night before?"

"No. I did it that morning. I kept the spare bedroom door shut. I wanted some privacy, and I didn't want Mason to feel like I was always on top of him. I also didn't want to wake him. It's tough working the night shift. Plus, his place is kind of small, and I knew it was a real inconvenience for me to be there."

"How long were you living with him?"

"About three months, maybe a little less. I'm sure he was anxious for me to get out."

"Were things tense between you two?" I asked.

"No. He was great. Like I said, though, it's a small place. It's barely big enough for just Mason."

"Is there anyone else who can confirm that you and Nalani were getting back together?"

Liam thought about my question for a moment, and then he said, "Kaylee might be able to."

"Who's she?"

"She's a friend of Nalani's. She was acting as a bit of a go-between for a while," Liam said.

"A go-between for you and your wife?"

"Something like that. I ran into Kaylee once, and we talked about the breakup. She admitted to me that she knew that Nalani had been having the affair."

"How was she acting as a go-between?" I asked.

"It wasn't like she was delivering messages or anything. She just told me that she thought Nalani had made a mistake and was regretting it. I didn't really care at first. Actually, I was kind of glad that she might be regretting it even though I didn't want her back. Then I started thinking about it more and asking myself what I would do if she did want to get back together."

"Did you call Kaylee and talk about that?"

"Not exactly, but I did call her a few weeks later and ask how Nalani was doing. I guess she told Nalani that I'd called because I got a call from Nalani a few days after that. That's when she told me that she wanted to talk."

"Does Kaylee know that you were moving back that day?"

"I didn't say anything to her about it, but maybe Nalani did."

"You said Nalani worked with her brother and sister-in-law. What can you tell me about them?"

"Koa is her younger brother. His last name's Opunui. He's the one who started the business, and then his wife, Moani, came to work with him once the company took off."

"Did Nalani get along with them?"

"For the most part, but she did resent that she wasn't one of the owners."

"Resent, that's a pretty strong word."

"Yeah, but I don't think it would lead to her getting killed over it. Nalani and Koa loved each other."

"Is there anyone else I should talk to?" I asked.

"I can't think of anyone."

"Based on what you've told me so far, the only person that could possibly be seen as a suspect is Gabriel Reed, unless it was a random crime."

"But that doesn't make sense. Nothing was stolen from the house."

"Let me just recap the timeline to make sure I have it right. You and Nalani decided to get back together. You were going to move back the morning she passed. You packed that morning, but Mason didn't see you leave. You called Nalani on the way to your house, but she didn't answer. You got to the house, saw her car in the driveway, wheeled your suitcase into the house, and that's when you saw her on the kitchen floor."

"That's right."

"Is there anything other than the affair that might make the police think you were the one to have hurt her?"

Liam looked away. He turned back to me after several seconds.

"I guess Alana told you."

"Told me what?"

"That I'd hurt Nalani before."

"She mentioned something about it, but I'd like to hear your version."

"We'd only been dating for a year or two, and I walked in on her with another guy. I went after the guy, and Nalani tried to pull me off of him. I moved my arm back to try to push Nalani away from me, and my elbow hit her in the face."

"You're saying it was an accident?" I asked.

"I would have never hit her on purpose. She screamed, and I immediately turned back to help her. That's when the guy ran out. We separated for a while then, too, but she was the one who made the decision to come back to me. She knew I didn't mean to hurt her."

Liam and I spoke for several more minutes, but we basically rehashed information that had already been discussed. I promised to give him an update after I'd conducted a few of the interviews. The one thing of note that he mentioned on the way out was that he was now staying at a hotel in Kihei. It was a fairly far distance from his house. I made a mental note to ask Alana if there was some legal reason Liam wouldn't be allowed back in the house. Perhaps it was more of an emotional reason. I doubted that I could return to the home I shared with a murdered spouse, even if I wasn't the one who committed the crime. I doubted I'd ever be able to get that image out of my mind.

I also found it odd that he hadn't moved back with his friend and former co-worker, Mason Howard. It was true that he said he didn't want to be a burden to Mason anymore, but I wasn't sure how much of a burden he would have been, especially since they were on different schedules. Maybe there was tension going on that he didn't want to talk about. It was worth following up with Mason on that.

There was also the new information that Liam was between jobs. It had certainly been a stressful few months for him, with the word "stressful" being the understatement of the year. He'd discovered that his wife was cheating on him. She'd kicked him out of the house that he co-owned with her. He'd had to live in a house that was apparently only large enough for one person, and he'd lost his job as an event planner. The guy's anxiety levels would have been through the roof. Was that the reason that he'd snapped or might have snapped?

I'm sure you noticed that I didn't question Liam on his assertions, both in Mara's office and at the bar, that he'd called Nalani on the way over to their house, as well as the fact that he'd brought his suitcase into the house. Alana had directly disputed those claims. I'd been the one to repeat them during our second conversation since I wanted to give Liam the chance to correct himself. He obviously didn't. So was Alana mistaken or was Liam intentionally lying to me to make his case more believable? I thought the answer to that question was clear.

I finished my Manhattan as Foxx slipped onto the seat opposite me.

"Is that your new client?' he asked.

"In a manner of speaking."

"And Alana hates the guy?"

"I don't know if I'd use the word hate. Actually, that is the best word. I don't think that I've ever heard her speak so badly about someone."

"She's okay with you working with him?" Foxx asked.

"It was somewhat her idea. How are things with you? Any news on Hani?"

"She sent me an email that her latest doctor's appointment went well."

"I think Alana was supposed to go with her. I wonder if she made it," I said.

"I feel guilty for not going. Do you think I should go?"

"Do you want to go?"

"I'm interested in the health of the kid and all. I just worry that I'll upset Hani if we're around each other."

I thought it was a valid concern, but I sensed that he was more worried about her upsetting him than the other way around.

"Why don't you give her a call tonight? I'm sure a phone call would go a long way," I said.

"Maybe. I'll think about it."

"By the way, what did you think of the guy I was talking to? You have a gut reaction?"

"Yeah. He's guilty," Foxx said.

"Why do you say that?"

"He has eyes like a weasel. Never trust someone with eyes like that."

"You could see his eyes from back at the bar?" I asked.

"No, but I got a close look at him when he passed me on the way out. I'm siding with Alana on this one. The dude did it."

Was Foxx's opinion scientific? Of course not, but there was something to be said about listening to your instinct. I'm a firm believer in the subconscious mind picking up on miniscule things that your conscious brain misses. So why was my gut instinct completely quiet when it came to Liam Hayes? I didn't know, but I was determined to find out.

6

THE PHOTOGRAPHER

I SAT AT THE BAR FOR A FEW MINUTES WHILE I SEARCHED FOR GABRIEL Reed's photography business on my phone. I was surprised to see that he had an art gallery in Lahaina just a few blocks from Harry's. I recognized the name of the place. I'd actually driven by it several times and always intended to go inside, but I'd never gotten around to it. I made the decision to jumpstart the investigation and headed over there.

I found it interesting that Gabriel Reed even had an art gallery. Most photographers try to stick to one genre or category of photography. It's usually not a good idea to paint yourself as a generalist. You tend not to attract the best-paying clients that way. How does the saying go? Jack of all trades but master of none. I knew from Liam that Gabriel was the commercial photographer for Nalani's place of employment. It didn't make sense that a commercial photographer would have an art gallery as well, so that meant that he also did work as either a portrait or landscape photographer, maybe both.

You're probably wondering why I spent so much time thinking about this since it probably had nothing to do with the case. Well, I consider myself an amateur photographer, which means that I've spent way too much money on cameras and lenses but still don't consider myself good enough to go pro. I probably could if I spent more time at it, but I don't want my love of photography to be ruined by paying clients. You're forced to do what they want and when they want it. No thanks. I'll pass.

Gabriel's gallery was a few blocks from Front Street, which is the main tourist road in Lahaina. That meant his rent was substantially less than the large number of galleries and art shops by the water. It also probably meant his sales were a lot less. The sign on the gallery door indicated his shop was about to close in a few minutes. I decided to go in anyway and hoped he'd agree to talk to me.

I entered the shop but didn't see anyone inside. I took a moment to walk around and look at the various large photos hanging on the walls. They all depicted various scenic shots of Maui, Oahu, and Kauai. The work was good but not mind-blowing. It's not hard to take a nice outdoor photograph when Mother Nature does all the work. None of the compositions seemed all that unique, and there was nothing in there that I hadn't seen a million times before since moving to the island. I guess the best word to describe his work would be "typical."

"Welcome to my gallery," a voice behind me said.

I turned to see the man who was obviously Gabriel Reed. Liam had done a decent job of describing him. He was about my height but maybe thirty pounds lighter. His blonde hair wasn't in a ponytail, though. It hung loose down his back. He reminded me of an 80s rock star. I assumed he felt he needed an edge to his look if he was going to compete with the other artists on Maui. It seemed like every island artist these days either had long hair, a shaggy beard, several tattoos, or all of the above.

"Are you the photographer?" I asked, even though I already knew the answer.

"Yes, this is all of my work. Does any of it interest you? We offer free shipping back to the mainland."

I'm sure you do, I thought, especially after seeing the huge prices for some of the photos. I knew enough about photography to know most of these prints cost him just a few bucks to make since he no doubt had his own color laser printer somewhere in the back. That meant the markup on these things was probably close to one thousand percent. I didn't begrudge him that. Everyone should be able to make as much money as they can.

"Your work is beautiful, but that's not why I'm here. I'm actually working for Nalani's family. I was hoping you'd have a few minutes to talk to me."

Sometimes it was a good idea to come by unannounced and watch how they reacted to my announcement that I was an investigator, even though my status as one wasn't quite official. In fact, I haven't even once taken the time to see what actually certifies someone as an investigator. Maybe there isn't even anything you have to do beyond having business cards printed. I did have one of those, but it still listed me as an architect.

Gabriel didn't disappoint me. His facial expression showed a mixture of surprise and then sadness.

"What do you mean when you say you're working for them? I haven't seen you at the warehouse."

"I don't work as an employee. They've asked me to assist the police in looking into her death," I said.

"So you're an investigator?"

"That's right."

"I'm not sure how I can help. I told that detective everything I know."

"You mean Detective Hu?"

"I think that was her name."

"She and I work together a lot. She's the best detective on the island," I said.

"What is it you want to know then?"

"I heard how much you cared for Nalani. If it's okay, I'd like to ask you some questions about the day before she passed."

"You mean got murdered," he said.

It was true there was a big difference between a person being murdered and a person simply passing from something like a heart attack or some kind of accident, but it wasn't like I could go up to someone and say, "Hi, heard your lover got murdered. Want to talk about it?" That actually brought up another issue I was struggling with while I walked to his gallery. Gabriel was the kind of guy who would steal another man's wife. It wasn't cool in my book, and I was doing my best not to stand in judgment of him and throw him serious attitude. Of course, his willingness to be involved with another man's spouse didn't mean he was a murderer as Liam had suggested.

"When was the last time you saw Nalani?" I asked.

"The night before she died. She came to my house, and I made us dinner."

That was interesting, I thought, since she'd supposedly decided by that point to reunite with Liam.

"Did she say anything about getting back with her husband?"

"Detective Hu asked me that, and no, Nalani never even hinted that she might be thinking about it. She hated her husband, and if he's saying they were getting back together, then he's lying," Gabriel said.

"Did she tell you why she hated him?"

"He was abusive toward her. He was always putting her down. She was never good enough."

"Did she talk about physical abuse, or was it all emotional?" I asked.

"She said he hit her years ago, but it was mostly emotional up until he murdered her. I'd say that counts as physical abuse. Don't you think?"

"What time did she leave your house that night?"

"Around nine. It wasn't that late since we had an early photoshoot at the warehouse the next morning. She was going to help me with it."

"This was for her brother's import-export business?"

"Yeah, that's where I was when I heard the news about her murder. None of us could figure out why she didn't show for work. Her brother and I tried calling her, but I never got an answer."

"Had you ever seen Nalani and Liam interact before?"

"No, I met her through the business. We'd actually known each other for some time before our relationship started."

"Did her brother and sister-in-law know about your affair?" I asked.

"I'm not sure. It wasn't something that we were public about. I certainly wasn't going to talk about it when I was doing jobs for them. I left it up to Nalani to tell them. I don't know if she did or not."

"How were they to work with?" I asked.

"What does that have to do with any of this?"

"I've heard that there was tension between Nalani and her brother over the business."

"Who told you that? Liam?"

"I'd rather not say."

"The guy doesn't know what he's talking about. I never heard her say one negative word about Koa or Moani. They're great people," he said.

"Do you know if Nalani filed for divorce from Liam?"

"She hadn't gotten around to it. We talked about it a few times. I'm not sure what the holdup was. I think she felt sorry for him."

"You two hadn't made plans for what would happen after she officially ended things with him?" I asked.

"Not really. Our relationship was serious, but I didn't want to pressure her. I knew she was going through a lot."

"A lot? Was there something other than her marriage that was causing her grief?"

"No. That was it, but her husband was constantly calling her. He was always harassing her and begging her to take him back. I even caught him following on several occasions. I was tempted to pull over and confront the guy, but Nalani always talked me out of it."

"He followed you several times, like more than three or four?" I asked.

"Try ten or more, and those are just the one where I caught him. The guy actually kept changing up his car. Maybe he was renting them. I don't know, but it was a constant nuisance."

"He followed you that many times?"

"Yeah, and it was always from the gallery. He wasn't very subtle about it, which made me wonder why he'd go to the trouble of changing cars. He's probably just incompetent. Maybe that's why he got fired from his job. You heard about that, didn't you?"

"I heard he lost his job, but I don't know why. Do you?"

"Nalani just said he'd been fired. She wouldn't tell me why. The guy's a loser."

"Just one more question. You said Nalani left your house around nine. Did you talk to her later that night?"

"No. The last time I said anything to her was when I walked her to her car. I still can't believe she's gone. When are the police going to finally get around to arresting her husband? It's obvious he did it."

"I appreciate your time, and I'm sorry for your loss," I said.

"You're not going to answer my question? When are they going to arrest him?"

"I'm sorry, but I don't know the answer. I do help the police, but they're not about to tell me if and when they're going to arrest someone."

"Well, they're idiots if they don't see he did it."

I thought about telling him I would share his opinions of the police with Alana, but I decided against it. Instead, I thanked him for his time and made my way out of the gallery. I was only a few steps away from the door when my cell phone pinged. I looked at the display and saw a text message from Alana. It said that her mother was at our house. It didn't end in an SOS, so I took it as her warning for me to stay away.

I walked back to Harry's since that's where I'd left my car. Instead of driving home, I went back into the bar to have a drink and kill some time. I didn't know why Ms. Hu had come by the house. Maybe it would be a twenty-minute conversation about the wedding, or perhaps it would be a two-hour discussion on how terrible I was and how Alana should run for the hills. I decided to split the difference and stay at Harry's for around an hour or so.

I ordered another Manhattan and made my way to a table in one of the back corners so I could spend the time thinking about what I'd learned from the Gabriel Reed interview. The news that Nalani had not mentioned anything to Gabriel about the potential reconciliation with Liam was certainly at the top of the list of revelations. It meant one of two things: Either Liam lied about his wife taking him back, or Nalani had postponed her decision to let her lover know it was over. Then I realized there was a third possibility. Nalani had agreed to get back with Liam, but she also intended to continue with the affair. Unfortunately, there was no way to know who was lying just yet.

The second thing that jumped out at me was Gabriel's claim that Liam had followed him and Nalani over ten times. It was also intriguing to hear that Liam had even gone through the trouble of acquiring different cars for his supposed surveillance on his wife and her lover. Did I believe Gabriel's story? I did, mainly because of Gabriel's theory that Liam had been renting other cars. It was an interesting detail that I thought was too good for him to have lied about on the spot.

Of course, there was always the possibility that the photographer was an accomplished liar. Many people were, and they were usually the ones I encountered on these investigations. I'd learned the hard way to never believe anything anyone told me until I had several pieces of evidence to back up the claim. I don't remember where I've heard the phrase "Trust but verify." Well, I no longer trusted, and I always verified.

The third and final item that I found intriguing was Gabriel's statement that Nalani didn't have any problems with her brother regarding the import-export business. Gabriel and Nalani had apparently been involved for months. It made sense to me that she would have mentioned something about the tension in the family business, especially since Gabriel also worked with them and knew all the players. It would be a natural thing to talk about. So, why hadn't she? Did that mean there was no disagreement and Liam was lying about it to deflect attention away from him? Possibly, especially since I saw no logical reason for Gabriel to lie about not knowing anything about the family disagreements.

All things considered, the interview hadn't boded well for Liam

Hayes. Of course, I didn't expect it to. It wasn't like I expected the wife's lover to have positive things to say about the grieving husband, especially if he thought that husband was a murderer. Nevertheless, Gabriel came across as a credible person to me, even if I thought his hair was ridiculous and his photographs tended to be a bit dull. Back to the photo stuff again, you ask? I know, but I just can't help my train of thought sometimes, especially when I'm trying to kill time waiting for my mother-in-law to leave my home.

7

FIVE THINGS

Foxx eventually came by my table, and we had a brief conversation about my interview with Gabriel. Foxx was always a good sounding board for these cases, and he often had great insight that would trigger subconscious observations I'd made earlier during my interviews. He agreed with me that the rental car thing sounded like a legitimate story. It also helped to verify his original theory that Liam was guilty, even though Foxx had based that entirely on the notion that he didn't like the way Liam's eyes had looked. Yeah, it was a superficial observation, but you'd be surprised how often those things tend to be accurate.

We also spoke a little about Hani and her mother. Normally, Foxx would have laughed after I told him the reason I was still at the bar but, as I've mentioned before, he's met Ms. Hu and completely understands my reluctance to engage her in conversation. Yes, I know exactly what you're thinking as you read this: we're both utter wimps for being scared of the lady. Trust me, though, you'd react the same way if you'd met her. She's a force of nature with a will of iron.

I looked at my watch and saw that it had been slightly longer than an hour since I'd received Alana's text. I said goodbye to Foxx and our wait staff and headed outside for my car. I popped the top back on the convertible and made the short drive back to my house. Maui the dog greeted me with his usual flair, which was to run up to me and do a dramatic fall and roll onto his back so I could scratch his belly. It was a move that was always executed so perfectly that it made me wonder if he practiced it while Alana and I were away. I was tempted to hold up a judge's scorecard with the number ten written on it.

I called out to Alana, but I didn't get a reply. Then I heard the shower running. I grabbed Maui's leash and took him for a long walk. I found Alana in the living room when I came back inside. She said hello, and I could tell from the tone of her voice that she wasn't in a good mood. Being a man, I immediately wondered what I had done to make her feel that way. It was still a possibility that I had committed some relationship infraction even though I hadn't seen her for several hours. Maybe I'd misinterpreted the text, and she was pissed at me for not coming to her rescue while her mother was here.

"Something wrong?" I asked.

"You know what's wrong," she said.

I didn't, though. That's why I asked.

"Your mother?" I guessed.

"She came by to give me a hard time for missing Hani's doctor's appointment. I called Hani and told her I couldn't make it. This case has taken over everything. Why can't my mother understand that?"

"I'm sure she does. She's just frustrated about Foxx, so she's taking it out on you."

"I know, but I shouldn't have to be her whipping boy. You wouldn't believe what she said about Foxx."

"What did she say?" I asked, and I immediately regretted not coming up with an excuse to swiftly end the conversation and leave the house for some made-up emergency.

"Do you think Foxx abandoned Hani?" Alana asked.

That was something she'd managed not to ask me since we'd found out months ago that her sister was pregnant. I'd wrestled with the topic myself several times. I never used the word "abandoned," though. Rather, I questioned if Foxx should have been willing to give the relationship another chance. He hadn't even considered it, at least that's what he'd told me during several conversations about Hani at our bar.

I'd gotten the impression that he actually liked her during their brief time together. Sure, Foxx was a philanderer, and Hani's undeniable beauty was definitely the reason he'd first gotten together with her. That, and the several glasses of wine they'd consumed before their first coupling. Sorry, I can't believe I just wrote the word "coupling." I think Foxx had grown to dislike her, and he'd been the one to break things off. In fairness to Foxx, he didn't know she was pregnant at the time.

Alana's question was interesting on multiple levels. It was clearly something that crossed her mind, yet she'd made the decision not to mention it to me before. I suspected that she was now using her mother's visit as an opportunity to toss it out there and have her mother take the blame for it. Ah, women, you can be so crafty and should never, ever be underestimated.

"Is this something you've thought of yourself?" I asked.

"No, I was just wondering what you thought of my mother's comment," she said.

Yeah, right, I thought.

"I have thought about it, and I think it would have been a mistake for Foxx and Hani to get back together."

"Why is that?"

"They've obviously got serious issues with each other. I think neither of them needs to be in a bad relationship. Better to end it now and just be there for the child."

"What are they?" she asked.

"What are you talking about?"

"You just said they have serious issues. What are the issues Foxx has with Hani?"

"You know what they are."

"I do?"

"Sure," I said.

"I don't think so. You've never told me, and I don't think I have the kind of relationship with Foxx where I could ask him myself."

"What do you mean? You guys are friends. Of course, you could ask him."

"I only see Foxx when I'm with you. Plus, Hani's my sister. It's not like he's going to talk openly about her in front of me. He's never done it once when I'm around, but I'm sure you two have spoken about it."

"Not that much," I said.

"Come on. You don't really expect me to believe that, do you?"

"Okay, it's come up a few times, but I don't see him nearly as much as I used to now that we live here. I usually just see him at the bar, and then we mainly talk about the business. It's not like he sits me down and says, 'These are the five things I don't like about Hani.'"

"So, there's five things?" she asked.

"No. It's just a number I pulled out of the air."

"Interesting that 'five' is the number you would pick."

"It's just a number. It doesn't mean anything."

"Sure it does. You could have said one or two, but you said five. Somewhere in your brain you think there are several reasons to dislike my sister."

"Why do I feel like a criminal you're interrogating?" I asked.

"We're just having a conversation."

"If you say so."

"You never answered my original question, though."

"I don't even remember what it was."

"Did Foxx abandon Hani?" she asked.

"I did answer it. I said I thought it would be a bad idea for them to give it another go when it seems clear they won't make it. You obviously disagree with me, though."

"I didn't say that."

"You didn't have to. It's pretty clear from your tone. You're judging him, and that's your right."

"I didn't say he abandoned her."

"No, but you did repeat your mother's comments, and I got the distinct feeling that you might think that, too. Maybe I'm wrong, though. It wouldn't be the first time."

"I think I was so shocked when Hani told me she was pregnant. I just assumed she and Foxx would give it another go. I didn't expect him to shut it down so quickly."

"Do you think he's not going to be there for the child? I assure you he will."

"I know he will," she said.

"Then why all the talk about abandonment, even if it started with your mother's concerns?" I asked.

Alana looked away, and it was obvious she was passing the interrogation she'd gotten from her mother onto me. I didn't like it one bit, but I was also keenly aware that this conversation could easily lead to a serious argument between us that could last for days. On reflection, I should have immediately dropped to my knees and begged forgiveness. Instead, I decided to dig a deeper hole for myself to crawl out of. Maybe my nickname should be "Moron" instead of Poe.

"What else did your mother say?" I asked.

"She wants us to hire Hani."

"Hire her? For what? To work at Harry's?"

"No. She thinks she should be our wedding planner. I told her I'd let the last one go and hadn't had time to look for another one."

"Okay, so you want me to be the bad cop and tell your mother no?" I asked.

"I already said yes."

"You said yes to hiring Hani?" I asked, since I was utterly convinced I hadn't heard what I'd clearly just heard.

"She's all alone and needs something to do. Hani's great at stuff like this. I'm not, and don't worry. I've already told her not to break the bank."

"You've talked to Hani about this?"

"Right before you got back. We had a brief conversation about it."

I thought about asking Alana if she'd reconsider an earlier suggestion I'd made about eloping to Las Vegas or just doing a simple Justice of the Peace ceremony in town. This wedding was supposed to be a celebration of our union, but it had turned into an ordeal that was beyond stressful. I was actually beginning to worry we wouldn't survive the pressure and make it to the altar. I'm sure I'm not the only one who has had those fears just before their wedding.

"How did your interview with David Lee Roth go?" Alana asked.

It took me a second to realize she was comparing the Van Halen singer to Gabriel Reed. Come to think of it, they did kind of look alike, at least in the hair department. I did appreciate her attempt at levity, and maybe this was her way of stopping our potential argument. Perhaps, she'd seen it coming, too. I gave Alana my rundown of the conversation, including Gabriel's claims that Liam had followed him multiple times, as well as his assertion that Nalani had said nothing about getting back together with her husband.

"He told me the same basic stuff," she said.

"Sounds like he has a consistent story then."

"Did you believe him?" Alana asked.

"I did. So what does that mean for Liam Hayes? Will you arrest him soon?"

"I met with the D.A. earlier today. She said we don't have enough to make an arrest."

"You're still convinced he did it, though?" I asked.

"Aren't you?"

"Maybe. It definitely doesn't look good for him."

"You don't know this guy like I do. He's capable of it."

I hadn't seen any of the crime scene photos, but it wasn't hard to imagine what Nalani looked like after having been stabbed multiple times with a corkscrew. I wasn't sure who would be capable of such a thing, but I also knew from experience that there were demented people out there.

I told Alana I was going to head upstairs to my home office and make notes about my conversation with Gabriel. I did that after each interview since it was always good to be able to reflect on their words at a later date. It was also my source material for these books. The biggest benefit, at least on this night, would be that it would take me more than an hour to jot my notes down. Hopefully, that would be enough time for both Alana and I to cool down from our talk.

8

THE CO-WORKER

I DECIDED MY NEXT STEP WAS TO MEET WITH SOMEONE WHO MIGHT BE able to verify some of Liam's claims and see how sincere their answers sounded. Liam had provided me with Mason Howard's phone number. If you recall, Mason is the friend and former co-worker who allowed Liam to stay with him after Nalani gave him the boot from their marital home.

I'd called Mason just after Alana had dropped the bomb on me that she'd asked Hani to be our wedding planner. Let me ask you something: If you were me, would you have been bothered by that? It wasn't like she'd gone out and hired some insanely expensive wedding planner who was about to bankrupt us, but I did think it was a decision that she should have run by me, even if it was just a formality.

It was yet another reminder that marriage was going to change our relationship in some ways that I hadn't anticipated. Hani was Alana's sister, so I never thought I could easily dismiss her since she was someone close to Alana. During the dating phase, though, Hani was just the nutty and self-absorbed sister of a girlfriend. Now, she was going to be my sister, too, or at least my sister-in-law. Legally, she and I were family, and that little epiphany ran chills through my body.

I couldn't very well complain that I didn't want a member of the family touching my wedding with a ten-foot pole. I was already having nightmares about having to listen to Hani throw in little digs about Foxx in between discussions about flowers and the song list for the reception. Speaking of that, Alana had already nixed almost all of my suggestions for the list since she said I had picked songs that would clear the dance floor. I know you've heard me joke before that I viewed myself as a prop for the wedding. Apparently, my little joke had turned into reality.

The discussion about Hani as our wedding planner was the main reason I'd fled the conversation with Alana and telephoned Mason. I wanted something to distract me from the oncoming hurricane that was Hani, even if that distraction was a gruesome murder investigation. I'd caught Mason at work since he was the night manager for the hotel. He agreed to meet with me the following night. My preparation for the interview the following day consisted of my usual routine of swimming laps in the pool, going for a long jog around the neighborhood, and taking the dog for a walk. It was an exhausting day, but such is the life of a guy living on Maui. I still can't believe I even considered staying in Virginia at one point.

The hotel was located in Kihei, as many hotels are. It's on the southside of the island and almost always has sunny skies and warm temperatures. The downside is that it's a long drive from my house in Kaanapali. I arrived at the hotel on time, though, and asked the reception desk clerk if he could let Mason know I was there. He picked up a walkie-talkie that was behind the desk and called Mason. I heard Mason say on the other end that he would be down in a moment.

The elevator doors opened five minutes later, and Mason came out to greet me. He looked to be in his mid-to-late forties. He was a little on the short side, maybe five-foot-seven. His round body seemed to emphasize his lack of height. We shook hands, and he suggested that we have our conversation in the hotel bar. I found it an odd location to talk about such a sensitive subject, but the bar was almost empty when we entered. There was only one person there, who was engrossed in the sporting event playing on the television screen behind the bar.

Mason led me to a table near the back of the room. It was by a window that overlooked the front parking lot. It was terrible as far as views go, but I assumed they'd given the best ones to the hotel rooms that people were willing to shell out big bucks for.

"Liam told me he hired you to investigate his wife's death," Mason said.

You and I know that's not technically true. I wondered if Liam had used the word "hired," and it was just another one of his lies. Perhaps, it was just an innocent assumption Mason had made when Liam had introduced the subject of talking to me about the case. I decided to let it slide and get to my main interview questions.

"How long have you known Liam?" I asked.

"We met here at the hotel, maybe six or seven years ago. I don't remember the exact time. The years seem to roll into each other."

It was an unfortunate observation I'd made myself. The years fly by the older you get.

"Liam said he was an event planner and you're the night manager. Is that correct?" I asked.

Mason nodded.

"Liam mostly worked days, but many events take place at night, so there were a lot of opportunities for us to work together."

"What kind of events did he plan?"

"Wedding receptions, small business conferences. Things like that. He was responsible for marketing the hotel for these events, and he'd also help manage them when they were booked."

"Sounds like a busy job," I said.

"It is, but most jobs in the hotel industry are like that. You work a ton of hours."

"Liam said he was let go. What happened?"

"He didn't tell you?" Mason asked.

"No. He just said that he'd lost his job. He didn't tell me the details."

"Why does it matter?"

"It doesn't, really. I was just curious. It never hurts to learn as much as you can about your clients and everyone who's involved."

I wasn't sure if Mason bought that excuse. I paused and waited to see if he'd give me a reason for Liam's dismissal. He didn't immediately respond, but then he spoke. Maybe it was an attempt to end the uncomfortable silence in our conversation.

"Tourism is down on Maui. The events really dropped off, so they had to cut costs somewhere. I felt really bad for him."

"It was pretty nice of you to offer him a place to stay when he and Nalani broke up. That must have been a real inconvenience," I said.

"It was no trouble. We were on different schedules anyway. We hardly saw each other."

"He wasn't there during the day?"

"I wasn't keeping track of him since I sleep during the day, but he was gone most afternoons."

"Do you have any idea where he'd go? Did your paths ever cross in the late afternoon or early evening?"

"I guess I just assumed he was out looking for work. Like I said, we didn't see each other much."

"Did he tell you that he and Nalani had decided to get back together?"

"He mentioned something about it. I wasn't really sure exactly what was going on."

"You didn't know what he was doing then when he moved out of your place?"

"No, I knew. It's just that he brought it up before, but nothing came of it. It seemed like they were going to get back together, then they weren't. I couldn't keep it straight sometimes," Mason said.

"Did Liam ever talk about the guy Nalani was seeing?"

"Not much. He just said that she was having an affair. I don't even know the guy's first name. I don't think Liam ever mentioned it."

"Just one more question. Liam said he went to see Nalani at their house. That's when he found her body in the kitchen. He said he came back to your house later that day to get his things and pack. Why didn't he just stay with you?"

"I told him he could. I saw him right before I was leaving for work."

"How did he break the news to you about Nalani?" I asked.

"It was terrible. He told me how he'd found her. That's when I said he could stay with me as long as he needed. I figured he wouldn't want to be alone, but he said no. He packed his things and left. I didn't speak to him again until he called me about your investigation."

"You've been of tremendous help. I really appreciate your time."

"That's all you need?" Mason asked.

"That's it. I think I might stick around and have a drink or two. Do you mind?"

"Of course not. The first one's on the house."

Mason led me over to the bar and told the bartender to get me whatever I wanted. He then said goodbye and headed back toward the elevators. I turned to the bartender. I wasn't really thirsty. I just wanted an excuse to stick around for a few more minutes.

"What can I get you?" the bartender asked.

"Do you know Liam Hayes?"

"Sure. I've known him for a couple of years."

"Do you know why he got fired?" I asked.

"Why do you want to know?"

I reached into my wallet and removed five twenty-dollar bills. I placed them on the bar in front of me.

"Two things: why did Liam get fired, and don't say a word of this to Mason."

"I saw the whole thing. Happened just a few minutes before my shift started. The guy totally lost it. He started screaming something about his old lady and this guy she's banging. He did it right there in the lobby in front of a ton of guests. The general manager fired him on the spot."

"Thanks," I said, and I slid him the money.

I exited the hotel and walked back to my car. I did a quick recap in my mind. Mason had clearly lied to me about the reason for Liam's dismissal. I had a pretty good idea that he'd been lying from the start since I hadn't heard anything about Maui suffering a drop in tourism. I'd initially chalked up Mason's fib to the fact that he wanted to cover for his friend, but then as the conversation went on, I really started to suspect it was a flat-out lie for ulterior motives.

There was also the B.S. about Liam being gone all day and Mason having no idea where he was. I doubted Liam was out looking for jobs as Mason had suggested. It seemed like most searches for that kind of job would be done over the internet or phone and not in person, unless it was an actual scheduled job interview. It seemed more and more likely that Liam was spending the days tailing Gabriel and Nalani, as our favorite photographer had said during his interview.

What did you make of Mason saying Liam never talked about Gabriel? The guy had a nervous breakdown at his place of employment, but he's not going to talk about it with a friend who is close enough to let him move into his house? That hardly seems likely. My bet is that Liam spent every moment he could complaining to Mason about the long-haired photographer who was having sex with his wife. Mason had to have known it made Liam look terrible, and it was yet another lie that Mason had told me. Maybe he assumed I'm just some gullible imbecile who would believe anything he said.

Of course, Mason wasn't the only one who tossed out a lie during our conversation. I'm sure you thought I had royally fouled up the chain of events when I described how Liam had found his wife dead and then returned to Mason's place to pack his belongings. I made the strategic decision that Mason would have just assumed I was repeating whatever Liam told me, and he was determined to vouch for his friend, whether it was the truth or not. It certainly confirmed that Liam had lied to me about moving back in with Nalani on the day she was murdered.

I felt pretty confident reporting to Alana that I was now utterly convinced that everything Liam Hayes had told me was a lie. Did that mean he killed his wife? It wasn't enough proof to convict him, at least I didn't think it was. There was only one conclusion to make, though. He was clearly hiding something, and the only thing I could think of was the truth about his wife's murder. The guy was so mad with jealousy that he'd acted like a raving lunatic and had followed his wife and her lover all over the island. It didn't take much of a stretch of the imagination to mentally picture him stabbing his wife with a corkscrew. Now all I had to do was help Alana prove it. Of course, that was easier said than done.

9

THE FRIEND

I WAS HALFWAY BACK TO THE HOUSE WHEN I RECEIVED A TELEPHONE call from Kaylee King. I'd called her a couple of days ago after Liam had given me her name as someone who could confirm that he and Nalani had gotten back together. She'd actually been the person that I'd called after my initial phone conversation with Mason. I hadn't gotten a hold of her, but I'd left a voicemail.

She gave me some vague excuse about being busy with something as the reason of her delayed return call. It didn't matter to me since I'd just assumed she didn't want to be interviewed, which I got. I certainly wouldn't be thrilled about it if I were in her shoes. She surprised me by asking if we could meet that night. It was already approaching eight o'clock, but I agreed to the meeting anyway. I really wanted to get as many perspectives on the case before sitting down with Alana again.

Unfortunately, Kaylee lived near Kihei, so I had to do a quick U-turn and head back to the area where I'd just left. I got to her apartment about thirty minutes later. It was a small complex with maybe fifteen to twenty units. I think the word I'd use to describe the place is "modest." It wasn't scary by any means, but it definitely wasn't nice either. I felt a little weird about driving my BMW into the parking lot since it was a decidedly nicer car than anything else there.

Kaylee told me that she lived in apartment 302, so I climbed a set of outdoor metal stairs that resembled something you'd see at a road-side motel. She must have been watching for me because she opened the door right as I walked up to it.

She looked about Alana's age, which would put her in her early to mid-thirties. I guessed her height around five-foot-seven or eight. She had dark-brown hair that fell just short of her shoulders. She had a beautiful face and a curvaceous body, and I did my best not to imme-diately look her up and down. I don't know why, but I wasn't expecting someone so attractive to open the door. I didn't assume she would be ugly. I guess I just didn't think about it, and I was caught completely by surprise when someone who could easily pass for a swimsuit model was suddenly standing in front of me.

"Hello, I'm Poe. Thanks for meeting with me."

"Of course. Please come in," she said.

Kaylee led me into her apartment. The door opened up into a medium-sized living room that was tastefully decorated. I saw a tiny kitchen in the back of the apartment. There was a hallway to the right side of the kitchen, which I assumed led to the back bedroom and bathroom. I sat down on a plush burgundy chair that was positioned to the side of a matching sofa. Kaylee sat on the side of the sofa that was closest to my chair.

"I was surprised when you called. I didn't think anyone was going to get around to talking with me," she continued.

"What do you mean? The police haven't spoken with you?" I asked.

"No, not a word. Are you working with them or did Liam hire you? He called me and said you might be contacting me."

"I work with Liam's attorney, so I guess you could say I'm helping her more than anyone else."

That wasn't exactly true, as you know, but I was worried she might clam up if I told her everything she said would almost certainly be repeated to the cops, or at least one cop in particular.

"How long did you know Nalani?" I asked.

"Since we were kids. I lived down the street from her, and we went to the same school."

"Does that mean you've know Liam almost as long?"

"We didn't meet him until high school. His dad was in the military, and they got transferred to Oahu. I think his dad ended up retiring a couple of years after that and then they moved to Maui."

"So, you were probably around for the entire relationship between Liam and Nalani?" I said.

"I was actually with her when she first met him. We were at the movie theater when she saw him. I remember because she'd told me he was cute, and then he showed up at our school the next day. She was so embarrassed."

Kaylee laughed as she remembered the event.

"Why was she embarrassed?" I asked.

"I'm not sure, really. I think she thought that he'd caught her staring at him, and then all of a sudden he was sitting near her in homeroom. She couldn't even look at him that first week."

"Did they start dating in high school?"

"Just for a short time. They didn't get serious until after school," Kaylee said.

"How old were they when they got married?"

"Nalani was twenty-four or twenty-five. I can't remember which."

"Were you happy for her, or did you not like Liam?"

"You're talking about the time he hurt her?" she guessed.

"I've heard mixed things about the story. I'm wondering if it was just an accident like some people say."

"How much of this are you sharing with Liam?"

"None, if you ask me not to. I'm under no agreement with him to report anything you say."

"Nalani never said if she thought it was an accident or not. I know she blamed herself for it."

"Why is that?" I asked.

"Because she'd cheated on him. She felt horrible about it. I think that's the main reason she got back together with him."

I wasn't sure if that made sense to me or not, but I pushed past it and continued with my questions.

"Was their early marriage good, or did they always have issues?"

"They had a weird relationship. It was like a roller coaster. He would be the best thing in the world one day. She couldn't stand him the next. I'm surprised they lasted as long as they did."

"Did you know about the affair between Nalani and Gabriel Reed?" I asked.

"Of course. She told me about him as soon as the relationship started."

"How long did it go on before Liam found out?"

"I don't remember exactly how long, but it was well over a year," she said.

"Liam told me it had only been going on for a few months."

"That's what she told him. Liam thinks he knew her, but he didn't. Not really. Nalani had other affairs that he didn't even know about. He still doesn't know about them."

"Were any of these guys still in the picture? Do you think they might have wanted to hurt her?" I asked.

"There was one guy. I never liked him."

"Who was he?"

"He had something to do with her brother's company. That's how she met him. Their affair didn't last long. I think he kind of freaked her out."

"What was his name?"

"It was Bryan. I don't remember his last name. Koa might."

"That's her brother, is that right?" I asked.

"Yeah. How is he by the way? I haven't spoken to him since Nalani died."

"I haven't met with Koa yet, but I'm sure he's torn up about it. Liam told me that he and Nalani had decided to give their marriage another try, but I also heard she was still meeting with Gabriel up until the night before she died. Did she ever tell you she was getting back with Liam?"

"She said they were thinking about it, but I hadn't heard for sure.

It wouldn't surprise me, though. She couldn't keep away from him for long. It was like they were addicted to each other."

"Do you think there was a chance she might have gotten back with Liam but might also have been trying to keep the affair going with Gabriel?" I asked.

"I could see her doing that. I hate saying this about my friend, but Nalani loved the chase. She couldn't get enough of guys pursuing her. I don't know if it was a low self-esteem thing or what. Liam was never going to be enough for her, but I don't think he ever got that. Nobody was ever going to be enough, not even this Gabriel guy."

"Speaking of him, did she get along with him up until the end? Do you know if she ever considered fully leaving Liam for Gabriel?"

"She liked him at first. She told me she found his confidence a turn-on, especially since that wasn't like Liam at all. Then she found out that it wasn't confidence. It was arrogance. She said she couldn't believe how self-absorbed he was."

That made sense, I thought. A lot of artists are that way. It's all about their work and nothing else. It's a tough trait to have if you're going to be in a relationship with another person. It also sounded like a terrible characteristic to have if the woman you're seeing is obsessed with you fawning all over her, as Nalani apparently was.

"Did they get in fights about that?" I asked.

"I don't know. I just know she wasn't happy about it. That's another reason I wasn't shocked when she said she might have been going back to Liam. She knew the Gabriel thing wasn't going to last. Liam was always the fallback guy."

I couldn't think of any more questions to ask, so I decided to wrap up the interview. I thanked Kaylee for her time and said I hoped she'd be willing to talk to me if I needed further clarification on something. She said she would. We stood, and she walked me over to the front door.

"Do you know if Alana is the one who has this case?"

"Yes, she does," I said.

I hadn't told Kaylee about my relationship with Alana since I tried not to throw that around when I interviewed people during these cases. I thought it might come out as pretentious, and I also didn't see how it would encourage people to open up to me.

"We all grew up together on the same street. We were best friends for a long time," Kaylee said.

"Are you still friends with the detective?" I asked.

"Not really. We drifted apart once Nalani and Liam got married. Alana wasn't happy about it, and Nalani said she made her choose between Alana and Liam."

"That didn't affect you, though," I pointed out.

"Maybe not, but I just felt weird trying to walk that line between Alana and Nalani. Do you know Alana?"

"I've met her," I said.

"I heard she landed the big one."

"What do you mean?" I asked.

"She's engaged to some rich guy from the east coast. It's funny how things turn out like that."

"How so?" I asked.

I immediately tried to figure out how Kaylee had heard what she'd heard. Yeah, Maui is a small island, but I don't go around throwing my money at everyone. I'm also the kind of guy who wears T-shirts every day. I don't exactly ooze money, at least as far as my appearance goes. Apparently, people were talking, though. I suppose gossip is an unstoppable force.

"Alana never cared about money, but it's all Nalani ever wanted. Alana got it, and Nalani never did."

"Do you know the rich guy's name?" I asked.

"I heard it once. Some funny-sounding name."

I smiled.

"Thanks again for meeting with me, Kaylee."

"Sure thing. What was your name again? Was it Poe?"

"Some people call me that. Why don't you call me by my real name: Edgar Rutherford?"

I could instantly see the look of recognition in her eyes.

"I know," I said. "It is a funny-sounding name."

I smiled again and exited her apartment. I didn't hear her door shut until I was halfway down the staircase. I suspected she was probably mad at me for not immediately telling her my connection to Alana, but I didn't care. If anything, it would give her something juicy to gossip about. How would she paint me, though? Would I be handsome or ugly, charming or obnoxious? I guess it didn't matter.

I walked over to my car, climbed inside, and backed out of the parking spot. I thought I caught a glimpse of Kaylee looking at me through the window. No doubt the BMW convertible only added to the rumor of Alana landing – how had she referred to me – "The Big One?" As far as the rumor mills went, it wasn't a bad thing to be called.

I did my best to collect all of my thoughts on the interviews with Mason and Kaylee as I made my way back to Kaanapali. The two interviews had contradicted each other on multiple fronts, and I was, unfortunately, back to my original starting place of not knowing whether or not Liam Hayes murdered his wife.

I did find Kaylee's comments about Nalani quite interesting. The woman sounded like a vain and deeply flawed person. She certainly didn't deserve the terrible fate that befell her, but a personality like that could easily attract numerous men who might want to do her harm after she inevitably rejected them once she got bored.

Alana and I were definitely going to have a lot to talk about once I got home, but I decided not to mention anything to Alana regarding Kaylee's comments on our relationship and the superficial judgment she'd bestowed on it. Nothing good could come from me repeating her words to Alana, and as they say, "Haters gonna hate."

10

THE WEDDING PLANNER

I SAW HANI'S CAR PARKED IN MY DRIVEWAY AS I ARRIVED BACK AT THE house. I parked on the street so I wouldn't block her vehicle. I didn't have the same aversion to Hani as I did to her mother, but I still considered driving back to Harry's and killing some time. I knew what her presence meant. I was in for a fun-filled evening of wedding planning.

I walked inside the house, and the dog didn't immediately run up to me. I assumed Alana had let him run around the backyard, or perhaps he'd escaped to the upstairs to avoid Hani as well. The dog simply didn't like her, which was saying something.

"Hey, Poe," Hani said.

I walked over to Hani and Alana, who were both sitting around the kitchen table. It was covered with brochures, color swatches, and fabric samples. Yep, I'd walked into wedding hell. I tried to judge the look on Alana's face to get an indication of how the night was going. She had a serious look, but I couldn't tell if that meant she was miserable or just concentrating on all of the choices before her. At least she wasn't yelling at the wedding planner and tossing her out of the house, so we had that going for us this evening.

I walked over to the kitchen island and placed my keys on the countertop.

"How did the interview with Mason go?" Alana asked.

"It wasn't just him. Kaylee King called me, so I went over to her apartment after I met Mason at the hotel."

It wasn't hard to catch the look Hani shot Alana. It wasn't so much an eye roll as it was that look you give when someone you think is a scumbag walks into the room. It was a combination of a head lean and then an eye shift where she sort of looked down to the ground and then back up to Alana. I don't know how women do that. I'd probably put myself in traction if I were to try that maneuver.

"You were at her apartment?" Alana asked.

"What did you think of her?" Hani asked before I could answer Alana's question.

I didn't understand the tone in Alana's voice when she asked about Kaylee's apartment. It wasn't like I'd gone there to sleep with her. Alana knew I conducted these interviews all over the place, mainly because that's what she did as a detective. Was there something going on with Kaylee that I didn't know about?

"I didn't really form an opinion about her. We talked about what she knew regarding Liam and Nalani getting back together."

"You must have formed some opinion about her," Hani said.

"She told me you guys grew up together, so I'm guessing there's something going on here that you're really getting at," I said.

Hani turned to Alana.

"Should you tell him or should I?" Hani asked.

"Tell me what?" I asked, and I joined them at the table.

"What did she say about Liam and Nalani?" Alana asked.

"She said Nalani hadn't specifically mentioned that she'd taken Liam back, but Kaylee also said that she wouldn't have been surprised. Apparently, Nalani was bored with her affair with Gabriel and had considered going back to her husband. Is that what she told you when you met with her?"

"I didn't talk to her," Alana said.

"Why not?" I asked.

"I can tell you why," Hani said, and she did another one of those things with her head and eyes.

I expected Alana to jump in after that comment, but she didn't. She went back to reviewing the brochures.

"You can't believe a word out of that woman's mouth," Hani continued.

I found her observation about Kaylee a bit on the hypocritical side since Hani wasn't exactly the beacon of truth and honesty. Nevertheless, that didn't mean she had it wrong in this case. Maybe Kaylee had lied to me the entire evening.

"Is that what you think, too?" I asked Alana.

"She's been known to lie before. That's why I didn't talk to her. What did Mason say?"

I filled her in on that interview. Alana confirmed that Mason had made similar comments to her, which only served to reinforce the prevailing theory that Liam had lied to both of us. I also told Alana about my brief talk with the hotel bartender and how he'd described Liam's outburst which had led to his dismissal from his job. I left out the part of how I'd convinced the bartender to provide me with that information.

"Just makes Liam look more and more guilty, doesn't it?" Alana asked.

"It doesn't look good for him," I admitted.

"That's all well and good, but let's get back to this," Hani said, and she indicated the stack of wedding stuff on the kitchen table.

I pulled a few of the brochures closer to me. They all featured various hotels and their spaces for weddings and receptions.

"Are these the top contenders?" I asked.

"Yes. Alana and I narrowed it down to those three hotels. Two are here in Kaanapali. One is in Wailea. The ones in Kaanapali have the advantage of being close to you guys, but I think the one in Wailea is a bit nicer. That one is also willing to give you a discount if you book more than twenty rooms."

I wasn't sure we'd be booking any rooms since I'd assumed all of the guests were Maui residents. I knew I hadn't planned on inviting anyone from Virginia, but maybe Alana had a guest list that was growing by the second. I looked at the brochure for the one in Wailea. It was the same hotel where I'd conducted the short case for Ms. Portendorfer. Maybe that was a bad omen.

"Well, we know this one will be expensive," I said.

"I have news for you, Poe. They're all expensive. Try not to concentrate on the budget, though. It's your wedding. It only happens once," Hani said.

If everything goes according to plan, I thought. I'm sure no one goes into their wedding assuming the ceremony will ultimately be a practice run for the next person they marry after their first divorce. Yeah, that's a morbid thought to have, but Ms. Portendorfer's adultery and news of Nalani's multiple affairs had left me with a negative view of the current status of marriage in our country. There was also Hani's comments about not worrying about the budget. I had mentioned more than once that I wanted Alana to have the wedding of her dreams. Now I was realizing that was a really dumb thing to say, especially with her sister as the wedding planner. Hani had expensive taste, especially when someone else was footing the bill.

"Is there one that jumps out?" I asked.

"I like this one. Alana likes the other," Hani said.

Apparently Alana liked one of the hotels in Kaanapali, while Hani favored the five-star resort in Wailea.

"Whatever Alana wants is good with me," I said.

"Can you go over the reception plans with him? There are a couple of quick calls I need to make," Alana said.

She stood and walked upstairs. I looked down again at all of the material on the table.

"I can't believe you pulled all of this together in just a day," I said.

"What do you mean?"

"This stuff. I can't believe you did this in just 24 hours."

"No, I didn't. I've been working on this for over a week. You'd be surprised how long it takes for people to call you back. You'd think they'd be anxious to talk to you since you're bringing them business, but I really had to stay on top of them."

"Your mother asked you to plan the wedding more than a week ago?"

"No. Alana asked me."

Hani must have noticed the look on my face because then she asked, "Oh, is that not what you were told?"

"No."

"Do you not want me to plan it?" Hani asked.

"I'm fine with it. You'll do great, and thank you for taking it on. I'm sure it's not easy, especially when the customer is a relative."

"Speaking of that, is there any way you can pay me half my fee upfront?"

"I don't even know what your fee is," I said.

She told me, and it was instantly obvious that I wasn't getting the friends and family discount.

"Will you take a personal check?" I asked.

"Of course," she said.

Apparently, she hadn't picked up on the sarcasm in my voice. I looked back at the stairs. Alana still hadn't come down. I turned back to Hani.

"Can I ask you something, but I need you to keep this from Alana?"

I saw Hani smile. If there's one thing she liked, it was secrets, especially when Alana wasn't in on them.

"Sure. You can ask me anything."

"Kaylee made some comments about Alana that were on a personal level."

"Like what?"

I told Hani about the "Landing the Big One" comment and the other references Kaylee had made regarding people gossiping about our financial situation.

"People love to talk, but you already knew that," Hani said.

"I don't care what they say about me, but does Alana know what they're saying?"

"Alana's not stupid."

"Of course she's not, but that doesn't have anything to do with whether she's heard these things or not."

"She has."

"Do you know that for certain, or are you just guessing?" I asked.

"We've talked about it, so, yes, I do know for certain."

"When did you talk about it?"

"Just before you bought this house."

"What about this house?" I asked.

"Just look around you, Poe. This place is breathtaking. It's not like people aren't going to notice, especially when everyone knows who you bought it from. It screams money. You have to know that."

As a side note, Alana and I had purchased the home from a famous professional athlete, whose name I refuse to utter for a variety of reasons.

"I don't want Alana to be miserable here," I said.

"She's not. She loves this house. It's just going to take her a while to get used to having nice things. We had nothing growing up. Now, all of a sudden, she's living in something like this. It just takes time to adjust."

"Is she going to lose friends over this?"

"If someone doesn't want to be her friend because she's successful, then what kind of a friend are they?" Hani asked.

"What about your mother? Is that why she doesn't like me?"

"My mother doesn't trust men, period, not after what my father did to her. It wouldn't matter if you were rich or poor, tall or short, old or young, she'll always be watching you out of the corner of her eye. That's just how she is. Don't let it get to you."

That was easier said than done, I thought.

"What about your father? Alana hasn't mentioned anything about him coming to the wedding," I said.

"That's because she doesn't want him there. I wouldn't bring it up if I was you."

"Does he even know she's getting married? Did your mother mention anything to him?"

"I doubt she has since she doesn't want him there, either. They rarely communicate anyway. She still hasn't forgiven him."

"What about you and Alana? Have you guys forgiven him?" I asked.

"I was really young when he left, so I don't remember him very well. Alana was older, though. It really hit her hard. Then we had to move in with Nalani and her family. It was tough, but we all grew really close. That's why Nalani's rejection of Alana was so hard. I can't believe she's gone. It just doesn't seem real."

"Do you think Liam did it?"

"I don't know, but if Alana does, then I'd probably go along with it. She's usually right about those things."

I tended to agree with that comment, but there was Alana's investigation of Foxx during my first trip to Maui. She was convinced she'd landed the guilty party then, too, and she'd gotten it wrong. I decided to shift the topic back to the wedding.

"So what does Alana really want? I'm good for anything. Does she want a big wedding? A small one?"

"I'm not sure. It's tough getting an answer out of her," Hani said.

"That's because they're big decisions, guys," Alana said.

Hani and I both turned to see Alana walking down the stairs.

"What about you, Poe? Which hotel do you like most?" Alana continued.

"The same one you like, of course."

"Then it's settled. I'll call the manager tomorrow and book it," Hani said.

She stood and then turned to me.

"Can I get that check before I leave?" she asked.

"Sure. Just give me a moment."

I climbed the stairs to my home office and wrote the huge check for the amount that Alana had apparently agreed to without my consent. I wasn't sure if this was a harbinger of things to come, or if she was just making snap decisions because she was stressed about the wedding and the investigation into the death of her former friend.

I thought I heard something move behind me, and I turned around to see Maui the dog stretching his back and yawning at the same time. I guessed he'd been hiding in my office all this time. What did I tell you before? He just doesn't like Hani.

"How are you doing, buddy?" I asked, and I bent over to scratch him behind his ears.

"What do you make of this wedding? Am I going to survive it?" I asked.

Maui yawned a second time. I guessed I was boring him.

11

GABRIEL

I sent Hani a text after Alana had gone to bed and asked her for the home address she and Alana had as a child. Sure, I could have asked Alana for that information, but then I would have had to answer a whole host of questions that I didn't want to get into with her.

The next morning Alana and I had a brief conversation about the wedding before she left for work. We spoke about some of the options Hani had given us. She said she was rethinking her decision on which hotel to use and was now considering the resort in Wailea. It didn't really matter to me, but I smiled and told her I thought it was a great idea. I didn't bring up the fact that I'd busted her when I learned she'd hired Hani much sooner than she'd let on. I was also still smarting from the sizable check I'd written my future sister-in-law, who I now realized was going to constantly be asking me for money in the years to come.

Something interesting happened, though, just as Alana opened the garage door to go out to her car. She turned back to me and said, "I have a confession to make. I actually asked Hani to plan our wedding a week ago."

"Was it still your mother's idea?" I asked, and I debated whether or not to let her know that I already knew that.

"She'd mentioned to me several times that Hani needed something to do. I asked her what she was really getting at, and that's when she brought up the wedding planner thing. She thought it would be a good distraction. I hesitated at first because I wasn't sure how you'd respond."

"Why didn't you just ask me?"

"It's a sensitive topic. You know that. Then there's all this tension between Hani and Foxx. I feel like they're making us pick sides. Don't get me wrong. I don't think they're doing it on purpose, but it's still happening."

"That crossed my mind as well, but I'm not sure what to do about it," I said.

"We need to figure out how to shut this down. It's only going to get worse after their child is born."

"What are we supposed to do?"

"Maybe we should have a group talk. Explain our position to them."

"Maybe, but that might not make much of a difference, and it might put them on the defensive if we're all in the same room. Maybe I should just talk to Foxx separately, and you talk to Hani."

"There's something else. I'm pretty upset that Hani asked you for money. That was never part of the discussion, and I'm going to ask for that check back. I'd just assumed she was doing it for free. I never would have charged her if it was the other way around."

I thought about saying that was because Alana had manners and class, but I knew she was already well aware of the personality differences between herself and her younger sister. I also thought about telling her that I found it beyond ironic that her mother had a problem with me because of my wealth, but she was apparently okay with Hani soaking me for money. Of course, there was nothing to be gained from saying any of this. Even though Alana probably agreed with me on all of these points, they were still her family, and my comments would do nothing but blow up in my face.

The end result of this pre-work discussion was that Alana and I agreed to become a united front once again. I told Alana not to worry about the money. I would pay Hani. She would deliver a spectacular wedding in return. Years from now, all we would remember was the fun we had at the event, at least that's how I hoped it would end up. Alana thanked me for my understanding, and I was glad that I'd scored major points with my wife-to-be.

After Alana left, I did my usual routine of swimming laps in the pool, taking the dog for a walk, and going for a long jog around the neighborhood. I really didn't have much planned for the day. The murder investigation had hit a bit of a snag, and I thought I'd spend the day just processing the information I'd learned. I knew I still needed to meet with Nalani's brother and sister-in-law, but I hadn't yet figured out my line of questioning for them. The only tension there seemed to have been between Nalani and her brother was the business, and I didn't see how that could result in her brother killing her.

After my morning workout routine, I climbed into the convertible and headed for the childhood home of the Hu sisters. I'd known the general area where Alana had grown up, but she'd never taken me there before. I didn't think that odd, mainly because there hadn't been a reason for her to drive by the place while I was with her. Ms. Hu had moved from that house years earlier, and both Alana and Hani lived away from their old neighborhood as well.

It took me about forty-five minutes to get there from our home in Kaanapali. I found the house without much problem. It was a small house, as most houses on Maui are. The neighborhood wasn't great, and I could see how a kid from this street would dream of climbing to higher levels. I'd hit the jackpot in terms of financial success, and I hadn't really done anything to earn that reward. Did that make me feel guilty? Sometimes, and now I felt a little like a jerk for not realizing more of what Alana had been going through. I don't mean to imply that she's been moaning about having access to lots of money now. She hasn't been, but I also understood that she's been taking a lot of grief from longtime friends who were apparently turning on her.

There was a dead-end at the end of the road, so I proceeded down there to make the U-turn and head back to Kaanapali. I spotted a house with yellow crime scene tape placed across the front door as I was halfway through the turn. I stopped my car and then backed up several feet to get a better view of the scene.

It was too much of a coincidence not to be Nalani's house. I knew many parents in Hawaii passed their homes down to their kids since land was scarce and everything was so expensive. Maybe Nalani had inherited her house, which meant this was the place where she'd been killed. Alana had told me the general part of the island where the crime took place, but she hadn't bothered mentioning the specific street or even the neighborhood, nor had she mentioned that she'd actually lived in that house before. I didn't think to ask her, either. It was sloppy work on my part, and I chided myself for not being more attuned to the case.

I was about to drive off again when my cell phone vibrated. I looked at the display but didn't recognize the number.

"Hello," I said.

"Yes, this is Gabriel Reed. We met the other day."

"Of course, what can I do for you?"

"Would it be possible for you to come by my gallery this morning? There's something I'd like to talk to you about."

"No problem. Can I ask what it is you'd like to discuss?"

"It's about Nalani. There's something you need to know."

"Okay, but you can't tell me now?" I asked.

"I'd rather do this in person. I'll see you soon," he said, and he ended the call before I had the chance to comment further.

I thought about calling Alana and telling her about the unexpected phone call from Gabriel, but I didn't really have any information to report. I made the decision to phone her after my meeting. I put the car in drive and made the long journey back to Lahaina. I parked at Harry's since it was free, and the only spaces surrounding

Gabriel's shop were overpriced parking lots aimed at exploiting tourists. I made the short walk over and entered the gallery. It was empty, so I walked up to the counter and called to Gabriel since I assumed he was in the back room. I didn't get a reply, though. I walked back to the front door and exited the shop. I looked down the sidewalk in both directions but didn't see him anywhere.

I made the decision to wait inside the gallery for a few minutes since I assumed he'd made a run for coffee or something like that. He still hadn't arrived five minutes later, so I pulled out my phone and called him. I heard his phone ring a second after that. It was clearly coming from the back room.

"Gabriel?" I called out.

I didn't get a response, though. The phone continued to ring. He'd probably just left his phone on his desk, but I also had this weird feeling that suddenly ran through me. I walked around the counter and headed into the back room. It was a large open space that consisted of several metal shelves that lined three of the four walls. The shelves were covered with wooden frames and what I guessed were large printouts of his photography work. A wooden fold-out table, which was covered with stacks of papers and photography equipment, was placed in the middle of the room.

That wasn't the main thing that jumped out, though. That would have been Gabriel's body lying on the cement floor just beside the table. His neck was twisted at a weird angle, and his eyes bulged out at me in this hideous glare. I ran over to him and felt for a pulse. There wasn't one. Then I noticed an overturned step stool that was beside his legs. I've stood on those things before. They fold up so you can store them easily. Unfortunately, that also means they tend to be unstable and wobbly when you stand on them, so I made the assumption that Gabriel had been reaching for something on the upper shelves and had taken a nasty tumble that resulted in his head connecting with the concrete floor.

I called 911 and then phoned Alana. She actually got there a few minutes before the ambulance did. I'd taken the opportunity while I waited for her to look around the back room. I'd been careful not to touch anything for fear of disturbing a potential crime scene, as well as leaving my fingerprints everywhere and having myself listed as a suspect. The person who reported the crime was often the perpetrator, and I had no wish for some overzealous cop to arrest me. No, I didn't think Alana would do that to me, but it's not like she's the only detective on Maui. Did all of this mean I thought Gabriel's death had been anything but an accident? No, it certainly looked like he'd been the unfortunate victim of a flimsy stool.

I was standing by the front door of the gallery when Alana arrived. I walked her to the back room but didn't go in with her so she could be free to make her own examination. She came out a few minutes later.

"You didn't touch him, did you?" she asked.

"Just to check for a pulse. I didn't move his body. His neck was angled like that when I found him."

"Why were you even here?"

I told Alana about my earlier phone call from Gabriel.

"I called him after I got here. I'm sure you'll see my number on his call log. That's why I walked back there. I heard it ringing from out here."

"He didn't say what he wanted to talk about?" she asked.

"Just that it was about Nalani."

"Did he sound stressed or angry?"

"No. His voice seemed pretty normal," I said.

"Did he mention Liam?"

"No."

"When was the last time you saw him?"

"You mean Liam? You think he might have something to do with this?" I asked.

"Gabriel said he'd been following him."

"I haven't met with Liam since that day at Harry's when he gave me the list of people to speak to. I'd thought about calling him later today, though."

"Don't. Not yet, at least."

"You really suspect this was foul play?"

"It's probably not, but you never know. Gabriel calls you and says he has something important to talk about, then he has an accident in his back office? Maybe it's more than a coincidence," she said.

I thought she was stretching it a bit. Accidents happen, and they never occur at convenient times.

We heard the sirens of the ambulance a moment later. It pulled in front of the gallery, and two paramedics rushed out of the vehicle. I stepped aside as Alana led them to Gabriel's body. They confirmed what we both already knew. He was gone.

I left the photography gallery so Alana could do her job. I walked the short distance back to Harry's. It was around noon, and I realized I hadn't eaten anything yet that day. Still, I wasn't hungry. I couldn't get the image of Gabriel's lifeless eyes staring at me out of my mind.

I entered Harry's and was immediately accosted by Foxx near the entrance.

"Thanks a lot, buddy."

"What's wrong?" I asked.

"You didn't think to tell me that you guys had hired Hani to be your wedding planner?"

"How did you know that?"

"Because she just left here. She said that she and I were going to be working closely together since I'm the best man."

"That's ridiculous," I said.

"You set me up."

"I'll fix it. Don't worry, she won't be bothering you about any of this."

"Why would you hire her to begin with? I thought you were already working with that lady I referred you to."

Foxx was referencing a woman he'd met at our bar who did wedding planning for one of the hotels in Kaanapali. She was the one who Alana had let go. Apparently, I'd forgotten to mention that to Foxx.

"Hani just marched right in here like she owned the place. You should have seen her," Foxx continued.

"I'm sorry. I'll talk to Alana. I promise."

My apology seemed to work somewhat because Foxx stopped yelling at me and walked back to the bar. I waited a moment and then joined him.

"And another thing. How do I even know that I'm the best man? You've never even asked me," he said.

Yep, I was dropping the ball on multiple fronts.

"Who else would it be?" I asked.

"Maybe that damn dog of yours for all I know."

It was an interesting proposition, but I doubted Maui the dog could be counted on to not lose the rings.

I reached behind the bar and grabbed one of Foxx's favorite beers. I twisted the top off and then dropped to one knee.

"Douglas Foxx, would you make me the happiest man alive and agree to be my best man?" I asked.

"You look ridiculous," he said.

"Trust me. I feel even more ridiculous than I look."

I stood and handed him the beer as I sat back down on the barstool.

"What do you say? Will you do it?" I asked.

He took a long pull on the beer and then placed it on the bar.

"Only if I don't have to do any work with that woman."

"You mean the mother of your future child?"

"I can't believe I ever got involved with her. You tried to warn me," he said.

"I'm sorry, but do you mind repeating that? I'm not sure, but I think you just finally acknowledged that I did tell you to stay away from Hani."

"Don't press your luck. You're not my favorite person right now."

"Well, maybe you'll find it in your heart to forgive me soon. By the way, you'll never believe what I just saw."

I then told Foxx about the discovery of Gabriel's body in the back room of his gallery.

"He fell off his step stool?" Foxx asked.

"Looked that way to me."

"Damn, what a way to go."

I agreed that it was, and then I shifted the topic away from Hani and dead bodies to our business. Foxx told me about a new business promotion he'd thought of, and I immediately agreed that it was a great idea. Sometimes you have to handle best friends and future spouses the same way. Just say yes and give them a huge smile.

My stomach pains finally won out over the emotional trauma I'd experienced by finding Gabriel on that concrete floor, so I asked one of our waitresses for a burger and fries. I didn't know if it was a depressing notion that I could eat so soon after what I'd seen. Maybe I was just getting used to the sight of a dead body after doing a few of these investigations. It's amazing what the human brain can adjust to.

While I waited for my food, I got a text from Hani confirming that she'd booked the hotel in Kaanapali that Alana had said she'd wanted the night before. I texted her back and said that Alana was now leaning toward the five-star resort in Wailea. She wrote me and said that hotel was clearly the best choice and that she'd move forward with booking that one. The name of that hotel made me immediately think of Ms. Portendorfer. She was undoubtedly gone from Maui by now, but I wondered if she'd vowed to be faithful to her husband after the episode with the stolen ring. Probably not, I thought.

I left Harry's after eating my burger and fries and went home. I took Maui for a short walk, and then I decided to burn off the calories from lunch by going for an afternoon swim. I changed into my swim trunks and jumped into the pool. I did something really stupid on one of the lap turns and tried to do that flip thing you see the Olympic swimmers do on television. It always looks so cool and graceful. It also looks fairly straightforward. In reality, though, it's a pretty damn hard thing to do, especially as you're heading for the wall of the pool while swimming at full speed. I'm not exactly sure if I managed a full flip underwater. It kind of felt like a half-flip, and my legs and arms didn't do what my brain had clearly intended them to do. The end result was that my head crashed into the side of the pool. I was immediately dizzy from the blow, and I rushed to break the surface of the water.

My head throbbed, and my vision blurred. I reached for the top of my head to feel for the damage. When I pulled my hand away, I saw blood on my palm and fingers. I was about to crawl out of the pool and go tend to my wounds in the bathroom of the house when a thought occurred to me. There was no blood on the concrete floor in the back room of the photography gallery. I had a gusher from bumping my head on the wall of the pool. Gabriel had fallen from a few feet and collided with concrete, yet there were zero cuts on his head. Even if he'd landed on the side of his head or face, you'd still expect there to be scratches. Granted, he was lying on the floor when I'd found him. Maybe the scratches were underneath him.

Alana came home a couple of hours later. She found me on the sofa with an ice pack on my head.

"What happened to you?" she asked.

I told her about my little pool accident and then asked her if she'd been there when the paramedics turned Gabriel over to put him on the stretcher.

"Yeah, I was there."

"Was that side of his head bloody?" I asked.

"I don't think so, but I wasn't really looking at it closely."

"But don't you think there would have been blood around the head, either way?"

"So now you think it wasn't an accident?" she asked.

"Will a medical examiner look at him?"

"Of course. I already ordered it. It probably won't be for a few days. I could ask them to rush it. Maybe they'd agree to that."

"There wasn't any blood anywhere else, so it wasn't like he was shot or stabbed," I pointed out.

"His neck was definitely broken."

"If he was murdered, then someone snapped his neck and then staged it to look like a fall off the stool. How hard is it to break someone's neck?"

"Not hard, if you know what you're doing," she said.

"Okay, but how many people know that. Could you do that?"

"Probably not. If I did, it would have to be to someone small like me. I'd never be able to do it to someone your size."

Well, at least I now knew she wouldn't be trying to break my neck during our marriage. She would have to settle on shooting me if she ever decided to get rid of me.

"Liam might have been able to."

"He's a good five or six inches shorter than Gabriel," I said.

"They could have been fighting first, which might have brought Gabriel lower to the ground so Liam could get his hands around his neck," she suggested.

I wasn't buying that, but I guessed the medical examiner's investigation would search for things like defensive wounds from a fistfight.

"Gabriel said on the phone that he wanted to talk to me about Nalani. He didn't say Liam."

"So? That doesn't mean Liam wasn't still stalking him. Liam's angry about the affair so he kills Nalani first and then goes after the guy she was sleeping with."

"Maybe, but what did Gabriel want to tell me about Nalani that he hadn't told me before?" I asked.

"I guess now we'll never know."

"Maybe we're looking at the wrong guy. Maybe it's someone else who loved Nalani and was angry that he got rejected."

"Why do you say that?"

"Kaylee King mentioned that Nalani had several affairs and that Liam only knew about a couple of them."

"Did she say there was a recent guy?" Alana asked.

"No. I got the impression that it was just Gabriel. Why do you think Liam listed her as a character reference?"

"What do you mean?"

"She was mainly Nalani's friend, not Liam's. He was bound to know that she'd side with Nalani and not him, yet he'd thought that she would back up his claims that he and Nalani were getting back together."

"You said Mason didn't know anything for sure, and Liam was living with the guy. Wouldn't he be more likely to know the truth since he was around Liam more?"

"I don't think so. He worked the night shift at the hotel, so he barely saw Liam. Plus, Kaylee was theoretically getting the inside scoop from Nalani herself. I would put more stock in what Kaylee says."

"You're forgetting that I know that girl. She loves to stir the pot. I wouldn't be surprised if she'd made up everything she told you on the spot."

"Does that mean you're going to go after Liam for this one, too?" I asked.

"I need to interview him for sure, but not until I find out what the M.E. says."

My cell phone pinged, and I looked at the display.

"Why does she text me and not you?" I asked.

"Hani?"

"Yeah, she says she booked the Wailea resort and cancelled the other one."

"I didn't realize we'd definitely decided on that one," Alana said.

"I just told her that you were leaning that way."

"That girl's getting out of control."

"You and your mother created this monster, not me."

"I'll talk to her," she said.

"When you do, please gently let her know that there's no reason for Foxx to be involved. All he has to do is stand beside me, hold the rings, and then give the toast at the reception."

"Don't tell me she's using our wedding as an excuse to bug him."

"You got it."

"I'll call her right after I call the medical examiner."

Alana walked into the kitchen to grab her cell phone, and I winced as I put the ice bag back on my head. What in the world ever possessed me to think I could swim like Michael Phelps?

So, what's your bet? Was Gabriel Reed murdered or did he simply fall off that step stool. Furthermore, if his death was foul play, then who did the deed? Was it Liam? Was it another jealous lover? Was there something else going on in Gabriel's life that had nothing to do with the murder of Nalani? I didn't have the answer to any of those questions. Maybe you don't either, but there was no sense in diving too deep into this one until the M.E. confirmed that it was actually murder.

12

YEP, IT WAS MURDER

ALANA MANAGED TO GET THE EXAMINATION SCHEDULED FOR THE following day. The medical examiner found no superficial injuries to Gabriel's head or face that would have been present if he'd really tumbled from the stool. The doctor was also able to determine by the way the neck was broken that it had resulted from a vicious twisting movement. I wish I could give you a better medical review than that, but I'm mainly repeating the layman's explanation that Alana told me over the phone as she left the medical examiner's office.

She also told me that she'd discovered that Gabriel had an assistant who he employed on a part-time basis. Alana had arranged to meet her at the gallery and invited me to join them. It wasn't often that I got to tag along, and I wondered if there was some special reason that Alana wanted me there.

I arrived at the gallery before Alana did. The door was locked, so I waited outside for the assistant to show. She got there a few minutes later. She looked to be in her early twenties. She was of average height and weight. She had light-brown hair that she'd pulled into a ponytail that was sticking through the back part of a red baseball cap.

"Are you with the police?" she asked.

"I'm not a police officer, but I'm here at the request of Detective Hu."

She accepted my vague description without asking any further questions. She pulled a key out of the front pocket of her khaki shorts to unlock the gallery door.

"Sorry I'm late," she said.

"No problem, I wasn't even aware we had a time scheduled this morning."

"My name's Brooklyn by the way."

"Cool name. I'm Poe."

"Also a cool name," she said.

I followed her into the gallery.

"This is the first time I've been here since Gabriel died. I can't believe it actually happened."

"How often did you work with him?" I asked.

"I helped him with his photo shoots. Sometimes we'd do several in a month. Sometimes just a couple. It really depended on the season. I'd also fill in here at the gallery if he couldn't be here."

"When was the last time you saw him?" I asked.

"The day before he died. We did a photo shoot at U'i Décor."

"Is that where Nalani worked?"

"Yes. They're probably Gabriel's biggest client."

"What does U'i mean by the way?"

"It means 'beautiful.' I always thought it was such a great name for a company," she said.

I heard the door swing open, and I turned around to see Alana enter the gallery. She walked up to Brooklyn and I.

"You must be Brooklyn," she said.

"Nice to meet you."

The two women shook hands.

"I'm Detective Alana Hu. Thanks for agreeing to meet so quickly."

"No problem. What was it you wanted to see here?" she asked.

"We'd like to take another look at the back room, and then I have a few questions I'd like to ask you."

The three of us walked into the back room. It felt a little weird being in the room again, especially since Gabriel's body had been on the cold concrete the last time I was here. My eyes immediately went to the exact spot.

"That's weird. Where did that come from?" Brooklyn asked.

"What are you talking about?" Alana asked.

"That stool. I've never seen it before."

The stool hadn't been moved since I'd found the body. It was still overturned and lying on the floor.

"That wasn't here before?" Alana asked.

"No. Gabriel was tall enough to reach the shelves, and I'd just use one of the apple boxes if I needed to get to the top shelf."

"What's an apple box?" I asked.

Brooklyn pointed to three wooden boxes that were on one of the bottom shelves.

"We use these things for photo shoots. They're great, really. You can put the camera on them if you're trying to get a low-angle shot. A lot of the time we just used them as a stool when we're on a shoot."

"Just to confirm, you've never seen this stool before this morning?" Alana asked.

"No. Maybe Gabriel brought it from home, though."

"Do me a favor and don't touch this. I need to get it dusted for fingerprints."

I could see the confused look on Brooklyn's face.

"Do you know if Gabriel was having any disagreements with anyone?" Alana continued.

"You don't think this was an accident, do you?" Brooklyn asked.

The girl was sharp, I'd give her that.

"We're not sure," Alana said.

"He complained a lot about this one guy."

"Who was it?" I asked.

"I don't remember his name, but he was married to Nalani."

"Liam Hayes," Alana said.

"Did you know Gabriel was having an affair with Nalani?" I asked.

"I did, and I told him to break it off."

"Why is that?" Alana asked.

"Because U'i Décor was our biggest client. If things ended badly between him and Nalani, we would lose them."

What did I say about her being smart? Apparently, this young lady had more brains than her older boss.

"You said he would complain about Liam. What exactly did he say?" Alana asked.

"That Liam was following him all the time. I think he was worried that Liam was going to get violent," Brooklyn said.

"Do you know if he ever did?" I asked.

"I don't think so, and Gabriel would have said something if he did."

"Did Gabriel ever tell you if he or Nalani were talking about ending things?" Alana asked.

"No. They never said anything, and they were both pretty flirty on the last photo shoot. I thought it was a little unprofessional, but he was my boss. What was I going to do?"

"How long did you work with Gabriel?" I asked.

"For about six years. I started interning for him after high school. We got along great, and he eventually hired me."

"We're going to need to go through his computer. Do you know if it's password-protected?" Alana asked.

"It is, but I have the password. The computer's out here in the front."

We followed Brooklyn back to the counter in the front gallery. There was a Mac laptop on one end of the counter. Brooklyn turned it on and typed in the password.

"What is it you need to see?" she asked.

"Mainly his emails," Alana said.

We watched as Brooklyn opened an internet browser and logged into Gabriel's Gmail account.

"You have his login information?" Alana asked.

"Gabriel gave it to me since this was his work email, too. I'd correspond with clients from time to time for him. Let me know if there's anything else you need."

Alana sat down on a stool in front of the laptop. She started scanning through the emails.

"Is there something special you're looking for? Maybe I can help you," Brooklyn said.

"Nothing in particular, but I'll probably know it if I find something odd. We may be a while," Alana said.

Brooklyn got the hint.

"Okay. Is it all right then if I take off? You've got my number. Just call me when you're done, and I can come back and lock up."

"That would be great. Thank you."

Alana waited for Brooklyn to leave. Then she turned to me.

"His cell phone is still on the back table. Why don't you go through it while I check out his emails?"

I walked into the back room and retrieved his phone. I pressed the home button to activate the screen.

"It's password-protected," I called out.

"Think Brooklyn knows that one, too?" Alana asked.

"Give me a second. I saw his wallet back here."

I fished his driver's license out of his wallet, which was on the table beside his Canon camera. I walked back to the front counter to join Alana.

"Anything jumping out at you?" I asked.

"Nothing yet."

Alana looked at me as I typed various number combinations into his phone.

"What are you doing?" she asked.

"I just tried his birthday, the month and the date. Didn't work."

"Okay, what now?"

"I'm trying the year he was born."

I typed the new number combination in and waited a moment.

"Nope, that didn't work either. What about the month he was born and the last two numbers of the year?" I guessed.

I typed that number in and turned the phone's display to face Alana.

"We're in. What do I get for that little display of hacking?" I asked.

"It would be impressive if not for the fact that I know you don't know the first thing about hacking."

"Yeah, it was lucky," I admitted.

I clicked on the text icon and searched through the various numbers Gabriel had corresponded with.

"Let's check out these text messages between him and Nalani," I continued.

There were dozens of messages back and forth, maybe hundreds of them. They clearly had a close relationship, but I already knew that. I found a few messages between Gabriel and Nalani that were sent the day before she was murdered. They backed up Gabriel's claim that he'd had dinner with Nalani at his house. Of course, that didn't mean she actually went there, or that he hadn't followed her back to her house afterward.

"Check this out," I said.

I held the phone toward Alana. I'm a little reluctant to describe what I saw since I don't want to offend sensitive readers. It was part of what I found, though, and I think it's important for you to know all of the information I discovered. The phone display showed a close-up photo of a woman's breasts.

"I assume that's Nalani," Alana said.

I looked back at the display and continued to scan through the correspondence between Nalani and Gabriel.

"Apparently, they were in to sexting. There's a ton of those types of messages in here. Unfortunately, they aren't very good."

"You're judging the quality of their sex writing?" Alana asked.

"Yeah, not only was this guy an average photographer, but he was also a mediocre writer."

"You're insane. You know that, don't you?"

"Oh, here's a picture of his penis. Want to see it?" I asked.

"No, I do not."

"You'd think people would delete these things," I said.

We spent another hour going through his phone and work computer. Other than the sexting messages, nothing jumped out as unusual. They were all about work assignments or personal plans, just the average things people talk about in their daily lives. The main thing that we got out of our little snooping session was that there was nothing to indicate that Nalani had remotely considered ending her affair with Gabriel.

Alana closed the internet browser on the computer and turned to me.

"There was something else I forgot to mention. After the medical examiner told me she thought Gabriel's death was murder, I checked out his clothing again."

"Why?" I asked.

"I was looking for things like tears or marks that might indicate a fight. I found something on the backs of his shoes. Scuff marks," Alana said.

"What could that be from?"

"My guess is Gabriel was murdered out here. Maybe the killer posed as a potential customer. He then walks up behind an unsuspecting Gabriel and snaps his neck. He catches him before he falls to the ground and then drags his body to the back room."

"Then he plants the step stool beside the body so it looks like an accident," I said.

"Exactly. That's why I want to dust that stool for fingerprints."

"You still think Liam did this?" I asked.

"What do you think? There's absolutely nothing on Gabriel's phone or email that shows he had any disagreements with someone other than Liam."

"That doesn't mean he didn't. Not everybody feels the need to put their issues down in writing," I said.

"I don't know, Poe. People use text messages these days to voice their disagreements more and more. It's a much easier way than actually talking to someone."

It was a good point she'd made, which meant we were back to Liam being the number one suspect, if he'd ever left that spot to begin with.

13

U'I DECOR

I GOT ANOTHER SURPRISE WHEN ALANA INVITED ME TO GO WITH HER TO meet with Koa and Moani Opunui, who were the brother and sister-in-law of Nalani. Alana said she wanted to question them about the photo shoot they did with Gabriel the day before he died. Perhaps we would get lucky and Gabriel would have mentioned something about any potential problems he was having. I thought it was a long shot, but I also got why Alana was doing it. A terrible crime had been committed, and she was desperate to do something, even if the lead didn't amount to much.

We climbed into Alana's car and made the drive from Lahaina to the middle part of the island where U'i Décor was located. We got an insanely awesome view of Mount Haleakala as we approached the warehouse where I assumed U'i Décor housed all of their merchandise. The dormant volcano crater was almost always hidden behind thick clouds, but today it was clear. It looked so close that I thought I could reach out and touch it, even though I knew it would take a few hours to drive to the top.

I turned my attention away from the volcano back to Alana as the warehouse came into view.

"Is Koa younger or older than Nalani?" I asked.

"Younger. He and Hani are the same age whereas Nalani and I were the same."

"So he was in the house when your family stayed with them?"

"Of course. He wasn't happy about us being there either since he had to move into his parents' bedroom so my mother could get his," she said.

"Did you guys stay in touch after you moved out?"

"A little. We were in different grades so we didn't interact a whole lot. I mainly just hung out with Nalani."

"Do you know when he and his wife started their business?" I asked.

"It was just after Nalani and Liam got married, so it's been a while. I know they really struggled at first, but now it's doing well."

Alana pulled into one of the parking spaces near the front office, and we climbed out of the car. We entered through the front door which took us to a large room that showcased many of the foreign products they sold. The work was a mixture of African and Asian art that ranged from large statues and decorative screens to smaller objects like vases and paintings. Most of it looked beautiful, and I'm sure they charged a decent chunk of change for their goods. I had no idea what it cost to acquire these items from their original homes or what it cost to ship them to Maui and beyond. The operation must have required an enormous amount of coordination.

"Hello, Alana."

I turned when I heard a man call out to Alana as he emerged from an office just off the back of the showroom. He was a tall guy, maybe even taller than me. He had a large stomach and thick arms and legs. He looked like he could have worked as a bouncer.

"Hello, Koa."

Koa walked over to us and Alana introduced me to him. She often referred to me as her associate when I would tag along during these investigations. Today, she introduced me as her fiancé.

"Nice to meet you, Poe. I've heard a lot about you," Koa said.

"Thank you. Alana's mentioned a few things about you and your wife. She said your business is doing really well. I'm glad to hear it."

"It's taken a while, but things are finally starting to come together."

"I guess you're on the road a lot," I said.

"Constantly. At first it was fun. I'd never really been off the island, but now the travel can get kind of tiring."

"I'm sure."

Koa turned to Alana.

"I'm glad you called me this morning. I was actually going to call you about something."

"Oh, what about?" she asked.

"Do you mind if we speak in the back? I don't want any customers who might walk in to hear this."

I assumed Koa wanted us to meet in his office. Instead, he led us through a door beside his office which took us into the warehouse space in the back. The place was enormous, and it had several huge rows of shelves that housed more merchandise.

"What did you want to talk about?" Alana asked.

"Liam came by to see me last night. He threatened me."

"How so?" Alana asked.

I wanted to jump in and ask how an average-sized guy like Liam would ever feel confident enough to threaten someone who looked like Koa. I kept my mouth shut, though, and played the part of the silent observer.

"He's upset that I won't let him back into the house. My parents left that house to Nalani and I. Liam's name isn't anywhere on the title."

"You still own part of it?" Alana asked.

Koa nodded.

"Moani wasn't ever interested in living there. Besides, we wanted to be closer to this place. Nalani was supposed to pay me for my half. She never did, though."

"Did you have an issue with Liam living there?" Alana asked.

"I never liked the guy, but you already know that. He was her husband, though, so I didn't say anything about him staying there."

"How did Moani feel about that?" Alana asked.

"I wasn't happy about it," a female voice said.

I turned and saw a slender Hawaiian woman approach. It was obvious who she was based on what she'd said. She stood beside Koa, and their shapes were a study in opposites. Koa looked at least a foot taller than her, and you could have fit several Moanis inside one of him.

Alana introduced me again as her fiancé. I guessed Moani wasn't impressed because she didn't say anything in return. She didn't even acknowledge my presence except to give me a millisecond glance before she turned her attention back to Alana.

"Koa's parents paid that house off. Liam didn't contribute one cent to it. Then he comes here and thinks he has the right to move back into the house? He's crazy," Moani said.

"You said he threatened you, though. Did he push you? Did he threaten to physically attack you?" Alana asked.

"He said we'd regret not letting him back in the house. How would you take that?" Koa asked.

"Why haven't you arrested him yet? It's obvious he did it," Moani said.

"It's not just my decision. The district attorney has to agree that there's a strong enough case."

"How isn't there enough evidence? He found her, and why was he even there at the house to begin with?" Moani asked.

"We're doing everything we can. She meant a lot to me, too," Alana said.

"Is that right? Funny, I don't remember seeing you around in a long time," Moani said.

Alana didn't respond to the verbal assault. Moani seemed to understand that she'd crossed a line, or maybe she was just afraid that she'd take it even farther if she stuck around. She gave Koa a look that I couldn't interpret and then walked back toward the front showroom. Koa waited for her to exit the warehouse, and then he turned back to Alana.

"I'm sorry about that. We both know you cared about Nalani. I know what went down."

"It's all right. It's an emotional time," Alana said.

"What was it you wanted to talk to me about? Is it about Nalani's case?" Koa asked.

"It might be. I'm not sure yet. We have reason to suspect that Gabriel Reed's death might not have been an accident."

"Do you think it's related to Nalani's death?"

"I don't know. That's why I'm here. Gabriel did a photo shoot for you the day before he died. Did you work with him that day?" Alana asked.

"I did. I'd just brought back some new stuff from Asia. Gabriel shot it for me so we could put the items on the website."

"Did he act weird that day?" I asked.

"No. Everything seemed normal with him, and I was with him most of the time."

"What about Moani? Was she there, too?" Alana asked.

"Not for most of it. She worked the showroom, and we were pretty busy that day. She only came back here a couple of times," Koa said.

"Did she ever talk to you about Gabriel?" Alana asked.

"You want to know if I knew about the affair."

"Something like that," Alana said.

"I didn't know at first, but I was okay with it once I found out. I figured it wouldn't last, but I was hoping Gabriel might be the one to make her finally leave Liam."

"Why didn't you like Liam? Was it just arguments over the house?" I asked.

"The truth is I never really liked him from the start. I couldn't figure out what she saw in the guy."

"Did Gabriel ever mention being threatened by Liam?" Alana asked.

"Not that I heard of. I really only talked to him when he'd come here for a shoot. He was a good photographer, and he'd always turn things around for us pretty quickly. I'm going to miss working with him," Koa said.

"If you think of something else, please let me know," Alana said.

"I will."

We said goodbye to Koa and exited the warehouse. Alana led me through one of the side doors that took us out of the building and into the parking lot. I assumed she'd avoided the showroom since she didn't want to have another run-in with Moani.

We got into her car and drove out of the parking lot. Alana pulled off to the side of the road after we got a couple of miles away from U'i Décor. I knew what that meant. We were in for a deep discussion.

"I know you haven't exactly jumped on the Liam-is-guilty bandwagon, but I just don't see who else this could be," she said.

"It's not so much that I think he's innocent. I just don't know that there's enough proof that he did it. You're right, though, when you say there doesn't appear to be anyone else that had it in for both Gabriel and Nalani, if the cases are even connected."

"How could they not be?" she asked.

She was right again. It was too much of a coincidence to think that two lovers could be murdered within days of each other and it not be connected in some way.

"Did you catch what Koa said when I introduced you guys?" she asked.

"I just remember him saying hello."

"He also said that he's heard a lot about you. How? I haven't said anything about you to him or Moani."

"I think that's just one of those things people say. It doesn't really mean anything," I said.

"I disagree. People say stuff like 'Nice to meet you' or 'How are you?' They don't say 'I've heard so much about you.'"

"Okay, but what does this have to do with Nalani's or Gabriel's deaths?" I asked.

"Nothing. It just pisses me off how much people gossip."

"This is really about Moani's comments that you weren't there for Nalani. You think your childhood friends are talking about you and judging you."

"That's because they are," she said.

"Probably," I said, even though I knew for a fact they were. "But you can't let that affect you."

"Everyone's looking at me and judging me for not having arrested Liam."

"That's because you're doing your job. You've not arrested a guy because the evidence isn't there yet. You can't give in to these people's emotions."

"We've got to break him somehow. I know he did it."

Alana put the car in drive and pulled back onto the road. I looked in my side view mirror and saw Mount Haleakala get smaller and smaller as we made our way back to the main road. It was a beautiful sight, and I wondered if that's why Koa and Moani had picked that area to build the U'i Décor gallery. Perhaps that's even how they came up with the name for the business.

14

CHECKMATE

ALANA ASKED ME TO HELP HER WITH THE INTERVIEW OF LIAM HAYES. Of course, she'd already met with him once before, but she thought he might be more open if I was there for the follow-up. She thought he could still be under the impression that I was on his side. I felt a little hesitant about the trickery, but the guy had lied to me on several fronts, even during our initial meeting when he thought he was hiring me to be his investigator. It wasn't the first time a client had lied to me, and I'd grown more than tired of running around the island and chasing false leads.

Alana called Mara on the way back from our meeting at U'i Décor and asked her to arrange the meeting with Liam since she assumed Mara would want to be present for it. Mara said she absolutely did, and she scheduled it to take place at her office the following morning. I arrived at the office a good twenty minutes before Alana did, which was part of her plan. Mara's assistant led me into the back where I saw that Liam and Mara were already preparing for the interview.

"Good morning, Liam," I said.

The guy didn't look good, which I understood. His skin was pale, and I could see dark circles under his eyes. I sat down beside him on the leather sofa. Mara was seated on one of the two matching chairs that were just off to the sides.

"Is she going to arrest me?" Liam asked.

He certainly didn't bother wasting time, did he?

"I don't think so. She wouldn't have scheduled this meeting if that was her intention," I said.

"How is your investigation going?" Mara asked.

"It's moving along. I've met with everyone on Liam's list. I just met with Koa and Moani late yesterday."

I turned to Liam.

"He said you threatened him. Did you do that?"

"Koa said that?"

"Yes. He said you came by his office and threatened him if he didn't let you back into the house."

"That's not true. I just asked him if I could stay there for a while. I know he owns it."

"Your name's not on the mortgage?" Mara asked.

"No. It was left to Nalani and Koa. I guess he owns it all now."

"I suspect Alana is going to ask you about your interaction with Koa. It sounded like it got rather heated, at least that's the way Koa described it."

"He thinks I killed her. He and Moani made that clear," Liam said.

"So why did you think they would let you stay there?" I asked.

"I didn't have a choice. I don't have anywhere else to go."

"Where are you staying now?" Mara asked.

"In a hotel near the airport, but I'm almost out of money."

I didn't think that was a very smart thing to say in the presence of your high-priced lawyer. I didn't know what kind of financial arrangement he'd made with Mara. Maybe he'd exhausted a sizable chunk of his funds by paying her retainer. Maybe he'd promised to sell some of his stuff to pay for her services. It certainly sounded like she had a choice to make. Either do this one pro bono or drop her client.

"Why aren't you staying with Mason?" I asked.

"I tried to go back there, but he said no."

"Why is that? I thought he was a friend?"

"He is, or at least I thought he was. This case has scared him off, though. He said he can't get involved."

"Have you had any luck with your job search?" Mara asked.

Apparently, she had heard Liam's earlier statement about being broke.

"I've had interviews with three different hotels. I thought the interviews all went well, but none of them said yes. I think my old manager must have called them or something."

"Why would they do that? I thought you just got let go because of the downturn," Mara said.

"I don't know. Some people just don't like to see others succeed," Liam said.

It was a true statement, as demonstrated recently by some of Alana's childhood friends, but I'm sure that wasn't the case in Liam's fruitless job search. I didn't blame him for not telling the story about his little meltdown in the hotel lobby, but it was just another example of Liam not telling the whole truth and nothing but the truth to the people he'd asked to represent him.

"Excuse me, Ms. Winters, but Detective Hu is here."

We all turned when we heard Mara's assistant announce the arrival of Alana. Mara stood and walked over to the door so she could greet Alana and shake her hand. The two women then walked back to the sitting area. Alana was wearing her light-blue suit. It was my favorite work outfit of hers since the cut of the fabric had a way of hugging her body in all of the right places. Was I a pig for checking out her body right before this interrogation? Maybe, but in my defense, I did try to be as discreet as possible.

"Thank you for agreeing to speak with me, Mr. Hayes," Alana said. "I just have a few questions, and I assumed you'd want your lawyer present."

Liam didn't say anything in response, and I could tell he was starting to sweat. I got a kick out of watching people get intimidated by my sweet little fiancée, but Alana does have a pretty good glare that she can toss out like the best prize fighter.

"I hope you don't mind, but I'd like to record this conversation," she continued.

Alana reached into her jacket pocket and removed a small digital recorder. She placed it on the table in front of the sofa and hit the record button. Alana turned to Mara.

"I'm not sure if you're aware of this, Ms. Winters, but the death of Gabriel Reed has been ruled a homicide."

I saw one of Mara's eyebrows raise.

"No. I can't say I've heard that news."

"During the course of my investigation into the murder of Nalani Hayes, I had the chance to speak with Mr. Reed. He claimed he and Nalani had caught your client following them and harassing them on several occasions."

"When you say harassing them, do you mean to imply that my client made physical threats toward them?" Mara asked.

"Not physical threats, per se, but Mr. Reed did say that Mr. Hayes had gone through the trouble of acquiring a variety of cars to help conceal the fact that he was following them. It seems he took this surveillance to extreme levels, which has raised my suspicions considerably. I was also made aware of the fact that Mr. Reed and Mrs. Hayes had dinner at Mr. Reed's home the night before she was killed."

"You suspect this means that Liam was aware of this dinner and followed Nalani home to do her harm?" Mara asked.

"I'm not saying that, but it does cast serious doubts on earlier claims by your client that he and his wife had reconciled. I also learned from Mason Howard, who Mr. Hayes was staying with, that he was completely unaware of this reconciliation. Furthermore, he claimed that Mr. Hayes' clothing was still in his house and unpacked at the time when Mr. Hayes was discovering the body of his wife. This directly contradicts Mr. Hayes' claims that he'd brought his suitcase back to his home since he was moving back in with his wife."

Mara didn't respond, and I knew Alana had taken her by surprise. I didn't know if Mara suspected that I was the one responsible for many of those revelations. She was a smart cookie, though, so she probably guessed I had uncovered some of it. That probably meant her follow-up thought was to realize I hadn't bothered to provide her with that information before this interview so she could prepare a proper defense for her client. Yeah, I'd sandbagged her, and it wasn't the first time I'd done that. Nevertheless, I had made it clear to both her and Liam that I was conducting my own investigation, and I wasn't technically working for either of them.

"I did follow them. I'll admit it, but I never threatened them. I never even got out of the car or spoke to them," Liam said.

"Did you switch cars to help hide yourself?" I asked.

"I borrowed Mason's car a couple of times. I even rented a car once, but just once."

"What did you hope to gain by following them?" Alana asked.

"I don't know. I just couldn't stop thinking about her. I couldn't believe she wanted to be with that guy."

"We spoke with Gabriel's assistant. She claims she saw you staking out Gabriel's photography gallery, too," Alana said.

That wasn't true, but Alana and I had made an educated guess that Liam had probably followed Gabriel back there a few times.

"Mr. Reed was murdered on Monday. Where were you that morning?" Alana continued.

"I was at the hotel," Liam said.

"Which hotel?" Alana asked.

"It's called Maui Sunrise. It's in Kahului."

I knew the place since I'd followed a previous client there. The name of the hotel wasn't an accurate description since most of the tiny rooms faced one of the busy roads near the airport that was on the opposite side of where the sun rose. The hotel had gained the distinct notoriety as being one of the cheapest places on the island, if not the cheapest. If Liam was staying there then it certainly spoke volumes about his financial status. I'm pretty sure the hotel charged customers by the hour, if you get my drift.

"Was anyone with you in your hotel room?" Alana asked.

"No. It was just me."

"And what were you doing?"

"I was watching television. There was a rerun of *M.A.S.H.* on," Liam said.

"You said earlier that Gabriel Reed was murdered. How did he die?" Mara asked.

"His neck was snapped," Alana said.

"And this attack happened in his gallery?" Mara asked.

"That's right."

"So you suspect my client drove to Mr. Reed's gallery and broke his neck as revenge for the affair with Mrs. Hayes?"

Alana didn't respond, and Mara turned to Liam.

"Mr. Hayes, would you have any idea how to go about snapping someone's neck?"

"No. That's not something I've ever thought about."

Mara turned back to Alana.

"Detective, I would wager that most people on this island have no concept of how to kill someone in that manner. There's a big difference between seeing something in an action film and knowing how to perform that killing maneuver in real life."

Alana ignored Mara's statement and turned back to Liam.

"Weren't you lying to me, as well as to your investigator, when you said you and Nalani had gotten back together?" Alana asked.

"You don't have to answer that," Mara urged.

"I didn't lie. We had gotten back together."

"Then why lie about the suitcase? I was at the house you once shared with Nalani. I know the suitcase wasn't there. I have the crime scene photos to prove it."

"I didn't think you'd believe me, so I made that part up. The rest is true, though. She called me the day before she died. She said she wanted to talk to me."

"She wanted to talk to you? That's different from your story that you two reconciled," Alana said.

"But that's what she wanted to talk about. She said she realized that she'd made a mistake with Gabriel. She asked if I could ever give her another chance."

"Let me be sure I understand you correctly: You'd followed your wife and her lover around the island for weeks; you even followed her the night before she died."

"But I didn't do anything to her. I didn't even get out of the car."

"That's enough, Liam," Mara said.

"So she calls you the day before she dies, the day you followed her to her lover's house, and says she wants to talk. You take that to mean she wants you to move back into the house, and you immediately forgive her for everything she's done to you?" Alana asked.

Liam couldn't control himself, and he was about to answer when Mara gently placed her hand on his arm. She leaned forward and whispered something in his ear that I couldn't hear, despite being just a few feet from him. Whatever she said, I knew it had shocked him because his eyes grew wide, and he nodded his head.

Mara turned back to Alana.

"My client no longer wants to continue this discussion."

"I'm sure he doesn't," Alana said.

She picked up her digital recorder from the table and turned it off.

"It's always a pleasure to see you, Mara," Alana continued.

Mara didn't respond.

Alana turned away from the group without saying anything to me. She exited the office, and I heard the little bell on the exterior door jingle as Alana presumably left the building. I was halfway tempted to leave with her, but I didn't want to miss the meltdown I was sure Liam was about to have. Of course, I expected Mara to throw me out first. She didn't do that, at least not at the level I expected her to. Instead, she was gracious about it.

"It's probably best if you weren't here," Mara said.

"Understandable," I said.

I stood and was almost to the office door when Liam called out to me.

"You betrayed me, you son of a bitch."

I stopped and turned back to him.

"You lied to her. You lied to me. Hell, you lied to your own attorney. Nalani was never going to take you back," I said.

"You don't think I've been through this before? Gabriel wasn't the first, but she always came back to me. She always got tired of them after the initial thrill wore off."

"There was no call from Nalani to you the night before she died. Alana has her phone records. So either you're doing a really bad job of trying to cover your tail, or your wife stopped at some convenience store to use a payphone instead of her cell."

Mara looked at Liam, but he didn't have an answer to my accusations.

"I'm not trying to set you up, Liam. I have nothing against you. I've actually defended you to Alana. I'm the one who poked holes in her theories, but you managed to fill all those holes back up by the lies you've told."

"I didn't do it!" he said.

He put his head in his hands, and I knew it was useless to speak anymore. Liam Hayes was done. Alana had captured the proof of his lies on her audio recorder. The district attorney had been right on the edge as to whether to agree to the homicide charges Alana was seeking. Liam had just been caught in a few lies that were pretty substantial. I couldn't imagine the district attorney not agreeing to move forward now. I assumed it was only a matter of hours before Liam would be behind bars.

I thought about calling Alana after I left Mara's office, but I figured she had her hands full. I didn't understand why Alana hadn't arrested him there in Mara's office, but maybe she wanted to get all of her ducks in the proverbial row before taking that step. I suspected she also wanted to pin the murder of Gabriel Reed on him, too. Maybe there were a few things she wanted to follow through on that case first.

Alana's plan for the interview had been a good one. I would bring up the confrontation between Koa and Liam so that Liam would be distracted by that line of thought. Then Alana would arrive and immediately start with the murder of Gabriel Reed. He wouldn't have been expecting that, and Alana assumed he'd immediately start panicking that he was about to be arrested for that murder. Then

Alana would suddenly switch gears and try to pin him down on the lies about Nalani. We'd changed the line of questioning on Liam three times, and he hadn't known which way was up.

I was a little wired, and I didn't want to go back to the house where I'd essentially have nothing to do, so I made my way over to Harry's instead. Foxx wasn't there, so I said hello to our staff, grabbed a drink, and sat down in one of the back corners to collect my thoughts on the Nalani Hayes investigation.

The case had started with the discovery of the brutal murder of Alana's old childhood friend. There was only one suspect: the jilted husband. Liam had initially claimed that he and Nalani were getting back together. His former co-worker and friend, Mason Howard, hadn't backed up that claim although he hadn't exactly disputed it, either. Interestingly enough, the victim's friend, Kaylee King, had stated that she wouldn't have been surprised since Nalani had a habit of always returning to her husband. She didn't have definite knowledge, though, that Nalani had left Gabriel and gone back to Liam.

Nevertheless, I now knew that Nalani hadn't made the decision to get back with Liam, at least not by phone call the night before she died. I also now knew that Liam had actually followed her to her dinner at Gabriel's house. It made sense that the romantic dinner could have been the tipping point to push Liam over the edge to murder.

Speaking of that, I've forgotten to mention to you readers that Alana had told me a few days ago that the corkscrew that had been used to murder Nalani didn't have any fingerprints on it. That wasn't exactly a surprise since most people would think not to leave fingerprints on the murder weapon. That meant Liam had either wiped the prints off after killing Nalani or he had worn gloves when he committed the crime.

Alana also said there had been a hand towel in the kitchen that Liam could have used, but it didn't have any traces of blood on it. I thought that probably disqualified it since I didn't see how Liam could wipe the fingerprints off a bloody corkscrew and not get any blood on the towel. Corkscrews aren't particularly long, which means the handle undoubtedly got blood on it, too. Of course, he could have used a different towel and disposed of it before the police arrived.

It would have also made sense if Liam's fingerprints were on the corkscrew, though. He acknowledged that it belonged to Nalani and him, but I doubted he would have had the presence of mind to think through that logical conclusion after murdering his wife.

There was something, however, that really bothered me. Unfortunately, it was a huge thing, and it had the potential to bring the whole case down, at least in my mind. That thing was the death of Gabriel Reed. There were two points brought up during the discussion with Liam. Mara had made the first one, and it had been a point I'd already considered. Both Mara and I doubted that Liam would have the knowledge and ability to break Gabriel's neck. It was more than that, though. The death had been staged to look like an accident. Granted, it wasn't the best attempt at staging the death, but it had been convincing enough to initially trick Alana and I, or at least give us enough reasonable doubt that we had to wait for the medical examiner's report.

If Liam had gone through the trouble of trying to stage an accidental death, why wouldn't he have also done the same to Nalani? Sure, his rage against her might have been substantially more than the anger he felt toward Gabriel, but I didn't think so. He loved his wife even though she'd put him through hell with her numerous affairs.

My guess is that he was even angrier with Gabriel Reed. Sometimes people focus all their anger on one person and blame that person for all of their problems. Yeah, Gabriel shouldn't have gotten involved with a married woman. I think everyone knows my stance on that, but his affair wasn't the reason for the marital strife between Nalani and Liam. It was really just a symptom.

The other big thing that jumped out at me regarding Gabriel's death was Liam's quick answer when Alana asked him where he'd been at the time of the murder. Liam had immediately answered that he was at the hotel and watching the television classic *M.A.S.H.* I knew for a fact that the show came on in the mornings since I'd watched it several times myself. They always played back-to-back episodes on one of those cable channels that specializes in shows that have gone into syndication. Sure, Liam could have known that *M.A.S.H.* came on around that time, and he could have used that as proof that he was in the hotel room when he was really in the gallery breaking Gabriel's neck. I tended to believe him, though, because he'd answered her question so quickly. He didn't even stop to think about it.

That left me with an obvious question: If Liam didn't kill Gabriel, then who did? That question brought up follow-up questions. If Liam didn't kill Gabriel for sleeping with his wife, why was Gabriel killed, and was it in any way connected to the death of Nalani Hayes? Did all this lead to another potential truth that Liam hadn't actually killed his wife? If someone could have been clever enough to try to stage Gabriel's death to look like an accident, then couldn't they have also tried to frame Liam for his wife's death? Was Liam just a sucker in all of this?

I was sure Alana was struggling with these questions as well. Maybe that's why she'd made the decision not to arrest Liam just yet. Maybe she was sitting somewhere going through all of this in her head like I was doing.

I pulled out my phone and called her. All I got was her voicemail, so I left her a message and ended the call. I was about to leave and head home when Hani and Foxx walked in the door. No, they hadn't put their differences aside and were about to have a pleasant lunch together. They were yelling at each other. It took me about three seconds to realize it was about my upcoming wedding.

"Poe told me all I had to do was stand there and look pretty," Foxx said.

"Well, you're going to need to get some work done if you want to pull that off."

"You didn't seem to mind how I looked when we were messing around."

At least he didn't use a different word to convey what we all knew he was really talking about.

Foxx turned when he saw me approach.

"There he is. Poe, tell her I don't have to do anything," Foxx said.

"Can I talk to you guys for a minute?' I asked.

"Sure, Poe, what can I do for you?" Hani asked, and she smiled as if she was completely oblivious to the chaos that she and Foxx were causing at the bar.

"Maybe we should talk over here," I suggested, and I led them back to the booth where I had been sitting when they stormed inside.

"Hani, what is it you're asking Foxx to do?"

"You said I didn't have to do anything," Foxx protested.

"One second, Foxx."

I turned back to Hani.

"What is it you want him to do?" I asked.

"I just wanted to go over the seating arrangement with him. I thought he might like to have some input," she said.

"It would probably be best if you went over that with Alana and I. Do you want to come over to the house tonight?" I asked.

"I can't deal with this," Foxx said, and he stormed off.

So much for us all handling this like adults. Then something that all guys fear happened. Hani broke out into tears.

"I don't know why he treats me like this," she said between sobs.

I looked up to the bar and saw Foxx staring at us. He didn't make a move to come back, though.

"It's all right, Hani," I said, and I pulled her toward me.

It was a bit tricky, considering how large her stomach had gotten.

"Why doesn't he want me anymore?" she asked.

"I don't know, but you'll make it through this. I promise."

I didn't know what else to say, but it didn't really matter since she pulled away from me and walked quickly out of the bar. She never once looked back to Foxx.

15

THE WORST MOMENT OF MY LIFE

I CALLED ALANA AGAIN AFTER I LEFT THE BAR, BUT I JUST GOT HER voicemail a second time. She was probably still at the police station, or maybe she was on her way to the Maui Sunrise hotel to arrest Liam Hayes.

My thoughts floated back to Hani's meltdown as I made my way home. I hadn't expected to see that this morning, and it made me wonder if Alana had ever gotten around to talking to Hani and asking her to keep away from Foxx. Hani was a pretty stubborn person, though. I could see her agreeing to Alana's request and then doing the exact opposite anyway.

I guess a part of me always assumed Hani and Foxx would work out their differences. Maybe they still would after the kid was born, but it seemed like that ideal point in their relationship was a million miles away. Of course, maybe they would never even reach that peaceful stage where they agreed to just be nice to each other.

Then another thought hit me. Maybe Hani's tears had just been for show. Maybe she was just trying to swing me over to her side and get me to pressure Foxx to take her back. I was a little depressed that I thought that of her, but these investigations had made me way more leery of people's intentions. The change in my outlook had been gradual, and I hadn't even really been aware of it until one day I realized I'd turned into a suspicious person.

I'd always been a fairly trusting person before. I assumed people were inherently good, and they'd usually do the right thing if given the chance. I suspect that I got that trait from my parents. They were good people, and they always thought the best of others, even when those people demonstrated they didn't deserve that trust. Maybe some of you readers think that's a naïve way to live your life, and it probably is. Maybe naivety is just a form of ignorance, and I don't mean ignorance as being synonymous with stupidity. That's how some people prefer to live their life, though, happily trotting through life with their blinders on. How does that saying go, "Ignorance is bliss?"

My time on Maui had been marked by extremes. I'd seen the best and worst of people. The best was obvious. It was the time I'd spent with Alana. She'd changed my life in a way I didn't think possible, and I couldn't believe we'd be married in a matter of a few months. I guess I'd always assumed I'd get married at some point, but that life status seemed to get farther and farther away as I stumbled from one bad relationship to another. Alana had changed all of that.

I actually thought of an old girlfriend as I made my way back to Kaanapali. I'd ended my relationship with Dorothy in the days before my first trip to Maui. I actually had her to credit for the big changes in my life. I probably wouldn't have gotten on that plane for the long flight to Hawaii if I hadn't been so depressed by the end of our relationship. It was a weird time in my life because I'd already considered ending that relationship for a while. It was clear that Dorothy and I were no longer compatible, if we had ever been in the first place. I still wasn't sure why I hadn't ended it sooner. Maybe most people are afraid of change, even when that change is positive.

I remembered the night I caught her with another guy. She'd actually made the decision to leave me for a car salesman. I'm sure you're accusing me now of exaggeration. You're wondering how someone could leave little old me for a guy who pedaled used BMWs. Well, trust me, it happened. That moment, however, was the defining moment of my life, and I owed all of the good fortune I'd had since then to the fact that Dorothy had stepped out on me with Chet. Yeah, I know, it's a horrible name, maybe even worse than Edgar. Funny how life happens like that.

I'd met Alana on my first day on Maui. It actually happened just a couple of hours after landing at the airport. I thought back to that moment I'd seen her in that Halloween parade. I hadn't realized it then, but I'm pretty sure I fell in love with her when I first saw her. Sure, it had started out as infatuation, but it hadn't taken long for me to determine she was someone really special. I still can't believe I'd actually considered going back to Virginia. What an idiot, but I would like to point out that I really only considered that for about twenty-four hours before I came to my senses.

As good as things have been with Alana, Maui hasn't been all sunshine and roses, or maybe I should say Birds of Paradise since we're in Hawaii. I don't need to go into the details of the bad stuff that was on the opposite end of the emotional spectrum. If you've read some of my tales before, you'll already know exactly the kinds of crazies I've dealt with during these cases. I've encountered everything from jealous lovers to greedy bastards to homicidal maniacs. No, our little slice of paradise wasn't immune to bad people.

That made me think about Liam, and I wondered how he was spending what was probably his last free day. Was he in full panic mode right about now? Probably. Maybe he was even wondering if he could purchase a last-minute flight off the island. Perhaps he was desperately trying to figure out how he could prove he hadn't killed Nalani and Gabriel. What if he had killed them, or just Nalani? What was going through his head then? Was there some part of him that thought he deserved jail, or had he rationalized the act by now?

I firmly believe the human brain is like a computer, and it has the capacity to be reprogrammed. I really think people can convince themselves of anything, and if they tell themselves the same lie over and over again, then that lie eventually becomes the truth to them. Perhaps the real truth goes so deep into the recesses of their mind that they can no longer access it. I have no doubt Liam felt that way about Nalani. She'd betrayed him, and she got what she deserved. At least that's what was going through his mind. Would the cold truth ever dawn on Liam in jail? Would he repent his crimes? Probably not.

I turned down the street in my neighborhood and was surprised to see Alana's car in the driveway. She usually wasn't home this early during the week, especially during a murder investigation. I entered the house and got my second surprise when the dog didn't immediately run to me. His ears always seemed attuned to the sound of the automatic garage door opening, and he always greeted me by the kitchen door, which led to the garage.

I walked through the kitchen and made my way to the sliding glass door so I could look out into the backyard. I assumed I'd see Alana and Maui out there, but I didn't. I turned around since I was sure I was about to see the dog walking toward me. There was the rare occasion when the dog would be fast asleep when I'd get home, and he'd trot over to me as he gave me a big yawn. He still wasn't there, though.

Alana wasn't in the kitchen or den, and she wasn't out back. That meant she had to be upstairs. I called out to her but didn't get a response. That's when I heard it: a dog whining. It wasn't something I was used to hearing, and it definitely sounded like Maui was in distress. It came from the front room, so I made my way there. I got the shock of my life as I turned the corner. Alana was on the floor on her side. Maui the dog was licking her face, but she wasn't responding. I ran up to her and kneeled down. Her face was a mess. Blood ran from her nose and mouth and onto the white carpet underneath her.

"Alana, what happened?" I asked.

I put my hand on her shoulder and shook her gently, but she didn't open her eyes. I leaned over and put my ear close to her mouth. I could barely hear her breathing.

"Jesus," I said.

I pulled out my cell phone and called for an ambulance. It was infuriating as I had to repeat my address three times. Why couldn't the lady just get it right the first time? I ended the call and turned back to Alana. I gently rolled her onto her back and examined her body. I didn't see any blood on her chest or stomach, so she didn't appear to have been shot or stabbed.

"Alana," I said again, but she wouldn't wake up.

I put my ear back to her mouth to make sure she was still breathing. The dog continued to whine.

I called Foxx and told him to get over to the house. He got there in less than ten minutes, which meant he'd probably pushed his SUV to over eighty miles per hour.

I heard the kitchen door open.

"Poe! Where are you?" Foxx yelled.

"I'm in the front room!"

Foxx rounded the corner.

"Oh, my God, what happened?"

"I don't know. She was like this when I got back," I said.

Foxx kneeled beside me.

"Who did this to her?" he asked.

I didn't answer him. I couldn't even think about that right now.

Foxx touched the side of her face.

"You're going to be all right," he told her.

It took an agonizing thirty minutes for the ambulance to get to the house. Foxx had called 911 twice since he'd arrived and screamed at the operator to get the ambulance there sooner. He kept getting up and running over to the window to look for the ambulance that apparently wasn't coming. I stayed beside Alana and held her hand. I kept telling her over and over again that she would pull through this. I watched her eyes the whole time and waited for them to open, but they never did.

Foxx ran over to the front door when we finally heard the sirens. He opened the door and raced out into the yard. He brought the paramedics into the house and over to Alana. They asked me what had happened as well. I told them I didn't know. They tried to get her to come to, but she wouldn't. They checked her body for injuries just as I had.

"She'll be all right," Foxx kept telling me.

The paramedics lifted her onto a stretcher and rolled her out to the ambulance.

"Come on. We'll follow them in my car," Foxx said.

We followed the ambulance to the hospital in Wailuku. There seemed to be a million cars on the road, and they all took their sweet time getting out of the ambulance's way. Foxx followed at a close distance the entire time. Neither of us said a word on the way to the hospital. I thanked God that I'd been able to reach Foxx since I didn't think I would be able to drive at a time like this.

During the drive, I wondered how long Alana had been lying there. Had she gone directly back to the house after the interview with Liam, or had I missed the attacker by just minutes? She hadn't answered the phone during either of my calls, so maybe she'd been unconscious that entire time. I didn't know.

I'd just spent the drive to the house thinking about how much she meant to me, and now she might be going away for good. How could things go from so good to so bad in one second?

I don't know how long Alana was in the bed at the emergency room before she finally woke up. Time seemed to have slowed down since I'd found her on the floor of our house. I asked her what had happened, but she was out of it and didn't respond to any of my questions. Maybe she wasn't even sure who I was. Her eyes had this faraway look in them. She kept complaining about how much her stomach hurt. Then she started vomiting blood. The doctor told me he thought she was suffering from internal bleeding.

I'd asked Foxx to call Hani, who could then call her mother. They arrived at the hospital just as the nurses carted Alana away toward the surgical suite. Hani and her mother showered me with questions, but I didn't have answers for anyone. That's when her mother started blaming me for Alana's attack. Why hadn't I been there to protect her? Was her beating related to one of my stupid investigations? I stood there and took it all. The truth is, I'd already been saying those things to myself. Her attack had probably occurred while I was killing time at Harry's. Some person had been beating the living hell out of her, and I'd been sitting in a bar and having a drink.

Hani put her arm around her mother's shoulders and led her to a chair in the waiting room. Foxx came over to me.

"Don't listen to her. It's not your fault," he said.

"Isn't it?" I asked.

"This case was Alana's before it was yours too. You had nothing to do with this."

I appreciated his words, but they definitely weren't sinking into my thick skull. I walked over to the hospital employee who was working the waiting room. I asked her how long these types of surgeries generally last. She said she didn't know but that she would try to get an answer for me.

I walked back to Hani and her mother.

"I'm sorry, Ms. Hu."

She looked up at me.

"I told her not to do that job. There were a thousand other things someone as smart as her could do. I'll never understand why she wanted to be a police officer," she said.

"She wants to help people, Mom. You know that," Hani said.

"Who did this to her?" Ms. Hu asked.

"I don't know. I tried asking Alana when she woke up, but I don't think she understood what I was saying."

"Do you think you can find him?" she asked.

"I won't stop until I do."

The four of us waited another hour, but we didn't get any updates. There was a monitor in the waiting room that listed the case numbers the patients had been assigned. Each number had a colored bar beside it which corresponded to a certain status in the procedure. For example, red meant they were still in surgery, while green said they were in post-op. Alana's number was still red. I must have checked it a thousand times, but it never changed colors.

A police officer arrived about two hours into the surgery. He seemed to recognize Ms. Hu for he walked right over to her.

"Ms. Hu, I'm very sorry for what's happened to Alana," he said.

He stuck his hand out, and she wrapped both of her hands around his.

"I have every confidence that she'll pull through this, though. She's a fighter," he continued.

The officer turned to Foxx and me.

"Which one of you is her fiancée?"

"I am."

"Can I talk to you a moment?" he asked.

I followed the officer out of the waiting room and into the hallway.

"I'm Captain Lucas Price."

"I've heard a lot about you, Captain," I said.

"And I've heard a lot about you as well. What are they saying about Alana?"

"Nothing much. We haven't heard anything since they took her back."

I then told the captain how I'd found her unconscious and how she'd vomited blood after getting to the hospital.

"I asked her who did this, but I got nothing," I continued.

"I think I can answer that for you. Liam Hayes turned himself in about an hour ago. He confessed to the murders of his wife and her lover. He also admitted that he was the one who attacked Alana."

His words were like a sledgehammer to my head. I hadn't spent more than a few seconds thinking about her attacker, but my thoughts hadn't ever gone to Liam. I wasn't sure why that was, though.

"I need to get back to the station, but would you please do me a favor?" he asked.

Captain Price reached into his jacket pocket and removed a business card, which he handed to me.

"Will you please call me on my personal number when she gets out of surgery? I'd like to know how she's doing," he said.

I could only nod at his request since my brain couldn't seem to command my mouth to speak. I watched the captain as he turned from me and disappeared around the corner of the hallway. Foxx came out of the waiting room a few moments later.

"What did he want?" Foxx asked.

I told him about Liam confessing to Alana's attack.

"That makes sense. He's the guy you and Alana had fingered for the murder of his wife, right?"

"Yeah, we'd just met with him this morning."

"How the hell do you think he got the drop on Alana, though?"

"I don't know. I don't even know why she was at home to begin with. I thought she was at work. I thought she was preparing to arrest him," I said.

"I guess he knew that and wanted to get his revenge," Foxx suggested.

Hani poked her head out before I could respond to Foxx.

"The doctor's here," she said.

We walked back into the waiting room and approached the surgeon.

"How is she?" I asked.

"She was banged up pretty badly. Her spleen was lacerated in several places. Unfortunately, we had to remove it," the doctor said.

I guessed the doctor saw the look on all of our faces because he then responded with, "Don't worry. The body can live without the spleen."

"I don't even know what the spleen does," Foxx said.

"It helps to filter your blood, so she will be more susceptible to certain infections like pneumonia," the doctor said.

"Do you expect her to make a full recovery?" I asked.

"I do. She'll probably need to stay here for several days, but she'll pull through okay. She's very lucky you guys found her when you did. She was bleeding out. She wouldn't have survived another hour."

"When can we see her?" Ms. Hu asked.

"She'll be in post-op for a couple of hours, and then she'll be moved to a private room. I would guess you could see her in another thirty minutes or so. Unfortunately, we only allow one person back at a time."

We all thanked the doctor, and he left the waiting room. Ms. Hu turned to me.

"You should be the first to see her."

"That's okay. She's your daughter. I'll wait until you and Hani have had a chance to go back."

"Nonsense. You're the one she'll want to see first. I know it."

Then she did something that shocked me. She walked over to me and hugged me.

"She's going to be okay," she said.

I don't know what it was. Maybe it was all of the emotions bottling up for the past few hours, or maybe it was just the realization that Alana was really going to be all right, but I broke at that point. I felt like an idiot, but I couldn't stop crying. I'm sure I embarrassed Foxx. I know I embarrassed myself. I hate admitting that to you, but it's always been my goal to tell you the truth in these stories.

We all took turns going to see Alana in post-op. They eventually took her to her own room. She was out of it for several hours, as I assumed she would be, but we all sat around the bed and just stared at her. No one said much of anything. No one needed to. It was obvious what was running through everyone's minds.

Foxx was the first to leave. I gave him the keys to my house so he could go over there and let the dog out. I told him I'd take a cab back later that night. Hani and her mother stayed a couple more hours, and then Hani announced she was taking her mother home. I stayed with Alana late into the night. She was asleep most of the time. She awoke around midnight.

"Poe," she said.

I was half asleep in a chair that I'd pulled over to her bedside. I stirred when I heard my name. It took me a few seconds to realize it had come from Alana.

"Hey, there," I said.

"What time is it?" she asked.

I laughed.

"That's the first thing you're wondering?" I asked, but I looked at my watch anyway.

"It's almost twelve."

"How long have I been out?" she asked.

"I'm not sure. I found you this afternoon."

"What happened?"

"You were attacked in our house. The doctor had to operate on you."

"Why? What did they do to me?"

I repeated what the doctor had told us after her surgery. She took it all in, at least I think she did, but she was probably still mostly out of it since she didn't have much of a reaction. Maybe the shock and anger would arrive tomorrow.

Alana looked down at her hand.

"Where's my ring?" she asked.

I looked at her hand, too. The engagement ring was gone.

"Don't worry about it. I'm sure they took it off before the surgery. They always do that. I'll ask the nurse to bring it to you."

I put my hand over hers.

"You scared the you-know-what out of me," I continued.

"I'm sorry about that."

"No reason for you to be. I'm just glad you're all right. We have a lot to do with our lives. So many adventures to enjoy. You can't leave me now."

Her eyelids grew heavy again, and she was asleep within seconds. I sat beside the bed for a few more minutes. Then I walked out of her room and made my way over to the nurse's station. I asked a nurse about Alana's ring. She checked the records and reported that there was no mention of a ring. She confirmed my thoughts that they would have removed the ring before surgery. They would have either brought it to Alana's room or given it to a family member before the surgery even started. Since neither of those things had happened, the nurse assumed that Alana hadn't arrived at the hospital with any jewelry.

I went back to Alana's room and saw that she was still asleep. I walked over to her bedside and kissed her goodnight. Then I walked out to the lobby where I called for a cab. It was after one o'clock in the morning by the time I got back to our house. I entered through the garage like I had the last time. Foxx still had my keys, but I could still get inside since we had one of those keypads on the outside trim beside the door that lets you punch in a code to get the door to open. Maui the dog greeted me this time. He ran up to me and did his dramatic rollover. It was such a routine thing for us, and it brought me more comfort than I could possibly imagine. Silly how little things like that can be such a big deal.

I walked upstairs to the master bedroom and checked the nightstand, which is where Alana usually kept her ring after taking it off before bed. The ring wasn't there. I hadn't really expected it to be. It seemed pretty obvious what had happened. The attacker had probably stolen the ring after hurting Alana, but why would Liam do that only to turn himself in a few hours later? It didn't make any sense.

16

AN INCONVENIENT TRUTH

I AWOKE AFTER SLEEPING ONLY A FEW HOURS. I TOOK THE DOG ON A walk to Foxx's house to get my keys back. I thanked him for his support the day before. We spoke for a little while, mostly just stuff about how we both hoped that Alana would make a full recovery. Foxx said he'd come by the hospital sometime in the afternoon. He also said he intended on calling Alana's mother and Hani that morning and offering to drive them to the hospital if they needed him to. It was a complete turnaround from their argument in the bar the day before, but I guess family emergencies can have a way of putting priorities in perspective. Not always, but sometimes.

By the time I got back to my house, there was a news truck parked in the street. There were two people, a man and a woman, outside the truck. The guy stood behind a large video camera that was on a tripod and was pointing at the front of my house. The woman held a microphone. She stood beside the guy, but then she looked at me as I approached. I did my best to ignore them and turned to head up the driveway.

"Do you live with the police detective?" the female reporter asked me.

"No. I'm just her dog walker."

"This is where she was attacked, isn't it?"

She took a step onto the driveway, and Maui the dog lunged at her. He would have wrapped his jaws around the poor lady's lower leg if I hadn't yanked back on the leash.

"Probably best if you stay off the property. The dog gets kind of territorial," I said.

Add news reporters to the shortlist of people Maui doesn't like. Of course, everyone hates the media these days.

I went back into the house and fed the dog. Then I changed into my swim trunks and swam laps in the pool for about twenty minutes. I'm sure you think I'm crazy for exercising at a time like this, but the physical exertion seemed to have a way of calming my mind. You can't concentrate on much bad stuff when every muscle in your body is concentrating on the physical task at hand.

I climbed out of the pool and sat on a patio chair after turning it to face the ocean. I watched the waves roll into the shore and tried to focus on their rhythmic sounds. I probably sat there for about thirty minutes, but I couldn't get Alana's attack out of my head. Someone had come into our home and tried to kill her. This was supposed to be the place she felt the safest, and now it would be a constant reminder of how dangerous the world can be. Granted, she already knew that being a police detective, but it's one thing seeing it happen to others. It's quite a lot different when the criminal shows up on your doorstep.

I went inside and took a long hot shower. I got dressed and went downstairs to eat some fresh fruit since I assumed the hospital food had the potential to put me in a room beside Alana's. You'd think they'd have healthy stuff there, but they almost never do. It's a universal truth about hospitals.

I tried to watch a little television before leaving for the hospital, but every local channel was talking about the case. A well-known detective had been assaulted in her own home, and it happened to be in one of the most exclusive neighborhoods on the island. The fact that it was directly connected to the murder of a woman and her lover by the estranged husband only added to the juiciness of the scandal. They aired an old photo of Alana when she was still a uniformed officer. The news also ran a photo of Liam Hayes. They'd taken it off the hotel's website where Liam used to work. Apparently, the hotel hadn't gotten around to removing him from their list of team members. Now they were being dragged into the mud as well.

I wondered if the news videographer had gotten a shot of Maui and I on the driveway and whether I would now be forced to watch myself a million times on TV for the next few days. That's when I made the decision to turn the TV off and not turn it back on for at least another week.

I finally got to the hospital around ten o'clock. Alana was awake when I walked into the room. She muted the television and turned to me.

"You're not going to believe this, but I just saw you and the dog on the morning news."

What did I tell you?

"Yeah, I ran into the news team this morning. They were camped in front of the house. Maui sends his regards by the way," I said.

Alana smiled.

"You know, he was the reason I found you," I continued.

"Remind me to give him an extra treat when I get out of here."

"Has the doctor been to see you this morning?"

"He left just a few minutes before you arrived."

She gave me the rundown on what she'd been told, which was pretty much the same thing that we'd heard immediately after her surgery.

"Do you even remember what happened?" I asked.

"Not really. Someone hit me from behind. It was pretty much lights-out after that."

I supposed that was ultimately a good thing.

"How did you even end up at the house? I'd assumed you'd be at work."

"I went back to the station after our meeting with Liam and Mara. The D.A. agreed with me that we had enough to charge Liam with

Nalani's murder. She didn't agree about Gabriel Reed, so I went back to his gallery."

"Why?" I asked.

"I figured Liam wasn't going anywhere, and I wanted another chance to go through Gabriel's emails and phone. I really thought we'd just missed something."

"Did you find anything?"

"No, and I felt a migraine coming on, so I thought I'd run back to the house and get my medication. I let the dog out the back. I left the door cracked so he could get back inside. I went upstairs to get the medicine. I came back downstairs, and I got hit a minute later."

"Did you see their face?" I asked.

"No. I didn't even hear footsteps behind me."

"If you were watching the news, I'm guessing that you know Liam Hayes turned himself in."

"I saw that. It's my fault. I got careless. I should have arrested him right there in Mara's office," she said.

"Please don't blame yourself for this."

"Did you have a chance to talk to anyone at the station? What are they saying about Liam?"

"Your captain came to the hospital last night, but we mostly just talked about you."

I then told Alana that her ring was gone, but I'd ask her captain to question Liam about it.

"That's weird. Why would he steal it?" she asked.

"I don't know. Maybe he was just trying to hurt you any way he could."

"I hope he fries for this."

"I'm sure he will. Two murders and a felony assault on a police officer. He's not going anywhere anytime soon."

I spent the rest of the day at the hospital. Foxx came by right after lunch. He asked Alana the same questions I had, and she gave him the same answers. Alana kept the television on all day, and I saw Maui the dog and myself a few times on the news. God, I looked grumpy as hell on TV. I needed to do something about that. Hani and her mother arrived in the late afternoon, and Alana got a third round of the same questions.

Alana's captain came by just after Hani and her mother left. Alana asked him about Liam, but he kept telling her not to worry about it and just concentrate on getting better. Did that stop her from asking questions and demanding updates on the prosecution? Of course not. He finally relented and tossed a little piece of information out to pacify her. He said Liam Hayes wasn't talking other than his initial confession that he'd attacked Alana and murdered Nalani and Gabriel.

I stayed with Alana until eight o'clock that night. I told her to call me if she got bored. I walked out to the parking lot. The evening air felt cool, and there was a steady breeze. I popped the top back on the convertible and made the long drive down the coast back to the house. There was something in the back of my brain that just wouldn't stop itching. It was like some little piece of information that was demanding to come to the surface. I tried to ease my mind to let the hidden fact come out, but it wouldn't arrive.

I walked outside to the backyard and assumed the position on the patio chair that I'd been in that very morning. This time the sounds of the waves did their trick. I finally heard the voice in my brain, and its message was clear: Liam Hayes didn't attack Alana. He didn't kill Nalani Hayes, and he didn't kill Gabriel Reed. He was a beaten man. Maybe his wife's constant affairs had done that to him over the years. Maybe it was his job. Maybe it was all of the above, and we just call that life.

The guy was a shell of a person, though. I couldn't see someone like that getting the drop on Alana. Hell, I couldn't even see him having the courage to drive across the island and sneak into our house. I remembered the way he'd looked at her in Mara's office. Actually, he could barely even look at her. He was so worried about what she was going to do to him. He'd completely given in to her authority. Sure, his attitude could have done a one-eighty afterward, but I didn't think so.

There was also Gabriel Reed. Liam had followed him all over the island. He'd switched cars a few times to keep Gabriel from recognizing him. He'd even gone to Gabriel's house and watched his wife have dinner with her lover. Still, he hadn't done anything to Gabriel. What would have been your response if you saw your spouse with their lover? Would you sit there and just watch, or would you burst in and read them the riot act? Maybe you'd do even more. Liam hadn't, though, so how was I now supposed to believe that he snuck over to Gabriel's gallery and snapped his neck like some cold-blooded assassin?

The only death I really saw as being plausibly committed by Liam was the death of Nalani. Still, I didn't think he'd done that one, either. He'd told Alana during the last interview that Nalani always came back to him. I believed him, too. It was the same thing Kaylee King had said when I'd interviewed her. She'd said Nalani and Liam had this weird, co-dependent thing. Nalani always would run back to Liam when the thrill of her lover's attention started to wear off. She loved being chased, both by Liam and her lovers.

Liam Hayes didn't do the crime. That was the inconvenient truth I'd come to understand while I listened to the ocean waves, but how was I going to prove it? I didn't know, but I wasn't going to stop until I did. Of course, this truth, if it was even the truth, brought up another disturbing reality: Alana's attacker was still out there. So was Nalani's and Gabriel's killer.

17

ON THE INSIDE

WE ALL WANT TO BE ON THE INSIDE, DON'T WE? MAYBE IT'S THE COOL group at school when we're kids. Then we become adults, and we want to feel like we have the best jobs and live in the best houses and drive the right cars. Human beings are social creatures, and they desperately want the approval and admiration of others. As someone once said, "No man is an island."

It's an unfortunate thing, though, that we judge ourselves and our success by our material achievements. If they aren't what we thought they would or should be, then we feel like we're on the outside. That's how Kaylee King felt, or at least how I thought she probably felt. I was about to change all of that, though. I was about to make her a player in the thing everyone on the island was talking about. She wouldn't be able to resist it, and that urge to be involved would overcome her fear.

I called Kaylee after my little revelation that I didn't think Liam was guilty of any of the things he'd confessed to. I didn't tell her that, at least not yet and not over the phone. She asked how Alana was doing, and her questions sounded sincere. Despite her initial criticisms of Alana and her new-found success, I thought Kaylee still cared for her. I guessed there was still some of that childhood friend-ship stirring around inside of her.

I asked Kaylee if she'd be willing to talk with me a second time, but this time I made the request that we conduct the interview at my house. Before she could answer, I told her that I hoped she wouldn't mind coming here since I was well aware of the fact that it was where Alana was attacked. I said I could understand she might not want to see where it had all happened. Was my reverse psychology obvious? Probably, but she ate it all up. She pretended to hesitate, but I was never in any doubt that she'd say yes.

We agreed on a time to meet the following morning. Kaylee arrived on time. I gave her a tour of the house and concluded it in the front room where the blood stains were still on the white carpet. I know what you're thinking right now. You're disappointed in me for being so manipulative and exploitative. Maybe I was being that way, but I was also desperate to discover the truth, and I thought Kaylee held the key to the first door of discovery.

I led Kaylee to the living room, which overlooked the ocean. We sat down on the sofa after I asked her if she'd like anything to drink. She declined.

"When do the doctors think Alana will come home?" she asked.

"I'm not sure, exactly. Maybe a week. Maybe two. She was beaten pretty badly."

"I can't believe someone would do that to her," Kaylee said.

I'm sure you caught that. Her use of the word "someone." She didn't say "Liam," which was another brick in building the wall of my theory.

"Liam confessed to the attack. Did you hear that?" I asked.

"I did."

"I think it's about time I get to the reason I asked you here. Liam gave me a list of people to talk to after I first took his case. This was back when he'd asked me to prove he didn't murder Nalani. People don't give you a list of others who will say they did the crime, but that's pretty much what everyone implied. Everyone, that is, but you. You're the only one who implied Liam might not be guilty. Even the guy he was staying with couldn't, or wouldn't, vouch for him. Mason Howard pretty much contradicted everything Liam said."

"But Liam said he did it. He confessed after he attacked Alana. That's what the media said."

"I think we both know they can sometimes get things wrong."

I paused a moment and then asked the main question I'd been wanting to get an answer to since last night.

"Nalani told you something, didn't she? That's why you came to Liam's defense. Maybe you didn't know for sure that he didn't do it. I'm guessing you don't know who did, but you had enough doubt that you wanted me to know he was probably innocent."

"She didn't tell me anything."

Her answer had been too quick. Usually when you ask a question like that, the person takes a few seconds to ponder if they could remember anything from previous conversations with their friend. Kaylee hadn't done that. She'd practically blurted out her answer before I finished talking.

"So why did you think he didn't kill her?"

"I believed his story when he said she'd taken him back. She always did," Kaylee said.

"There's still Gabriel's death. It's the thing that doesn't fit. Nalani and Gabriel were into something dangerous, weren't they?"

"What do you mean?"

"Gabriel's neck was snapped, and his body was staged to make it look like an accident. The news doesn't know that. Just a few people do. Now you do, too. Does that sound like something Liam would know how to do?"

Kaylee didn't answer me, and she did that subconscious thing of looking away to avoid my gaze.

"What did she tell you?" I asked.

She still didn't respond.

"I don't know why Liam would confess to something he didn't do, but it's got to be a pretty big threat if he'd rather be in jail than face what's out there. I understand you're scared, but no one will know what you tell me."

"How do they know I'm not already here?" she asked.

"You're just a good person visiting the fiancé of a hurt childhood friend. You should probably go see Alana today at the hospital. I'm sure she would appreciate it."

"I don't know who killed them. I swear."

"What did Nalani say?" I asked.

"She was going to end things with Gabriel. She just didn't know how."

"Was she afraid of Gabriel?"

"She wasn't afraid he would try to hurt her, not directly, but she said he wouldn't listen to her."

"About what?"

"She said he knew something, and it was going to get both of them killed."

"Do you know what it was?" I asked.

"No. I asked her, but she said I was better off not knowing. Now, I'm glad she didn't tell me."

"So when you heard Nalani had been killed, you thought it was this thing that she'd referred to?"

Kaylee nodded.

"Do you think Liam is involved?" I asked.

"I don't think so. She would have mentioned his name. All she talked about was Gabriel. She said he was arrogant and reckless. It had something to do with money. He thought they were going to get rich."

"Did you say anything to Liam or Gabriel after Nalani was killed?"

"No. I was too scared. I didn't talk to anyone but you. I didn't even want to do that, but then you said you were working with Liam. I figured you were trying to prove his innocence, and I didn't think he'd done anything wrong."

"Has anyone come to you since Nalani and Gabriel died? Anyone you don't recognize?" I asked.

"No, and I've been watching. I hardly leave the apartment. It took a lot just to come over here."

"When did all of this start?"

"A few weeks before she was killed. She just started acting weird. She wouldn't talk about it at first. I thought it probably had something to do with Liam, but then she finally admitted it was this thing with Gabriel."

I thanked Kaylee for coming to the house and her courage to tell me what she knew. I'm guessing you thought it wasn't very much, but it made all the difference in the world to me. Gabriel had some money-making scheme, and he'd gotten Nalani and himself killed in the process. Everything had pointed to the jilted husband who hadn't done himself any favors by stalking his wife and her lover across the island.

Alana hadn't mentioned any of this to me, which meant she didn't have a clue about it. Someone thought she did, though. That's why she'd gotten jumped in our house. This person or persons thought she was getting close to figuring it out. What had she done, though, that would lead them to that conclusion? Was it somewhere she'd gone, or something she'd inadvertently said to the wrong person?

I called Mara Winters' office and asked to speak with her. I'd been on hold for almost ten minutes when she finally got on the line.

"I'm sorry for the long wait. I couldn't get off the other line. How is Alana?" Mara asked.

"She's going to be fine. She's a tough lady."

"She is that. Please send her my best. I'm going to try to come see her in a few days, but I'm guessing she's inundated with people right now."

"I'll let her know."

"What can I do for you? I'm guessing there's another reason you called than to give me an update on Alana."

"There is. I'd like to know if you can set up a meeting between myself and Liam Hayes."

"Do you really think that's a good idea under the circumstances?" she asked.

"I'm not going to jump across the table and try to strangle him, if that's what you're worried about."

"No. I don't think you'd do that, or maybe you would considering what he did to Alana. The thing is, I'm not Mr. Hayes' attorney anymore. I dropped him after it became apparent he'd been lying to us all."

I didn't bring up the fact that I thought it had more to do with the dramatic reveal of his lack of finances.

"I don't think he did it, Mara."

"Attack Alana?"

"Or kill his wife and her lover. I think he was framed. Actually, I don't even think they set him up until recently. I think his past and his obsessive behavior are what made the police zero in on him. I really don't care about him, though. I just want to find who did this to Alana."

"And you think he knows?" Mara asked.

"He confessed for a reason, and it wasn't because he was guilty."

"What do you think is really going on? You must have a theory."

I told her about my earlier conversation with Kaylee King and her comments that Nalani told her Gabriel was into something dangerous.

"Does Alana know any of this?" she asked.

"No, and I want to keep it that way for a while. I don't want her stressing about it, not until I have this thing all figured out."

"I don't have any pull with the police now that I'm no longer his attorney. You're going to have to contact the department and try to set up the meeting yourself."

"Who do I talk to over there?"

"I don't think it really matters. I doubt they're going to let you anywhere near him, not after what he said he did to Alana."

I ended the call and walked into the kitchen to get my car keys. I made the decision to visit Alana first and try to figure out this jail-house interview thing later. My car keys weren't on the kitchen counter where I usually left them. That's when I remembered they were already in my pocket from my earlier walk with Maui the dog. I usually kept the house unlocked when I'd take him around the neighborhood. The recent attack changed that, though. I reached into my pocket and felt a piece of paper first. I pulled it out and saw it was the police captain's business card with his personal number. If he couldn't get me in to see Liam, then no one could. Would he buy my theory, though, or would he laugh me out of the station? I was about to find out.

18

TEXT MESSAGES

It took considerable prodding on my part to convince Alana's captain to let me speak with Liam Hayes. He had all the objections that both Mara and I knew he would. I think the ultimate reason he said yes was because of his close relationship to Alana. He knew what the implications were if they'd arrested the wrong man. The killer was still out there, which meant Alana's life could still be in danger. His one and only stipulation was that he had to be in the room with me. I objected at first, mainly because I thought the presence of a police captain would intimidate Liam to the point of him refusing to talk. Captain Price held firm, though, so I had no recourse but to agree to his terms.

I drove to the police station and had to wait over an hour for them to bring Liam to one of the interview rooms. A police officer led me into the back where I found Captain Price standing outside the room.

"I'm not going to have any trouble today, am I?" he asked.

"You have my word. I won't cause you any problems."

"A guy just doesn't confess to crimes he didn't commit. I've done this job for a long time. It just doesn't happen like that."

I didn't respond to him because there was no way I was going to convince him of anything there in that hallway. I needed to talk to

Liam first. Captain Price led me into the room. Liam was already inside. He was seated at a metal desk that was pushed up against the back wall. One of his hands was on his lap. The other was handcuffed to a metal ring on the top corner of the table. His eyes widened when he saw me. I walked over to the table and sat across from him. Captain Price stood a few feet from me, presumably close enough to grab me if all of my actions had been an elaborate charade just to get close to Liam to attack him.

"Alana survived the attack. Did they tell you that?" I asked.

Liam nodded.

"Why didn't you shoot her or stab her? Why give her the chance to pull through?"

Liam didn't respond.

"I can't even begin to tell you how I felt when I saw her there on the kitchen floor. Blood all over the tiles. I was sure she was dead," I continued.

"She should have left me alone," he said.

"I knew it was you, even before the police told me. Do you know how?" I asked.

"It was the meeting at Mara's. You saw how angry I was."

"It wasn't just that. It was her ring. I spent a small fortune on that thing. If it had been a robbery, the person would have taken the ring. There were other valuables in the house, too. I have several expensive watches, for example. Nothing was taken, though. That meant the attack had to be personal. You were the only guy who wanted to hurt her, so it had to be you."

"She should have left me alone," he repeated.

I turned and looked at the captain. It wasn't hard to interpret the look on his face. He finally believed me, at least he looked somewhat open to the idea. I turned back to Liam.

"Alana wasn't attacked in the kitchen. It was in the bedroom, and her ring was stolen. How did you get both of those details wrong?"

Liam looked at me, then over to the captain, then back at me.

"I first hit her in the kitchen, but I dragged her body into the bedroom."

"Why would you do that?" I asked.

"I don't know. I just did."

"You're wrong again, Liam. It wasn't in the bedroom, either. It was the front room. You weren't there at the house. They gave you a few of the details, like the fact they beat her versus shot her, but they left out the small stuff. They probably didn't think anyone would question whether you really did it or not."

"I don't know what you're talking about," he said.

Captain Price walked over to the table.

"Who attacked her if you didn't?" he asked.

"She should have left me alone," Liam said for a third time.

"I can think of only one thing that would make a man confess to three crimes he didn't commit. It would be a threat to his life or someone he loves. Since you don't have any kids and Nalani is gone, I'm assuming they told you they'd kill you if you didn't take the blame," I said.

Liam didn't respond.

"Your wife and Gabriel got in way over their heads with something. What was it?" I asked.

He still said nothing.

"What was it, Liam?" I asked.

"I don't know. I swear I don't know."

"They got killed for it, and Alana got attacked in her own home because someone thought she was getting too close. What was it?"

"I don't know, but it had to be Gabriel's doing. Nalani wasn't into anything illegal. I would have known about it. There was nothing."

"Who convinced you to confess?" Captain Price asked.

"I never saw the person. Someone texted me a photo of Alana. She was lying on the floor and bleeding. They said she was dead and that the same would happen to me if I didn't confess. They said they'd come over to the hotel and kill me, so I knew they were watching me."

"Do you still have the text?" Captain Price asked.

"No. They told me to delete everything off my phone, so I did. I barely even remember the photo of her. I was so scared I couldn't look at it for very long," Liam said.

"So you never talked to the person?" I asked.

"No. It was all by text. They also sent me photos of Nalani and Gabriel."

"These were photos of the crime scenes?" Captain Price asked.

"Yes, but I didn't get them until after the text about Alana's attack. I would have brought them to you if I'd gotten them before."

"You really have no idea what this is all about?" I asked.

"No. I would tell you if I did. I shouldn't even be telling you any of this. They said they have someone on the inside who will kill me if I talk to the police."

"How do I know any of this is true? Maybe you're just trying to save your ass. You've offered us no proof, and it doesn't take a genius to intentionally get the details of your crime wrong," I said.

"I don't know how to prove it. I told you I deleted the messages."

"I think your interview is over," Captain Price said.

He turned to me.

"Unless you have any more questions for Mr. Hayes."

I shook my head.

"You have to protect me. They said they'd kill me if I talked," Liam said.

"You're going back in. You can't get your story straight. Why should I believe anything you say?" Captain Price asked.

"They're going to kill me. I haven't done anything wrong," Liam said.

Captain Price ignored Liam's pleas. Instead, he led me out of the room and walked me back to the lobby of the police station.

"It won't be hard to verify his story. The phone company will have a record of those text messages, if he's telling the truth, that is."

"Thank you for setting this up," I said.

"You're convinced he's telling the truth this time?"

"I am, but it doesn't matter what I think. Does it?"

I didn't bother debating the pros and cons of Liam's story. It was either true or it wasn't. Either way, it needed proof. Maybe the text messages would prove me right, but they still didn't answer the question of who really attacked Alana.

I exited the building and walked to my car. My next stop was the hospital to visit Alana. I thought of Liam on the drive there. Liam Hayes was either a coward or a liar. I voted for the former. He'd gone to jail to save his own skin while allowing the person who murdered his wife to go free. Of course, he could have been making all of this up, as Captain Price apparently believed. I didn't think so, though. He'd botched the facts of the assault, and his comments about the threatening text messages seemed to correlate with what Nalani had told Kaylee King. Gabriel had gotten himself mixed up in something bad, and he paid the ultimate price for it.

Alana was sitting up in bed when I walked into the hospital room. She looked at the clock on the wall.

"You're a little later than you said you'd be."

"Sorry. I got sidetracked," I said.

"It's okay. It's just that this place is beyond boring."

"That's actually a good sign."

"How's that?" she asked.

"It means you're getting better. You aren't just sleeping through the day, so now you have the energy to get bored."

"I hadn't thought about it like that."

"Embrace the boredom. You're on the road to a full recovery."

"What kind of trouble are you getting in today?" she asked.

"No trouble. Just some errands. I'm yours the rest of the day. Is there anything you'd like me to get for you, maybe a magazine or a book?"

"Don't B.S. me. I've seen that look on your face. Your mind's a million miles away."

"No, it's not," I protested.

"It's this case. Isn't it?"

"How could it be? Liam confessed. Case closed."

Alana looked down at her hand, then back to me.

"Why did he take my ring?" she asked.

"Who? Liam?"

"He beats the living hell out of me. Then he thinks to steal the ring before he leaves the house?"

"You have some theory about that?" I asked.

"I've been thinking about it all morning."

"And?"

"I don't think he attacked me. I think it was someone else."

"I thought you said you didn't see your attacker?"

"I didn't, but it was a sneak attack, similar to the one that took out Gabriel Reed. I don't know if Liam has that in him," Alana said.

"You told me on my first case that every person has murder in them."

"And I still believe that, unfortunately. I'm just not sure Liam would have attacked me the way he did. I think he would have shot me in the back. He certainly wouldn't have the courage to attack me with his bare hands."

"The same with Gabriel's death?" I asked.

"Yeah. I don't think he did that one, either."

"Beautiful and brilliant. Is it any wonder that I proposed to you?"

"You've already thought of this, haven't you?"

"It's the reason I was late. I was in a meeting with your captain."

I told her about the jailhouse meeting with Liam and his claims that he'd been sent the photos of the attacks along with a threat to confess to the crimes or end up like the previous victims.

"What did the captain think?" Alana asked.

"I'm not sure. If I had to bet, I'd say he was leaning in the direction of Liam lying about the entire thing."

"Don't underestimate the captain. He takes a while to come to a conclusion, but that's because he's usually thought it out pretty thoroughly."

"We'll know soon enough. He's trying to get the phone records to prove the text messages were real."

"If it was Gabriel who put all this into motion, what do you think it's all about?" she asked.

"I have no idea, but I'm guessing Nalani's death was a warning. Gabriel apparently didn't get the message."

"Maybe they thought he was going to the police, and they needed to shut him up."

"Probably," I said.

"Don't think I don't realize you've kept this theory hidden from me. It's my case."

"I'm sorry, but maybe you haven't noticed that you're in the hospital. I didn't want to stress you out."

"I thought I just got through telling you how bored I am. Let me help. It will give me something to think about."

It was then that I realized just how addicted to the hunt Alana was. Maybe she was even worse than me.

"Okay. Let's talk it through. What was Gabriel doing?" I asked.

"I don't know, but it's why I went to his gallery. I figured there had to be something there."

"But you didn't find anything," I said.

"I know, but maybe I wasn't looking for the right thing."

"Maybe there's just nothing there."

"You should go back yourself. Give the gallery one more search. If you don't find anything, then search his house, too. Just do me one favor: Don't tell the captain any of this."

"Why not?" I asked.

"Because he won't approve of you doing it. He'll insist on assigning another detective."

"You have good people in there. Well, all accept that one bozo."

If you've read any of my previous books, then you'll know exactly who I was referring to. He's a detective who I've had a few run-ins with. Alana doesn't like him either.

"I do have some good detectives I work with, but none of them are as insightful as you. Besides, you already know more about this case than any of them. It would take too long to bring them up to speed," she said.

"I'll try to go to the gallery tonight then, after I've left here."

"You should go this afternoon. Save yourself the torture of Hani coming over here."

"You've spoken to her today?"

"Yes, and she said she's bringing the wedding stuff here. She said this is the perfect time to get my undivided attention."

"You should tell her no if you need to rest."

"It's okay. I'm actually looking forward to it. Besides, I'd like to start planning something good for a change."

"In that case, don't worry about the budget. The sky's the limit. Anything you want."

"Don't forget, though, I'm still lead detective on this. If you find anything, I want to be the first to know."

"Absolutely. You'll be the first. I swear."

19

THE RING

I CALLED BROOKLYN FROM THE HOSPITAL AND ARRANGED TO MEET HER at Gabriel's gallery in Lahaina. I arrived around four in the afternoon. The little town was packed with tourists, as it usually was, so I parked at Harry's and made the short walk to the gallery. I saw Brooklyn through the large windows in the front of the building, so I knocked on the door and walked inside.

"Thanks for coming out here again," I said.

"No problem. However I can help. Is that detective going to be okay? I heard she was attacked."

"She's going to be fine. They have pretty good doctors at that hospital. They did a good job of patching her up."

"I'm so glad to hear that. I was really worried about her."

"How did you hear about it?"

"It's all over the news. It's all anyone is talking about. I'm glad they caught the guy who did it."

"I'm sure it's a relief to everyone," I said.

"What is it you wanted to look at?"

"I saw the detective earlier today, and she asked me to have another look around the gallery."

I could see the look of confusion in her eyes.

"Okay, but why? I thought Nalani's husband confessed to killing Gabriel," she said.

"He did, but they think there's something more to it than that."

"Like what?"

"I can't really get too far into it. I hope you understand," I said.

She hesitated a moment but then seemed to accept my explanation.

"What is it you need to look at? Do you need to go through his computer again?"

"I do. Can you log me into his email account?" I asked.

I followed Brooklyn to the computer. She started typing his login information for the Gmail account. That's when I noticed it. The huge diamond ring on her finger. I hadn't seen it before, but maybe she hadn't been wearing it the last time. It had to have cost a small fortune. I'm not an expert on jewelry, but I do know a lot more about diamond rings after having spent weeks shopping for Alana's engagement ring.

"Nice ring. I assume congratulations are in order," I said.

She hesitated a moment and then looked down at her hand.

"Oh, it's not an engagement ring. Sometimes I just wear it on that hand."

Brooklyn slipped the ring off her left hand and put it on her right.

"For a second, I forgot it was there. I usually don't wear it at work," she continued.

I found it an odd response. I doubted a woman would wear a ring on her left hand if it wasn't an engagement ring, unless she was going out at night and didn't want guys hassling her.

"Do you mind me asking what you're going to do now that Gabriel is gone?"

"I'm thinking about starting my own photography business. A couple of his clients have already asked me about taking over for him."

"Is U'i Décor one of them?" I asked.

"They are."

"That's good, right? Didn't you say they were his number one client?"

"They have a ton of work, but I just hope I'm good enough to keep up with it all."

"I'm sure you'll do great."

"I'm not even sure I want to do it. All Gabriel did was work."

She finished logging onto Gabriel's email account.

"There you go," she said.

I took the mouse from her and started scanning through the emails.

"I was thinking of running down the street to get a quick bite. Do you mind if I come back in a little while like last time?" she asked.

"No problem. I'll be fine here," I said.

Brooklyn left, and I spent the next hour trudging through Gabriel's emails. Nothing jumped out at me, which I assumed would be the case since Alana hadn't been able to find anything, either. It had been a long shot, though, and part of me only did it because I couldn't think of anything else to do to discover what kind of trouble Gabriel had gotten into.

I closed his email account and walked into the back room where I'd discovered Gabriel's body. I looked on the shelves and saw several of his large photography prints. They were landscape shots of the various islands. There were also several canvas bags, both large and small, that I assumed held his photography gear. Most of them were on the lower shelves. I opened the first bag I came to and saw a variety of Canon prime lenses. I owned a few of these lenses myself. Most of them cost between two and three thousand bucks, so he probably had around twenty grands' worth of lenses in this one bag alone. Photography can certainly pay well if you get the right client.

I opened the next bag and found a few different camera bodies. The narrow doors on the sides of each camera body were open. I knew that's where the camera cards get inserted, so I found it a bit sloppy for him to leave those covers open since it allows dirt to potentially get inside the camera. Sure, the bodies were safe in his bag, but it was still careless since all sorts of grit can get into those bags when you're shooting in places like the warehouse of U'i Décor or some sandy beach with a scenic waterfall in the background.

I checked the other camera bags and found an assortment of other pro gear like strobe lights, zoom lenses, colored filters, a light meter, and various circular reflectors that were either gold, silver, or white. He had a great collection of equipment. Maybe Brooklyn could buy the stuff from his relative or whoever it was who stood to inherit his belongings.

I walked into the front of the gallery and waited for Brooklyn's return. I took the opportunity to look at the photographs hanging on the wall. It had to have been difficult to sell these. There was so much competition in Lahaina alone for selling artwork to tourists. Every shop seemed to either have a painting or photograph or some sculpture they were trying to unload. If I had to guess, I would say that most tourists probably just ended up buying a T-shirt or baseball cap with the word "Maui" or "Lahaina" written across the front. Twenty-dollar T-shirt or two-thousand-dollar photograph of a waterfall? Which would you choose?

I turned when I heard Brooklyn open the door.

"They are beautiful, aren't they?" she asked.

"He did gorgeous work. He had such a great eye," I said.

Forgive me for lying, but no one should ever talk bad about the dead. Unless they're a serial killer, of course.

"What will happen to all these prints now? Does Gabriel have a relative on the island?" I asked.

"Not that I know of. Both of his parents are dead, and he said he was an only child. I don't know what happens now. I don't even know if he has a will."

"Will you try to keep the gallery?" I asked.

"No chance of that. Gabriel was already three months behind on the lease. He didn't tell me about it, but I was here the last time the landlord showed up. It got pretty ugly."

"How so?"

"The landlord said he'd lock us out and sell all the photographs and Gabriel's gear to pay the back rent. Gabriel told him he'd have the money soon, but I don't think the landlord believed him."

"How's that possible? It seems like you guys were always busy," I said.

"We did a lot of work, but none of it paid very much. It's really hard to make a living as a photographer these days, especially on this island. Everybody thinks they can do it, and a lot of businesses are content to use their iPhones to take the photos. Nobody seems to care if it's just going on the web. Gabriel's probably got fifty-grands' worth of equipment back there, and it's been replaced with a five-hundred-dollar phone that everyone carries around with them," she said.

"I thought you guys had a lot of corporate clients."

"Not really. U'i Décor was our main one, and they were really the only ones who paid on time. Most of the work we did recently was weddings and portraiture."

"And this gallery? It wasn't bringing in money?" I asked.

"I suspect the gallery is what really did Gabriel in. He said he always dreamed of having one. The rent was too high, though, and we're too far back from Front Street for the tourists to find us."

"It sounds like you're in a tough spot."

"I am, and Gabriel still owed me for the last two months. I'll never get that money now."

"Do you own your gear, or did you just use Gabriel's?" I asked.

"It was all his. I can't afford the equipment, but maybe I can find a way to buy it from his estate."

"I can give you the name of a lawyer if you like. Maybe she can advise you regarding his estate," I suggested.

"Thanks. I'd really appreciate that."

I thanked Brooklyn for letting me into the gallery again, and I left after wishing her good luck. I had the feeling that a lot of his gear was probably going to disappear once she realized it was easier to walk off with it than apply for a business loan at the local Maui bank. No one would ever know, no one except me, and I certainly wasn't going to tell anyone.

I did find her comments on Gabriel's business pretty interesting on multiple fronts. My initial impression of the quality of his work was that it was average at best. I didn't see how he'd ever convince tourists, even wealthy ones, to part with that kind of cash to buy a photo that wasn't even as good as something they'd see on a Hawaiian calendar at a local drugstore.

Was I being harsh? Sure, but I didn't say that out loud. You're the only one who knows how I felt. Apparently, though, I'd been right. His gallery was failing to the point that he couldn't pay the rent. The decision to open the gallery had probably been made by his ego. Every artist dreams of having a gallery. It seldom ever works out that way, though.

Brooklyn was right as well. Art was dying in multiple genres. First, the internet killed the music business. Then cell phones killed off photography and video. Nothing's valuable anymore when everyone can do it, even if they can't do it nearly as well as the pros. Granted, there were still some businesses that wanted to hire someone who knew what they were doing, but it also seemed that his corporate work wasn't cutting it, either.

As I mentioned earlier, most photographers specialize in certain areas. It looked like Gabriel was trying them all just to get his head above water. He'd even turned to shooting weddings. I don't mean to imply there's anything wrong with that. There isn't. Weddings are obviously special events, and couples love having quality photographs to remember that time. However, most couples don't have the money to hire someone really good, not after forking out thousands for the dress, the venue, and all the free food and booze their guests will wolf down. The photographer often gets the short end of the stick. That's why this sector of the business tends not to attract the top talent. It's kind of viewed as slumming it if you're a photographer. Sorry to say that, but it's the truth. That meant if Gabriel had turned to it, he must have been in a tough place.

I also found it interesting that Brooklyn said he hadn't paid her in a couple of months. She'd told me the first time I'd met her that she'd started out as Gabriel's intern. That meant he couldn't have been paying her very much when he eventually hired her. No one goes from being the unpaid help to being a highly paid employee. She was probably making minimum wage at best, and she probably only agreed to do it since she was learning valuable photography skills, at least I hoped she was. He couldn't even afford to cover that low cost, though, and he'd stiffed her along with the landlord.

All of this evidence pointed to the fact that Gabriel was broke, yet he'd told the landlord that he was about to come into enough money that he could pay the back rent. Did I think that Gabriel had landed a big corporate client or some high-paying fashion photography job? Probably not. In all likelihood, he was referring to whatever illegal plan he'd been cooking with Nalani.

I walked back to Harry's and decided to slip inside to check on everything before heading back to the hospital. Foxx wasn't there, so I headed into the back office and logged onto the internet. I searched for Gabriel Reed's photography business. I realized after seeing the search results that I hadn't been as thorough as I should have been last time. There were three websites that could have been his. I'd selected the first one on the Google search results which showed his corporate work, one of which was U'i Décor. There were other clients, as well, including a luxury car dealership and a helicopter tour company.

I went back to the Google search and selected the next item that popped up. This business was called GR Photography, and it was a website dedicated to his wedding work. There were photography samples featuring over a dozen couples. I could tell they were real couples and not models. I don't want to sound mean, but you can usually tell when the wedding has been staged for marketing purposes since the couple is always gorgeous and everything looks too perfect. These couples were the real deal. The website offered five different wedding photo packages that ranged in price from one thousand dollars to five thousand. It became pretty apparent to me that Gabriel did a lot more wedding work than Brooklyn had let on.

The third website to show his name was the one for his gallery. It had numerous samples of his landscape work. It also showed behind-the-scenes photos of Gabriel and Brooklyn in various scenic locations on Maui and some of the other islands such as Kauai and Oahu. The website also had a long biography of Gabriel. I read it and learned that he was from Arizona. It featured the usual talking points of how he'd always dreamed of being a photographer and how he wanted to dedicate his life to capturing the beauty of the Hawaiian Islands. I found his writing to be as bland as his photography. Yes, it became obvious to me as I was scrolling through his work that I really didn't like Gabriel Reed.

I thought Brooklyn's best bet was to drop the landscape and corporate stuff and concentrate on the weddings. People are always going to be getting married. Furthermore, if they make the journey to Maui to recite their vows, then they have some spare money to spend. You have to go where the money is, as the old saying goes.

I logged off the internet and walked back into the bar to get a drink. Foxx had arrived and was talking to one of the bartenders.

"Hey, buddy. How's Alana doing today? I haven't had a chance to go see her yet."

"Major improvement. You may want to hold off your visit until tonight. I think she's probably up to her eyeballs in wedding stuff right now. She said Hani was coming by this afternoon to go over everything."

I could see a subtle shift in Foxx's mood. What was that all about?

"Everything all right?" I asked.

"Nothing's wrong. Can I talk to you a second, though?"

"Yeah, but I thought that's what we've just been doing."

"You know what I mean. Let's go back there."

Foxx pointed to one of the back booths.

"Sure thing," I said.

We walked to the back of the bar and slid into the booth.

"What's on your mind?" I asked.

"I need you to be honest with me about something."

Time for another sidebar. How many times have you been approached like that from a friend or family member? They say they want you to be honest, but I've found that they usually don't. What they really want is for you to tell them that everything is okay. I didn't know what Foxx was about to say. I just knew I almost certainly didn't want to hear about it. He's a good friend, though, and he had been there for me in a big way just a couple of days ago.

"What's on your mind?" I asked.

"I've been a dick lately, haven't I?"

"In what way?"

"This whole Hani thing. I haven't handled it well."

"I wouldn't agree with that. It's a pretty big deal. Your life is about to change in a major way. You're just adjusting to that. It's what anyone would do."

How's that for a noncommittal answer?

"I don't know. I've been kind of mean to her."

"Foxx, you and I both know that Hani is an expert at pushing people's buttons."

"Sure. I know that, but I still should have handled it better," he said.

"Okay, so start now. Commit to the notion that you aren't going to let her get to you. Smile and be nice. Make getting along your top priority with her."

"I was thinking of proposing," he said.

I was so stunned by his words that I was absolutely sure I hadn't heard him correctly. My brain started processing other options for what he might have actually said, but I couldn't come up with anything else. I couldn't even mutter the request for him to repeat himself. I think I just sat there and looked at him like an idiot.

"I was wondering if you could tell me where you bought the ring for Alana. You had it custom designed, didn't you?" he asked.

He just mentioned engagement rings, so I must have heard him right the first time.

"Foxx, have you lost your mind?"

"What are you talking about?"

"Why in the world would you propose to Hani?" I asked.

"Because she's having my kid. Isn't that what guys are supposed to do in situations like this? I mean, how much of an ass am I to not even consider it?"

"I thought you were actually being kind of mature about it. You didn't immediately just propose. You thought it over and came to the conclusion that you and Hani weren't a good fit. Just because things worked on a physical level doesn't mean they were going to work on an emotional level. That's way more important for a lasting marriage, at least I think that's what's supposed to make a marriage last. I haven't done it yet."

"It just seems like I should give it a shot. The kid deserves to have two parents."

"The kid does have two parents," I said.

"I mean two parents who are married."

"And if things don't work out like you know they won't, then you've just put the kid through a messy divorce."

"I don't know that. Maybe I'm jumping to conclusions. Maybe things would be okay if we just gave it another try."

"She works every last nerve in your body. I'm pretty sure that's a direct quote of yours."

"Why are you trying to stop me from doing the right thing?" he asked.

"I'm not. I'm offering an alternate point of view."

Foxx didn't respond, and we both sat there staring at the table between us.

"Is this because of the thing with Alana?" I asked.

"What do you mean?"

"It's gotten everyone emotional."

"Maybe."

"When something like that happens, it's sort of an emotional punch to the side of the head. You realize how fragile life is, and you start questioning all of your decisions."

"You don't think I should propose?" he asked.

"I'm not saying that. What I am saying is just don't rush into anything. Wait for the emotions to settle and then see what you want to do. Maybe you'll still want to propose. If you do, I'll take you to the jeweler myself. The guy was great."

"How much did it cost?"

"More than you'll want it to, but don't worry. You can afford it."

"How are things going with you guys? Have you settled on a place to get married?"

"I'm not sure. Alana was leaning toward this place in Wailea. Maybe she's changed her mind, though. Hey, when do you find out the sex of the kid? I've been wanting to buy him or her a present to welcome them to the world."

"Hani wants it to be a surprise, so she's refusing to find out."

"Can't the doctor let you know on the side?"

"I already tried that, but Hani made him swear not to say anything to me either."

"Are you hoping for a boy or a girl?" I asked.

"I've thought about that a lot, and I can't decide. Part of me wants a boy because I'd have a much better idea of how to raise him, but then I'd be afraid he'd turn out just like me."

"What's wrong with that?"

"Come on, Poe. You've been around for a lot of the stuff I've done. We're both lucky we're not in jail back in Virginia. You really want a kid to turn out like that?"

"I think you're exaggerating a little bit, don't you?"

"Not really. Think about it some more. You've probably blocked the really bad stuff we got into."

"But if it's a girl, then you'll probably be even more worried since you know how guys think," I said.

"Yeah, but then they'd get one look at me. You really think some guy's going to treat her wrong after I tell them what I'd do to them?" he asked.

"I see your point. Well, either way, I know the child will be loved, and he or she should have a pretty amazing life."

We spent the next half an hour or so talking about the places we wanted to take the child on the island. Then we expanded to the rest of the world and realized this kid was going to live on an airplane for all the cities and sights we wanted him or her to experience.

I realized then that I'd spent most of my time trying to referee the fights between Hani and Foxx, and I hadn't really contemplated how this birth was going to affect Alana and I. We were going to be his or her aunt and uncle. Sure, our level of responsibility wasn't anywhere near the level of a parent, but we had a certain role to play in their life. I intended to fulfill mine to the maximum level. I also had the good fortune of being independently wealthy, so I had plenty of spare time on my hands. I would need to put that time to good use.

Foxx told me he'd probably see me at the hospital later that evening, so I said goodbye for now and headed out to my car. I drove past Gabriel's gallery on the way to the main road which would take me back to Alana. My mind naturally drifted back to the investigation, and one of Brooklyn's comments popped up. She'd said that Gabriel didn't have much of a life. I somewhat disagreed with her since he'd obviously had time to wine and dine Mrs. Hayes. However, he had met her through his work, so maybe he was a workaholic after all.

That observation led to another one. If all Gabriel did was work, then most of the people he would associate with were his clients. Did that mean his money-making scheme had to be with one of them? Was one of his wedding couples up to no good? Was it one of his corporate clients? Had he heard or seen something that he wasn't supposed to? If so, how had he intended to cash in? Of course, I could be completely wrong. Maybe it was a neighbor. Maybe it was one of Nalani's friends. The possibilities were endless, and the multiple searches of his gallery had turned up nothing.

20

FLASHY

ALANA'S MOTHER WAS AT THE HOSPITAL WHEN I GOT THERE. LUCKY ME. She was sitting in a chair by the window. She shot me this look as I walked into the room that let me know she was just as pleased to see me as I was to see her. I'd thought we'd had a breakthrough of sorts in the hospital waiting room. She'd shown me real compassion, and I'd hoped she'd come to the conclusion that I wasn't such a bad guy after all. Apparently, I'd been wrong.

"You just missed Hani," Alana said.

"Did you guys have a chance to go over the wedding details?"

"I think we covered everything. I made a lot of decisions. I hope you don't mind."

"Not at all."

"Hani's doing a wonderful job. I told you she'd be a great wedding planner," Ms. Hu said.

"We're so grateful for your recommendation," I said.

Alana glared at me, but I'd said it with such conviction that I almost fooled myself into believing it.

"You also missed another visitor," Ms. Hu said.

I turned to Alana.

"Who came to see you?" I asked.

"Moani did. We haven't seen her in forever," Ms. Hu said.

"That's nice. What did she have to say?"

"She spent most of the time crying," Ms. Hu said.

Apparently, she was going to answer all of Alana's questions for her.

"That's not true. She barely cried. She told me how glad she was that I'd pulled through."

"She's certainly done well for herself," Ms. Hu said.

"How so?" I asked.

"You should have seen all the jewelry she was flashing. Who wears that many diamonds to the hospital?" Ms. Hu asked.

"It wasn't that much jewelry, Mother."

"Still. She sure wants the world to see that she's made it. It's tacky, flaunting your success for others."

"It was one ring and one necklace. What's the big deal?" Alana asked.

"Whatever you say, Alana, but I don't like it."

I wasn't sure how to respond to this discussion on what was and what wasn't acceptable to wear to a hospital while visiting an old friend, so I kept my mouth shut. It was obvious, though, that Ms. Hu had a thing against anyone who had some level of money. Was it jealousy? I guessed so since I didn't know another word to describe it.

"I'll leave you two alone. I need to be getting home anyway," Ms. Hu said.

She stood and walked over to Alana.

"I'll be back in the morning," she continued.

She kissed Alana on the forehead and then walked past me without saying a word.

"Have a good evening," I said after Ms. Hu left the room.

Alana laughed.

"She means well," she said.

"How do you figure?"

"Don't worry. She'll eventually warm up to you. It just takes her time."

"It's been two years. How much time does the lady need?" I asked.

"Maybe a decade or so. Maybe a little less."

"Are you serious?"

"Of course not," she said, but I thought she probably was.

"I guess I have that day to look forward to. She looks at me like I'm an IRS agent or something."

"Come on. It's not that bad."

"We'll agree to disagree. So, did Moani have anything interesting to say?"

"She just wished me a speedy recovery. We talked a little about Nalani and Liam."

"Did she have anything insightful to add?" I asked.

"Not really. She didn't like Liam. In fact, I don't know anyone from Nalani's childhood who liked him."

"By the way, was her jewelry that obnoxious, or was your mother exaggerating?" I asked.

"It was...impressive. I guess that's the best word. I'm not sure if you'd call that flashy or not."

"Everybody has their thing. For some people, it's cars."

"Or huge houses by the water," Alana said, and she smiled at me.

"Wait a minute. A house is an investment, not some obnoxious statement to the world that you're doing all right."

"If you say so, but can't the same be said for jewelry? Isn't that supposed to go up in value?" Alana asked.

"I assume so, but I've never tried to sell jewelry."

"The point of all of this is that you need to buy me more diamonds. It's an investment."

"I figured there was some ulterior motive to this conversation," I said.

"How did things go at the gallery? Did you find anything I missed?"

"Unfortunately, no."

I told Alana about my fruitless search of Gabriel's emails, as well as my search of the back room that revealed nothing but his gear and more of his photography work. I did point out the revelation that Gabriel had been broke and couldn't afford the rent on his gallery or the paycheck to his one and only part-time employee. I also told her about my theory, if that's what you'd call it, that Gabriel's probable illegal scheme had most likely been with a client of his.

Alana suggested that we search his website to see who his clients were. I told her that I'd already done that and didn't come up with much of interest beyond U'I Décor, the car dealership, and the helicopter tour company. Sure, there were probably more clients than that, and I realized I'd been neglectful when I didn't ask Brooklyn to provide me with a thorough list of their clients. Before we called her, though, Alana asked me to get her iPad off the table so we could search through Gabriel's social media accounts. The business accounts seldom had privacy settings on them, so we should be able to access everything on them.

We found a total of six social media accounts for his photography businesses. He used just Facebook and Instagram, and he had accounts for his wedding, corporate, and landscape sectors. He'd done a good job of separating the genres and not confusing his potential clients. He'd been a jack of all trades, at least in the photography business, but he'd presented himself as an expert in each of his categories. For example, his Facebook account of his wedding business featured many blog entries he and Brooklyn had written about the various stages of wedding planning, as well as the importance of hiring an experienced photography team to capture your once-in-a-lifetime moment. He also had many behind-the-scenes photos of him and Brooklyn at weddings across the island. I recognized some of the resorts, including the one where Alana and I were considering getting married.

The social media accounts of his corporate business were pretty sparse in comparison to his wedding business. Perhaps it was because his corporate work wasn't that much, or maybe there was just a ton more stuff you could talk about on weddings but not that much about corporate work. Maybe companies like the car dealership and helicopter tour company simply didn't care that much about social media, and Gabriel had realized it was a waste of his time to have a big presence in that marketing effort.

The landscape photography business had a small Facebook presence, too, but the Instagram account was by far the busiest. That made sense considering Instagram was a photography platform. Gabriel had a ton of behind-the-scenes photos of himself taking shots of waterfalls, beaches, and palm trees. There were even shots of him in the volcano crater of Mount Haleakala. Brooklyn was also prominently featured. She'd clearly been heavily involved in his business. I was scrolling through the photographs when Alana asked me to stop.

"Go back to that last one," she said.

"What did you see?"

I scrolled to the last photo and saw an image of Brooklyn standing on the beach at sunrise. She was holding a Canon 1DX camera against her chest. Women notice jewelry. I notice camera equipment. Clichéd? Of course.

"Let me see the iPad," Alana said.

I handed it to her and watched as she expanded the photograph with her fingers.

"That's interesting," she continued.

"What is?"

"Look at that ring on her finger."

"What about it?" I asked.

"It's on her right hand."

"Funny you should say that. It was on her left hand when I saw her earlier today. I mentioned something to her because I thought she'd just gotten engaged."

"What did she say?" Alana asked.

"It was weird. She slipped it off and put it on her other hand. I thought maybe she was just playing at being engaged. Does that make sense?"

"I don't know, but I do know I've seen this exact ring before, and it was on the person's left hand. I was intrigued because it was unlike any engagement ring I'd seen before."

"Was it in a magazine?" I asked.

"No. It was on Moani's finger. She took my hand in hers, and it shocked me because she hadn't been very nice to me the last time we ran into each other. I looked down at our hands and saw that giant rock on her finger. I was tempted to say something, but I didn't want her to know that I'd noticed it."

"Unlike your mother," I said.

"Now be fair. My mother didn't say anything either, not until Moani left."

"You're sure Brooklyn has the exact same ring?" I asked.

"I'm positive. It's a very distinctive ring."

"So they just bought it from the same jewelry store."

"Maybe, but it looked custom-made to me. Didn't you say earlier that Brooklyn was complaining that Gabriel had stiffed her on her last few paychecks?"

"Yeah."

"So how does someone who is counting every paycheck afford a ring like this?"

"Easy. Someone gave it to her."

"Did she say that?" Alana asked.

"When?"

"When you complimented her on the ring?"

"No. She just said she usually didn't wear it at work."

Alana pointed back to the iPad.

"Like she's doing on this beach while she's working?"

Alana scrolled through all of the photographs on the landscape Instagram account. We found several shots of Brooklyn. It was diffi-cult to tell in some of those, but the ones where we could see her hands clearly, she was wearing the diamond ring.

"So she wore the ring way more often than she thought she did. What does any of this mean?" I asked.

"Two things. One, when someone compliments a woman on her ring, she always says something like, 'Thanks, my boyfriend got it for me,' or 'My fiancé got it.' It's just what women do. You're not going to admit that you bought it for yourself, but we've just established that Brooklyn probably didn't get it for herself."

"So?"

"You're not getting this. There's only one circumstance that I can think of when you wouldn't say who got you the ring, and that's when no one is supposed to know who got it for you."

"Oh, wow, Koa's having an affair with Brooklyn?"

"You're getting slow in your old age," she said.

"Cut me some slack. It's been an emotional couple of days."

"Koa got his wife and mistress the same ring. I don't even know what to say about that."

"Do you think Brooklyn knows?" I asked.

"Let's find out."

Alana went to the social media account for Gabriel's commercial work. It only took a few seconds to find behind-the-scenes photographs of Brooklyn at one of the U'i Décor shoots. There were three shots of her. Her hands were clear in one of them. She wasn't wearing the ring.

"Yep, she knows," Alana said.

"That's pretty ballsy. Koa gives her the ring and tells her not to wear it around Moani because she has the same exact one."

"That's why Brooklyn had it on her left hand. Koa probably told her he'd marry her one day. Poor girl thinks he's actually going to leave his wife for her."

"Poor girl? She's the one having the affair. Serves her right."

"Her? What about Koa?" she asked.

"Him, too. He'll probably get caught. It's only a matter of time before someone notices what he did."

"Maybe not. Maybe he'll break things off before it comes to that."

"Gabriel was sleeping with Nalani, and Brooklyn is sleeping with her brother, Koa. Boy, they really knew how to service that business account."

"Stop it. That's disgusting," Alana said.

"Hey, I'm not the one cheating."

"Unfortunately, all any of this means is that Koa and Nalani were lousy spouses."

She was right, of course. We'd inadvertently uncovered a bit of a scandal, but it didn't mean anything in the grand scheme of things.

21

THE BACK-UP PLAN

I stayed with Alana until around eight o'clock in the evening. The doctor came by just as I was about to leave and told her he thought she'd be out of the hospital in another four days. She disagreed and said she thought she could go home in the morning. She made the case that she could heal faster if she were in her own home. The doctor tried to stress the seriousness of her injuries, but he may as well have been talking to the wall. It's hard to convince a Hu woman of something when they have their mind set.

I was almost to Lahaina when my phone rang. It was Captain Price.

"Good evening, Captain. I'm guessing you're calling about Liam's phone records."

"Good guess, and you were right for believing him. He did receive threatening text messages. Everything was exactly as he said, including the photos of Alana, Gabriel Reed, and Liam's wife."

"Have you spoken with him since we last talked?"

"Not yet. I've been busy trying to track down the number that called Liam. It was a dead end, though. Burner phone that was bought at a convenience store in Kihei. We checked out the store, and they don't have a working security system, so we couldn't get an image of the person who bought the phone."

"You have been busy since we talked."

"Have you discovered anything on your end?" he asked.

"Nothing that relates to this case. I've spent most of my time at the hospital."

"Well, the next time you see our girl, tell her to take it easy. She's already called me twice today."

"Is that right?" I asked.

"She called about Liam's phone records, so I'm guessing you filled her in on our little interview. I just got off the phone with her fifteen minutes ago. She requested that we pull the phone records for Gabriel Reed."

"She must have just called you after I left her room. When do you think you'll get his records?" I asked.

"Probably not until tomorrow."

"Alana mentioned several days ago that she had Nalani Hayes' phone records. Is there any way you can send them to me?"

"What is it you're looking for?" he asked.

"I'm not sure, but maybe something small will jump out that she might have missed. Alana was looking for proof that Liam was lying about getting back together with his wife. Alana didn't know at the time that it was Gabriel Reed who was up to no good."

"Tell you what. Swing by the office tomorrow morning, and we'll take a look at them together."

"Okay, thanks. I'll see you tomorrow."

I got home and took the dog for a long walk. I realized that I hadn't really learned much that day. Sure, I had confirmation that Liam had been threatened, but I already knew in my gut that he was telling the truth about that. I also had come to the conclusion, thanks to Alana's keen eyes, that Brooklyn had taken her boss' lead and was probably fooling around with one of her clients. I assumed that Moani was completely in the dark about it. I couldn't see her willing to wear the same ring that her philandering husband had given his mistress. She probably would have shoved it down his throat.

I'd also learned that Foxx was having some sort of emotional crisis brought on by Alana's attack. Did I think he'd change his mind and decide to marry Hani? I didn't know, but I wasn't willing to put down any money on the bet. Foxx can be an impulsive guy, and his emotions often won out over his brain. I hoped he didn't pop the question and then decide to take the ring back before they made it to the altar. Their relationship, such as it was, was already pretty turbulent. I shuddered to think what would happen if Foxx made Hani a jilted bride.

I made the decision sometime during the long walk with Maui that I didn't feel like waiting for the morning to review Nalani's phone records. I understood why the captain didn't want to send them to me. I was a civilian, and he didn't want me to get into the habit of thinking I could do whatever I wanted to do. I supposed I was lucky that he'd even bothered to call me to let me know I'd been right about Liam.

I walked back into the house and called Alana.

"Hey, just realized it's after nine. I hope I didn't wake you," I said.

"Nope, I'm just here, bouncing off these four white walls."

"I got a call from your boss. Seems like you've been going behind my back and working."

"How am I going behind your back? You never asked me not to call anyone."

"But I asked you to take it easy," I said.

"Making a phone call is strenuous?"

"All right, I won't argue the point. I'm calling because I need your help."

"At last. What are we going to do?"

"Do you have Nalani's phone records here at the house? I asked the captain for them, but he won't let me see them unless he's with me."

"Go into my office. There should be a printout of them on my desk."

I walked up the stairs and found them exactly where she said they would be. How are women so much more organized than men?

"Give me a little while to look through these, and I'll call you right back," I said.

"Okay, but call me back. I want to be involved."

I took the records into my office and sat down on the gray sofa I had pressed against the wall on the opposite side of the room from my desk. There were several pages of records. Three of the pages listed all of the incoming and outgoing phone numbers from the last month. The other pages were transcriptions of all the text messages she'd sent and received.

I decided to tackle the calls first. Alana had created a separate sheet where she'd handwritten the names and numbers of Nalani's friends and co-workers. I compared those numbers to the ones on the sheet from the phone company. Most of her personal calls, at least the ones that I assumed were personal, were to Gabriel and Kaylee, with about eighty to ninety percent of them being to her lover. They apparently couldn't get enough of each other. The other calls were to Koa and Moani. Those obviously could have been either work or personal. I also saw a few calls to the main number for U'i Décor.

One of the things that jumped out at me were the calls to Liam. There were none, at least not for the last month that she was alive. I did see where he had made several calls to her, but I guessed they'd gone unanswered based on the length of the call. It was another nail in the coffin of his lies that she had planned on taking him back.

I checked the text messages next. There were several numbers listed under those sheets. Most of her messages were sent and received by the same people as the phone calls, which made sense. She had several text exchanges with Koa, Moani, and Kaylee. I read the transcriptions for those. The Koa and Moani messages were almost all exclusively work related. They spoke about certain sales orders, as well as inventory reports on various goods. I found it a bit odd that there wouldn't be any communication about family-related stuff, such as a dinner invitation, or just a casual inquiry as to how the person was doing or feeling.

The text messages with Kaylee King were all that way. There were several exchanges about how stressed Nalani felt about her crumbling marriage to Liam. Kaylee certainly came across as a caring friend. She offered her advice and encouraged her to stay strong. Nalani also brought up Gabriel a few times, but they were all positive messages about how Nalani was looking forward to going out with him on some romantic date.

I checked Gabriel's text messages last. I pretty much already knew what I'd find since I'd read the text messages between them from the time I searched Gabriel's phone when Alana and I were at his gallery. It took me about thirty seconds before I realized something was wrong. I walked over to my desk since that's where I'd put my phone when I'd entered the office. I called Alana.

"I was just getting ready to call you. Did you find anything?" she asked.

"As a matter of fact, I did. Do you remember when I was describing Gabriel's and Nalani's text messages?"

"How could I forget? You kept trying to show me shots of their body parts."

"Someone altered them," I said.

"What do you mean?"

"This transcription is slightly different from what I saw on Gabriel's phone, at least the part from the day before she was killed."

"They changed what was written? How could they do that?" she asked.

"No. Not what was written, but they did delete some of the lines of text. I remember because I was paying particular attention since Liam had claimed that Nalani called him to get back together. I wanted to see if there was any indication that she was going to break things off with Gabriel."

"There wasn't, though. Didn't they even have dinner that night at Gabriel's house?" she asked.

"Yes, and that's what the text messages talked about."

"Okay, so what's the missing text?" she asked.

"There's a line in these phone records from Gabriel where he says he has something for her. Then he says it's the thing they talked about."

"Does he ever say what it is?"

"No, and she doesn't even ask him, so she obviously already knew," I said.

"She didn't say anything in response?"

"No, which is kind of weird especially when someone tells you that they have something for you. You'd think they'd respond somehow, but she didn't."

"Maybe she got distracted," Alana suggested.

"I don't think so because she responds to other things around the same time. I think someone deleted those specific lines for a reason."

"Okay, but what reason?"

"It has to be related to why they were killed. Why else would you delete it? It's not like they're inflammatory."

"But why delete just Gabriel's end of the conversation?" she asked.

"Because the killer couldn't get to Nalani's phone."

"Sure he could. It was on the kitchen counter if I remember correctly."

"Yeah, but the killer didn't know about the texts then. Gabriel was killed after Nalani. By the time the killer knew about the thing Gabriel had, whatever that was, Nalani was already dead, and her phone was in your possession."

Alana didn't respond, and I assumed she was trying to figure out if she thought I was on the right track.

"That's interesting," I said, and I walked back to my desk.

"What's interesting?" she asked.

"I just noticed my card reader on my desk. I plugged it into my laptop so I could download the most recent photos I took of the Iao Valley to my backup drive."

"And this is relevant how?"

"Remember when I said I searched through all of Gabriel's stuff?"

"Yeah."

"I don't remember seeing any compact flash cards or a card reader in his bags. They weren't on that table in the back room either," I said.

"What's weird about that?"

"I'm an amateur photographer, and I have at least four cards in my camera bag. I actually have one of those waterproof cases that holds the cards. Gabriel had every piece of gear known to man, yet he didn't have any cards in any of the bags. There's one more thing. He had multiple camera bodies in one bag, and all the side doors were open."

"The side doors?" she asked.

"It's where you insert the compact flash card. At first, I thought he was just being lazy since you don't want to leave those little doors open. I don't think he did, though."

"You think someone else came into his gallery and took all the cards?"

"Exactly."

"It also explains why he was killed there. It's a much more public place than his house, which is kind of in the middle of nowhere. That always bothered me."

"Maybe the killer came to the gallery and demanded the return of the card. Then he killed him," I said.

"So what's your guess? What was on that card?"

"Don't know, but it had to be proof of someone doing something they weren't supposed to be doing. Why else would the person want it enough to kill Gabriel?"

"Back to the text messages. Do you think Gabriel was referring to that evidence when he told Nalani he had something for her? Do you think that's why she was killed? The killer went to her first?"

"Maybe. It would explain why Nalani didn't respond to that text. She knew what it was about, and she was afraid. Kaylee said as much. She said Nalani told her that Gabriel was going to get them both killed."

"It also explains why that line of text was deleted on Gabriel's phone by the killer. They knew what it meant, too. Unfortunately, we don't have any way of knowing what was on that camera card," she said.

"Not necessarily. Gabriel said he had something to give her. Maybe he did that night before she died. He could have easily backed up that card to a DVD or thumb drive. Did her house look ransacked?" I asked.

"No, but she could have had the backup on her person or maybe in her bag. They might have found it pretty quickly."

"What about Gabriel's house? He could have made multiple back-ups. I would have."

"I searched his house pretty thoroughly. I didn't notice anything out of the ordinary. Nothing looked disturbed."

"So it's gone, whatever it is," I said.

"Looks that way. At least we know it probably was connected to his work. That should narrow the list of suspects considerably."

I looked at my watch. It was pushing ten o'clock.

"It's getting late. You should go to bed," I said.

"I'm too wired now."

"All the more reason to end the call. You need to rest."

"What are you doing tomorrow?" she asked.

"Other than coming to the hospital?"

"You know what I mean."

"I don't know. I think I've run out of options."

"We'll think of something," she said.

I wasn't so sure I agreed with her, though. I said goodnight and told her again to go to sleep. I hoped I could do the same, but something told me that sleep would be a challenge that night.

22

THE SEARCH

THE MORE I THOUGHT ABOUT THE MYSTERIOUS PHOTO, OR WHATEVER IT was that Gabriel had wanted to give Nalani, the more I became convinced that the killer hadn't taken it, at least not from Nalani. Unless he or she had been somehow secretly listening in on their cell phone calls, I didn't think they would have known about it when they went to Nalani's house to kill her. So if Gabriel had given it to her that night, then chances were it was still at her house, but no one had thought to look for it.

I got up early in the morning and drove over to Nalani's house. My car is pretty conspicuous, and I knew it wouldn't blend in with the rest of the cars in that neighborhood. I thought about borrowing Alana's car, but it was owned by the department. I didn't think that would go over too well if someone saw me. I decided not to try to hide the car by parking down the street, so I parked in the driveway and walked up to the front door like I belonged there. I'd learned to pick a lock on my second case, and I felt pretty confident that I could get inside the house in a couple of minutes.

The first rule of picking a lock is to see if the door is, in fact, locked. I turned the doorknob, and the door swung open. Did I find that odd? Of course, and I suddenly wished I had a gun as I imagined some masked man waiting for me on the inside. I walked into the house and saw someone had definitely searched the place. The front door opened to the den, but I could also see into the kitchen since the house had an open floor plan.

There was a long, narrow table pushed up against the wall near the front door. It had three drawers that ran just under the lid of the table. All of them were open, and their contents were on the floor. There was a large bookshelf against the far wall of the den. All of the books had been pulled from the shelf and were also on the floor. The cushions of the sofa and matching chair were either on the arms of the furniture or on the floor. The area rug in front of the sofa had also been overturned.

I looked into the kitchen and saw that all of the drawers and cabinets were open. Everything had been tossed and was either on the kitchen floor or the countertop.

I walked into the back and searched three bedrooms and two bathrooms. Everything was a wreck. It looked like the thief had been very thorough in their search. Nevertheless, I spent about two hours in the house going over everything again. Maybe they might have missed a clever hiding spot. For example, I turned the potted plants upside down, hoping that Nalani had thought to wrap the DVD or thumb drive in a plastic bag and hide it in the dirt. She hadn't, though, and all I managed to do was make more of a mess.

I walked back through the bedrooms a second time. It was obvious which one was the master, so that meant the other two rooms had to have been for the kids years ago. They were both tiny, and I couldn't imagine how they'd fit three kids in one of them. That had been what Alana had told me. She, Hani, and Nalani had all stayed in the same bedroom for one year while Ms. Hu took the other small bedroom. I felt guilty as I realized that my childhood bedroom had been three times this size, and I had it all to myself. I then thought of our bedroom at the new house in Kaanapali. It was as big as Nalani's den and kitchen combined, and it had an insane view of the Pacific Ocean.

I walked back to the front of the house and went into the kitchen.

I looked at the blood stains on the floor. It looked like someone had spilled gallons of red wine on the tiles. Nalani hadn't just been stabbed to death with that corkscrew. She'd been butchered. Maybe that didn't make much of a difference since death was death. I don't know if that makes any sense, but I realized as I looked at the floor that the killer had attacked Nalani with a ferocity I hadn't realized before.

That made me think of Alana's attack. She'd been beaten badly, and I knew at that moment just how lucky I'd been not to lose her. Sure, I'd known that before, but that fact drove even deeper into my mind as I stood by the blood stains that seemed to cover the entire kitchen floor. It was no wonder Alana had been so shaken after viewing the crime scene. She'd been standing in the middle of the house where she'd lived as a child and was looking at an old friend whose life had been cut short by a madman. How had Alana handled it as well as she did? The woman's courage continued to amaze me, but women have always been tougher than men. Haven't they?

Alana had become such a source of strength for me since I'd met her. She was the person I inevitably turned to during a crisis or even when I just needed to vent about something. I did my best to return the favor, but Alana didn't usually need me to lean against as much as I seemed to need her. I guessed every couple was like that. We all have our strengths and weaknesses, and we each seem to take on various roles in the relationship as time goes by. I don't think they're even conscious choices. We just naturally gravitate to them, and there's this unspoken understanding between the man and the woman.

I was about to head for the door when something entered my mind. We all have someone we turn to in times of trouble, which meant Nalani did, too. I'd thought that person had been her best friend, Kaylee King, and she had fulfilled that role to a certain extent. But what if there was someone else who was the true source of strength for Nalani, someone who she returned to again and again?

I took one more look around the house. I wasn't going to find anything there, if it had even been there to begin with. The killer seemed to constantly be one step ahead of me. I exited the house and walked down to my car. I didn't see any neighbors looking at me through their windows, and the cops weren't there, so apparently no one had called 911 when they saw a stranger walk into the house.

I decided to drive to the hospital and check in on Alana. I felt impatient to talk to her, as I often did, so I called her from my car and told her about Nalani's house being searched. While I was describing the wreck that I'd found, a second idea occurred to me. Maybe the killer didn't find the drive because someone else had already grabbed it. If that was the case, and I was more than willing to admit that it was a longshot, then there could only be one person who had it.

I asked Alana to pull a favor for me since I doubted her boss would agree to my request a second time. I told her to tell him that she'd check herself out of the hospital and conduct the interview herself if he didn't let me in to see Liam Hayes. Her blackmail scheme worked, or maybe Captain Price was finally starting to see things our way. Either way, Alana called me back within just a few minutes and told me to head directly for the police station instead of coming to the hospital to visit her.

I arrived just ten minutes later since the police station was fairly close to the hospital. Captain Price had already moved quickly. I met him in the lobby, and he told me that he had Liam moved to the same interrogation room where I'd met with him before. We talked as we made our way to the back.

"Alana said something about Nalani's house getting tossed. How did you find that out?" he asked.

"I saw it from the window. It wasn't hard to see. The place was a wreck."

"Through the window? I'm sure," he said.

We entered the room, and I saw Liam handcuffed to the table again. I wasn't sure why they kept doing that. I didn't think the guy was brave enough to attack anyone. I also knew he was too terrified to be on the outside. Therefore, he had no intention of trying to escape.

I sat down in the same chair as before. Captain Price assumed the same position behind me. Maybe he still thought I wanted to pounce on Liam.

"You know why I'm here, don't you?" I asked.

Liam said nothing. I'll admit that I didn't think he knew why. I just wanted to throw him off balance from the very beginning of the interview.

"You haven't been very honest with me. I keep discovering more and more lies," I continued.

"I told you the person sent me those texts. What else do you want?" he asked.

"That part was true. I'll give you that. The phone records back you up."

"See. I wasn't lying," he said.

"No, not about that part, but about earlier stuff."

Liam said nothing, and I thought I could see the wheels in his head spinning and trying to figure out how much I'd learned.

"I'm sorry about your wife. I think everyone has been concentrating on catching who did that to her. No one, including me, gave you any time or space to grieve. I know you loved her, maybe even more than anyone else did. I just came from your house. I saw the kitchen floor. I saw what they did to her."

"No, you didn't. Her body wasn't there this morning. You didn't see her face. You didn't see her eyes. She was everything to me. Do you know what it feels like to lose someone like that?" he asked.

"No, but I saw Alana beaten half to death."

"You still have her, though. I have nothing. Everything has been taken away from me."

"Help us catch them. Help us make them pay."

"I don't know who they are. I already told you that. It was just a text message," he said.

"Your house was turned inside-out. What do you think they were looking for?" I asked.

"How should I know?"

"My guess is it's something that Gabriel had. It would almost certainly be a photograph of something."

"I have no idea what he was into. How would I? I couldn't stand the guy."

"True, but someone told you."

"I never even talked to Gabriel," he said.

"Not him. Your wife. She called you. She needed your help."

"You searched her phone records. You saw she didn't call me. I admitted that I lied about us getting back together."

"That was true. Her call didn't have anything to do with that, but she still called you for something else. Maybe she used her work phone. Maybe she used a carrier pigeon. Who gives a damn? She got a hold of you, though."

"You don't know what you're talking about," Liam said.

I turned to the captain and looked at him for a long moment. Then I turned back to Liam.

"Okay, Liam. You can play dumb if you want, but the texts Captain Price found prove you didn't murder your wife or Gabriel Reed. You're being released today. The paperwork is already in motion."

I stood and turned to the captain a second time.

"Thanks for letting me talk to him again."

"Is that true?" Liam asked.

"Is what true?" Captain Price asked.

"I'm being released?"

"You'll be out of here within a couple of hours," he said.

Did I think that was true? I didn't know. Maybe it was. Maybe it wasn't. The captain and I hadn't even discussed it, nor did we determine any kind of strategy for this meeting. I had been winging it, but he was perceptive enough to understand what I was going for. I could understand why Alana liked him.

"You can't do that," Liam protested.

"Why not? We're not going to hold an innocent man," Captain Price said.

"You know what the threat was. You read the texts. They'll know I talked to you if they see me get out of here."

"That's not my problem, Mr. Hayes. We're not bodyguards."

"I'll be dead within an hour," Liam said.

"You want help? Then answer Mr. Rutherford's questions."

"You went over there that morning, Liam. I know it wasn't because you were getting back together. I get that, so what did Nalani want to give you? She must have told you something. She called you because she was scared. Gabriel had dragged her into something dangerous. She went to his house that night. I doubt it was some kind of romantic dinner. I think it was to talk him out of whatever it was he was doing, but she couldn't. He was desperate for money, and that makes people do all kinds of stupid things. So she did what she always does. You said it yourself. She always came back to you. She needed you to get her out of the mess, but you couldn't. She was in too deep, and it was too dangerous."

"I wanted to help her, but I couldn't do anything," he said.

"What was it she got caught up in?" I asked.

"I don't know. She didn't tell me. I told her I didn't want to know. I just knew someone was trying to kill her."

The man was a coward. I couldn't understand why he wouldn't have tried to protect his wife, even if she'd left him. Their history alone warranted his assistance. All he had to do was pick up the phone and call the police. He'd done nothing, though, but stare at her dead body on that kitchen floor. He was still doing nothing but trying to save his own skin. The man disgusted me.

"What did she give you, Mr. Hayes?" Captain Price asked.

"She didn't give me anything. She was dead when I got there."

"You took something, though. You already knew what it was. You found it and pocketed it before the police arrived," I said.

"I didn't even look at it. I still haven't looked at it," Liam said.

"Was it a drive or a DVD?" I asked.

He didn't respond.

"What was it?" I yelled.

He did a small jump in his chair, and I knew I'd rattled him.

"It was one of those little memory sticks. She had it in her jewelry box. That's where she always kept her valuables."

"Where is it now?" Captain Price asked.

"It's in Mason's house. I hid it inside a toilet paper roll under the guest bathroom sink. There are several rolls. It's the one on the bottom, all the way in the back."

"Is Mason connected to any of this?" I asked.

"No. He just gave me a place to stay. I didn't tell him any of this."

"Who do you think killed your wife? You have to have some idea," Captain Price said.

"I don't know who killed her. I'd tell you if I did."

"This isn't the first time your wife had brought it up, whatever it was. She's the one who told Gabriel, and he pushed it farther than she expected he would," I said.

"She didn't give me any details. She just said she needed help at the end. I don't even know what it was about. It could have been anything," Liam said.

"I don't believe you," I said.

Liam turned to the captain.

"You can't let me out. They'll kill me."

Captain Price ignored him. He looked over to me.

"I'd like to talk to you outside," he said.

I nodded, and we walked into the hallway. Captain Price took another look at Liam through the small window in the door. He had started to cry. I could tell by the look on the captain's face that he was just as disgusted at Liam as I was. He turned back to me.

"Do you think his life is really in danger?" he asked.

"He made a good point. They'll know he talked to the police if he shows up on the streets. They probably don't know he took the drive, but they'll figure he confessed to the threatening text messages. I still think he knows way more than he's saying."

"He's terrified, but I don't think we're going to get anything more out of him, not unless you have irrefutable proof to throw in his face. What do you think is really going on here? What did his wife get into?" Captain Price asked.

"I don't know. I'm guessing Gabriel thought he and Nalani would pay Liam off to go away. That would solve all Liam's money problems, but Gabriel had no idea how dangerous these people really were."

"I'm surprised he didn't try to flee the island after Nalani was killed."

"Maybe he didn't have the means. The guy was apparently stretched pretty thin," I said.

"So, what now?"

"We need to go get that drive," I said.

"If this Mason guy hasn't already gotten rid of it."

"I doubt he even knows it's in his house. He works the night shift at a hotel, so he's probably home now."

"I'll drive you over there myself. You can call him on the way. Wait until he finds out the key to solving a double murder is hidden in his toilet paper."

I found myself in the car with the police captain five minutes later. It was a surreal moment for a guy who had only moved to the island a couple of years ago. I called Mason on the way over to his house, but I didn't get an answer. For a moment, I was worried that the killer had figured out the same thing we had and that we'd find Mason dead.

I texted Alana and told her about the conversation with Liam and where we were currently headed. She wrote me back and said she couldn't believe she was stuck in the hospital room. I was halfway tempted to call the doctor and tell him to post nurses outside her room to keep her from sneaking out.

I tried Mason one more time, but I still didn't get an answer. I didn't have any problem with letting myself into his place by means of a picked lock, but I didn't think that was the best thing to suggest in front of the captain, especially considering he was Alana's boss. We got to the house, and I called Mason a third time as I climbed out of the car. We walked up to the front porch, and Captain Price banged on the door.

"Mason Howard, are you home?" he yelled.

There was no response, so he banged on the door again.

"Mason Howard!"

The door opened a few seconds later. Mason was wearing a wrinkled white T-shirt and gray shorts. His hair was messed up. It looked like he'd just crawled out of bed.

"Mr. Howard, my name's Captain Lucas Price. I'm with the Maui Police Department. May we come in?"

Mason stepped back and pulled the door open wider.

"What is this about?" he asked, and he turned to me. "You're that investigator guy I spoke with."

"Sorry to bother you, Mason. I tried calling earlier," I said.

"I turn my phone off when I go to sleep."

"Probably a good idea, but we need to get inside your guest bathroom right now."

I walked past Mason and headed for the back of the house.

"What's this about?" he asked, and Mason followed us to the bathroom.

"Your friend, Liam Hayes. He left something here," Captain Price said.

"In the bathroom?"

"We'll explain in a moment," I said.

I opened the door but found a spare bedroom.

"The guest bath is the next door," Mason said.

I continued to that door and went inside. I kneeled on the floor and opened the cabinet. There were several rolls of toilet paper, as Liam had said. I pushed most of the rolls to the side and grabbed the three on the bottom row in the back. The first two rolls had nothing inside the cardboard tube. I found the thumb drive in the third one. It was a black drive with the name Lexar on the outside.

"How did that get there?" Mason asked.

"Your friend put it there," Captain Price said.

We walked back to the front of the house.

"That's all you guys needed?" Mason asked.

"Yes, and we're sorry that we had to barge in like this. I hope you have a pleasant day," Captain Price said.

I thought his words were a bit on the odd side. After all, we'd just stormed into the guy's house and raided his toilet paper supply to find a hidden drive. The entire affair was insane. At least Mason now had an interesting story to tell when he got to work that night.

The captain and I walked outside to his car. My phone pinged just as I opened the door. I looked at the display.

"I think we know who that is," Captain Price said.

"Yep. It's Alana. She wants to know if we found the drive," I said.

"Why don't we do your fiancée a favor and open this drive at the hospital so she doesn't feel so left out. I'm sure they have a computer there we can borrow."

It was a kind gesture on his part, but I wasn't sure I agreed with him. I didn't want to stress Alana out anymore, but maybe her blood pressure would go through the roof if we kept her from the action any more than we already had. I called Alana on the way back to the hospital and told her we were coming there with the drive.

She'd arranged for one of the nurses to bring a laptop to her room by the time we arrived. She extended her hand as we entered, and I knew it was a futile gesture to try to plug the drive in myself. I handed her the drive, and she inserted it into the USB port. A folder popped onto the screen a few seconds later. I leaned closer to the screen as Alana double-clicked on the folder. I saw two subfolders. The top was labeled "DCIM" and the bottom said "MISC."

"Those are Canon camera files. Click on the top folder," I said.

She double-clicked on the file labeled "DCIM," and two more subfolders appeared.

"Click on the top one again," I said.

Alana double-clicked again and several photos immediately appeared. They were shots of products that I assumed were from U'i Décor since everything looked Asian. The objects in the photos were mostly statues of various designs. Some looked like they were from China, while others were clearly from India.

"It looks like he took double photos of everything," Alana said.

"He set the camera to shoot a raw file and a jpeg simultaneously. I do the same thing. All pro photographers are going to want to shoot raw since it gives you more data to adjust the photo."

"So why the jpeg then?" she asked.

"He can drag those files to a data DVD or something for the client to throw on their website or social media account. It's just a convenience thing."

We took a few moments to scan through all the photos. They represented about ten different statues. Each object had been shot in the warehouse, and we could see the rows of product shelves behind them.

"These all look like product shots. I don't see anything that could remotely be used to blackmail someone," Alana said.

"There certainly isn't anything here that would be worth killing someone for," Captain Price added.

"We have to be missing something. It doesn't make sense that Gabriel would want to give this to Nalani," I said.

"Unless it was just a photographer-client thing, and Liam took a drive that he thought was important. Maybe he grabbed the wrong drive. Maybe Gabriel had never given her anything to begin with, and Liam just assumed this is what Nalani was worried about," she said.

"Nalani Hayes was dead by the time her husband arrived. It wasn't like she was around to tell him anything," Captain Price said.

Alana turned to me.

"Liam hid something for no reason," she said.

I looked back to the digital photographs on the laptop screen. It certainly looked like Alana was right. I'd wasted the entire day on a wild goose chase.

23

A STUDY IN PHOTOGRAPHY

I STAYED WITH ALANA FOR ANOTHER COUPLE OF HOURS. I'D ASKED Captain Price if I could keep the drive so I could make a copy of it on my home computer. He'd said no and left with the drive himself. However he'd allowed me to shoot the photographs with my phone so I'd have some form of visual reference of them.

"The more I think about this, the more convinced I am these are just photos from a client job. I don't buy that U'i Décor has anything to do with this. I lived with Nalani and Koa for a year. They never had any problems with each other," Alana said.

"Yeah, but you were just kids then. You don't know if anything changed."

"True, but I don't see how it could ever get bad enough that Koa would kill his own sister. That is what we'd be ultimately saying, isn't it? If Koa was involved in the blackmail scheme, then he's responsible for two deaths, not just one, as well as the attack on me. I just don't see it."

I eventually left the hospital and decided to stop at Harry's on the way back. My initial excuse had been to check on the business, but that's all it was, an excuse. I really just didn't want to be alone, and I figured I could use a drink or two. I sat at the bar for a good hour and nursed one Manhattan. The ice melted and I didn't even finish the drink. I kept staring at the photographs on my phone. They were clearly U'i Décor products, but I didn't see how they could be a threat to anyone. Liam must have grabbed the wrong drive or he'd simply gotten confused and made the incorrect assumption that it was a drive that Nalani had wanted to give him.

The more I looked at the photographs, the more convinced I became that something was wrong. There were actually a few things wrong. The first was the lighting. It absolutely sucked. I know you've heard me be very critical of Gabriel's work, but there's a difference between being an average photographer and an incompetent one. He'd clearly used the overhead sodium vapor lights of the ware-house. They cast an unattractive red glow on the statues. That was certainly not the type of light one would use when trying to capture an attractive product shot for a marketing website or brochure. A pro would use their own lights. I knew Gabriel owned several light kits since I'd seen them in the back room of his gallery. It was hard to comprehend that he wouldn't have brought them for the shoot.

The other thing that jumped out at me was the background, which consisted of the many rows of shelves in the warehouse. It was true that Gabriel could have used an editing program like Photoshop to remove the background, but he'd made the work ten times harder for himself by not using a solid-colored background like a bluescreen or even a white card. He'd have to individually trace each statue by hand to remove the warehouse background for each photograph. If he'd used a bluescreen, then he'd literally just be hitting one button.

I got up from the bar and went into the back room to log onto the work computer. I went to the U'i Décor website and clicked on their product page. I saw several examples of their various products, including statues and vases. They all had different natural back-grounds that showcased all of the beauty of Maui. I clicked on one of the images so that it would become larger on the screen. I studied the image closely and saw that there was nice light on the object itself. It certainly didn't have a red glow to it, and that red glow would have been almost impossible to edit in Photoshop from the surface of the statue or vase, especially the objects that had white in them. They would have definitely picked up the red from the sodium vapor lights.

There was something else I noticed. The objects on the website most likely hadn't been shot in front of a bluescreen. How did I determine this? Because the lighting matched in both the foreground object, which was the statue or vase, and the background, which was a beach or waterfall in most of the online photographs.

Let me explain. It's pretty difficult to get the lighting perfect when you're shooting an object or person inside a studio and then replacing the background with an outside image. A photographer is going to use indoor, controlled lights to create beautiful light on the subject matter. In the case of a product shot or portrait, that light is almost certainly going to be even light, meaning there will be little to no shadows. Natural backgrounds, however, will have shadows, unless you shoot them at high noon, which is the absolute worst time to shoot a photograph since the light is so unattractive. That's why photographers shoot in the early morning or later afternoon light. It's just prettier.

Here's the challenge, though. If you use even light on the subject but the background has long shadows from the morning or evening light, then you have two images that don't match. An observer may not be able to figure out what's wrong with the edited photograph, but their brain will register that something isn't quite right. They'll inevitably end up getting distracted when they should just be gazing at the image and deciding they need to buy it.

I didn't see even a hint of inconsistent light styles between the image and the background in all of Gabriel's online product shots. I came to the conclusion that he hadn't shot them in a studio. Rather, he'd most likely loaded the statues and vases into the back of his vehicle and taken them all across the island so he could photograph them in natural settings.

I opened up a second page and typed in the address for the website that featured Gabriel's landscape photography. I compared the images he was selling as wall art to the product shots on the U'i

Décor website and noticed something interesting. They were the same locations and almost the exact same framing. For example, Gabriel had shot an image of an Indian god in front of a beach at sunset. There was a matching photo on his landscape website with the exact same beach at sunset. All he'd done was remove the Indian god statue and snapped another photo. It was a great way to get double the bang for his buck, and he most likely had Brooklyn there assisting him. She was probably getting paid by the hour or by the day, so he was able to use her for two different business ventures but only have to pay her once, or not at all based on Brooklyn's comments to me the last time I saw her at the gallery.

Back to the photographs on the drive that Liam had taken. I'd proven that everything about those shots was wrong: bad lighting, bad backgrounds, bad composition, too. They couldn't be professionally shot. That meant one of two conclusions. Option one: Gabriel didn't shoot them. Option two: Gabriel shot them, but he never intended to use them professionally.

Here was another interesting thing I thought about. It's pretty hard to do something badly once you get good at it. I was pretty good at photography myself. I'd learned the rules of composition and lighting, so most of my photographs - including portraits - were pretty good to look at. It pained me, though, to look at other people's photographs, especially shots of their friends and family members. They either have miles of headroom, meaning the space between the top of the subject's head and the top of the frame, or they have something weird in the background that conflicts with the subject, like a light pole or sign in the background that appears to grow out of the top of the person's head. They also have no idea of how simple positioning in relation to the sun can make a big difference between pleasing light on a person's face versus harsh light that makes them look ten years older.

My point is that I know this information so well that it becomes instinctive and I don't have to think about it anymore. Gabriel had to be the same way. He'd have to consciously decide to take a lousy photograph, and it would probably pain him to do so. The photographs on the drive were pretty bad, so the only conclusion that I could come to was that Gabriel had been in a mad rush when he shot them. Why was he in a rush? I didn't know, unless he was shooting something that he knew he shouldn't be shooting.

"Hey, buddy, got a minute?"

I looked up and saw Foxx standing in the doorway.

"Yeah, what's up?" I asked.

Foxx walked into the room and sat on the chair in front of the desk.

"Thanks for the talk the other day. You really saved my ass."

"What do you mean?"

"Talking me out of the proposal. I don't know what the hell I was thinking. You're right, though. It probably was all that emotion from Alana's attack."

I didn't think I'd talked him out of the proposal. Rather, I'd just suggested that he postpone it and give himself a bit longer to think about it.

"Does this mean you're not going to propose?" I asked.

"Hell, yes, that's what it means. But I have decided to approach her in a whole new way. No matter what she says or does, I'm going to smile and say yes, unless she demands for me to move in with her or something."

"I suspect that's the best way to handle it."

"Anyway, I won't be needing the name of your jeweler, after all."

"What do you mean?" I asked.

"Remember, I wanted to buy a ring?"

"Oh yeah, well, now you're also saving yourself some big bucks. When you said custom ring, I wasn't sure you knew what kind of money you were getting yourself into."

We spoke for a few more minutes. He asked about Alana and then invited me to have a drink with him before I headed home. I told him I'd be out to the bar in a minute. Foxx left the room, and I turned back to the laptop.

Something jumped out at me that I'd missed the first time since I'd been spending all my energy judging lighting and backgrounds. I didn't see any of the objects from Liam's drive on the product page of the website. They might have been brand new products, though, and Koa or Moani just hadn't had time yet to put them on the website. That was even more evidence that these shots hadn't been done for professional purposes.

I closed the web browser and walked to the bar to join Foxx for that drink. I ordered another Manhattan. This time, I finished it. Foxx encouraged me to have another one with him, but I said I was too tired. I got home and took the dog for a long walk. I took a hot shower afterward and went immediately from the bathroom to the bedroom. I was exhausted, and I felt like I could sleep for at least twelve hours. I looked at the empty bed, and my thoughts drifted to Alana. She still had a few more nights to spend in that terrible hospital bed. It was weird sleeping without her. Funny that I had spent most of my life sleeping by myself. Now, I had a hard time sleeping without Alana at my side.

I looked over to Alana's nightstand and remembered that her engagement ring had been stolen. I reminded myself that I needed to call the insurance company and file a claim so I could buy her a replacement ring. It had been custom-made, and I laughed to myself as I pictured Foxx going to the same jeweler and ordering a similar ring for Hani. I collapsed on the bed and was asleep almost instantly. I woke up less than ten minutes later. I knew exactly why Gabriel had taken the photographs, and I was pretty sure I knew what they represented.

24

THE JEWELER

I spent the morning thinking about jewelry and came up with my own theory about the investigation, which I'm willing to admit could be completely wrong. What is my theory? Well, before I get to that, I'd like to explain how I ended up at a particular jewelry store later that morning. It hadn't been a stroke of luck as it might appear to the casual reader. Rather, it was a decision I made after contemplating the nature of jewelry stores and the buying habits of the American consumer. Sound boring? Just indulge me for a moment if you will.

I think there are four levels of jewelry stores, and they each cater to a different group of clients. The first level is targeted to the masses. This is where the average guy goes to buy the engagement ring. He doesn't want to drop more than a couple of grand on the thing, so he buys the solitaire diamond with the simple setting and pops the question at the local restaurant. Maybe he puts the ring in the champagne glass because he's heard that's a romantic thing to do. Maybe he does it at his house after sprinkling rose petals all over the floor. You get the point.

The second level is for the guy who is doing a bit better financially. Maybe that's because he's older and has gotten a couple of job promotions and a few cost of living increases under his belt. This guy has five grand or so to spend on the engagement ring, or maybe he's upgrading his wife's original ring. Now they have a couple of kids, and he wants to get her something nice to show that he still cares. He still relies on those cheesy television commercials to tell him where to shop, but he's old enough or smart enough to know which one to pick over the other.

The third store is for the guy who owns his own company and is doing really well. He can afford to drop fifty grand on the ring. That might sound outrageous to most people, and it probably is when you consider you're just buying a rock that came out of the ground. It's not like you're purchasing a cure for cancer. Nevertheless, the dude is pulling in a substantial amount of money each year, and his girl-friend knows it. He's not going to get away with buying her a simple ring. It has to have the fancier cut, like an Asscher cut, and the size better be two carats or more, preferably more. That doesn't even include the setting, which better have multiple smaller diamonds as well. This customer thinks he's made it, and he has in a way. What he doesn't know is that there is a fourth level of store that caters to people with real money.

I'll refer to this level of jewelry store as "insanity." You're not going to find anything for sale under seven figures. You'll also see armed guards on both the inside and the outside of the store. You certainly aren't going to find this fourth level on Maui. In fact, you probably won't find it anywhere on the Hawaiian Islands. You really need to travel to a large metropolitan city like New York, London, or Paris to buy jewelry of this caliber.

You will find the other three levels of jewelry stores on Maui, though. There are a ton of the level one and level two stores in the tourist places like Lahaina and Kaanapali. For some reason, jewelry is one of those items that tourists seem to love to shop for while on vacation. They think they're getting a great deal because the manager hangs a "Fifty Percent Off" sign in the store window. They don't realize that the sign never changes, and they aren't ever getting a good deal. Maybe they do know that, though, and they simply can't help themselves.

Although I'm by no means an expert on jewelry, I know enough to avoid those tourist traps. Thanks to my parents, I also have a fair amount of money, so I headed for level three when it came time to purchase Alana's ring. There's really only one place to go if you're looking for stuff in that price range. It's located just ten minutes from my house, and it's owned by an older gentleman who has sold custom-designed jewelry for decades.

I went into my home office and logged onto the social media page for Gabriel's landscape photography business. I found an image of Brooklyn holding one of the cameras. The diamond ring on her right hand was facing the camera that had taken the photograph of her. I right-clicked on the image and downloaded it to my desktop. I then imported the photograph into my Photoshop program and enlarged the section of the picture that showed the diamond ring. I cleaned up the image as best as I could and then printed it on my color printer.

I said goodbye to Maui the dog. Yes, I speak to him all the time, and I made my way over to the jewelry store. I arrived just as the owner walked over to the door to flip the "Closed" sign to "Open." The gentleman's name was Fred Banks. I guessed his age at around seventy-five years old. He was a little on the short side, but he seemed even smaller since he walked and stood with a small hunch to his posture.

I walked through the door, and he instantly greeted me by name. He should have, considering all the cash I've dropped in this place.

"Mr. Rutherford, it's a pleasure to see you again."

"The pleasure is all mine, Mr. Banks."

We walked over to one of the display cases.

"Are you looking for a particular piece today, or are you just browsing?" he asked.

"Neither, I'm afraid. I was hoping you could help me with something, though."

"If I can."

I reached into my pocket and removed the printout of Brooklyn's diamond ring.

"I'm wondering if you've seen this ring before. It's a gorgeous piece, and I can't think of another jeweler on the island who would sell something this beautiful."

He took a quick glance at it and then looked back to me.

"I'm sorry, but I've never seen that before," he said.

"Are you sure?"

"Positive."

"Would you mind looking at it again?" I asked.

"I know every piece I've ever bought and sold. That isn't one of them."

He said this without looking at the printout again, which I found both interesting and telling. I'm sure you did, too.

"Is there another store on the island that does custom pieces like this? It might not be custom, but I'm guessing it is."

"There are a few shops in Lahaina that might sell something like that."

"They do custom work?" I asked.

"I'm not sure. You should swing by there and ask them."

Was he trying to get me out of the store? Probably.

"I was wondering if you could do something for me. I was thinking of buying Alana a diamond tennis bracelet to match that necklace I bought from you a while back. Do you have anything like that in the store?"

"I have a few pieces you might like," he said, and he led me over to another display case.

I looked at each piece, and they were indeed beautiful. I had zero intention of buying them, though, not unless he played ball.

"These are gorgeous, but they don't perfectly match the necklace," I said.

"We could create something for you. It would take a few weeks or so, but then it would match. Is it a special occasion? Do you have a deadline?"

"It's not your typical special occasion, but it is a celebration of sorts. Alana is getting out of the hospital, and I wanted to present her with something special."

Mr. Banks' facial expression suddenly changed.

"So that was your fiancée on the news the other day. I saw the name Alana, but I didn't know if it was the same woman."

"There's only one police detective named Alana on the island, at least as far as I know. I appreciate your offer to make me something, but I'm just going to wait until I see those other two jewelry stores you mentioned. Maybe they already have something that will work," I said.

Mr. Banks looked at the printout in my hand.

"Where did you get that photograph?"

"I think this ring is connected to the case Alana was working on when she got attacked. They even stole the ring I bought from you. I called the insurance company just before I left the house to come here."

"Would you like to order a replacement ring today?"

"No, not yet. Maybe there's still a chance I can get it back. It's not likely, though."

"Is she going to be all right?" he asked.

"She's still in the hospital, but she'll pull through. We're both still shaken. The attacker left her for dead."

Mr. Banks paused a long moment. Then he asked, "May I see the photograph again?"

I handed him the paper.

"I think I may have been mistaken. I may have been shown a similar design before. It might have been hand drawn, which is why I didn't remember it at first."

He handed the printout back to me.

"So you made this ring?" I asked.

"No. I wasn't able to help the customer."

"I thought you could do custom work?"

"We can, but we aren't able to take every job that comes our way. For instance, we don't cut the stones here. I have a person on the mainland that can do that for me, but the customer in this case didn't want to ship the stones off the island."

"Why would you need to cut the stones?" I asked.

"They don't come out of the ground already shaped like a solitaire or an emerald cut. They must be shaped by an expert."

"Raw stones? How often are you presented with something like that?"

"Almost never. Of course, there are other concerns when a customer presents you with one. I was quite busy at the time, and I had to pass on the job."

"Did you recognize the man?"

"No. I can't say I'd seen him before, and I haven't seen him since then."

I slid my phone out of my pocket and quickly logged onto the U'i Décor website. I navigated to the page labeled "About Us" and found a photograph of Koa. I held the phone's display in front of Mr. Banks.

"Is this the gentleman?" I asked.

"Yes. That looks like him."

"Thank you, Mr. Banks. Your service continues to impress me."

"About that tennis bracelet, are you sure I can't order a few for you to look at? Your fiancée certainly deserves a welcome home gift after everything she's been through," he said.

"I think you're right. She does deserve one. Yes, please call me when you have one for me to look at."

"Very good," he said.

I folded up the printout of Brooklyn's ring and slipped it back into my pocket.

"One more thing, Mr. Rutherford. I trust there's no reason for anyone to know about myself and that other customer. I did turn the job down, after all."

"Of course. You and I only talked about Alana's tennis bracelet. I can't wait to give it to her. She'll be so excited."

"Wonderful. Have a good day, Mr. Rutherford."

"You as well, Mr. Banks."

I left the store realizing that I'd probably just committed to buying a twenty-thousand-dollar tennis bracelet just to learn what Koa had inside those statues. I thought I knew already, but it was good to have confirmation.

My next trip would be to the hospital to visit Alana and tell her I was pretty sure I knew how Gabriel was blackmailing Koa with those photographs. I decided to leave out the part of the story regarding the tennis bracelet since I wanted the gift to be a surprise. Plus, I didn't want her to accuse me of bribing the guy when I saw it as a simple business transaction since I was getting a nice piece of jewelry out of the deal. It was something that was sure to delight my wife-to-be. That is ultimately the number one priority, is it not? Happy wife, happy life.

25

TOTALED

I ENTERED THE HOSPITAL ROOM AND FOUND ALANA ON HER CELL PHONE. She motioned for me to come to her.

"He just got here. I'll let him know," she said into the phone.

Alana ended the call and turned to me.

"That was Captain Price. He got Gabriel's phone records. He said they prove a few of his text messages had been deleted by someone," she continued.

"Such as the text about Gabriel wanting to give something to Nalani?" I asked.

"Yes, but there was more than that. Get this. Gabriel sent several photos to Koa, and those photos matched what we saw on the drive Liam found at his house."

"Not surprising, but it was a stupid move on Gabriel's part. Those photos got him killed," I said.

"Why?"

"Because they were proof."

"Proof of what?" she asked.

"That Gabriel knew what was going on. I suspect Nalani was the one to tell him. She probably had it all figured out, but she made the mistake of letting Gabriel know what was happening.

Gabriel was desperate for money, so he probably convinced her to identify which products were being used, and then he took photos of them."

"I still don't understand. Were they illegal artifacts or something?"

"Close. It wasn't the statues themselves. It's what is inside them."

"Koa is smuggling drugs into this country?" Alana asked.

"Maybe. He could be moving all sorts of stuff in through U'i Décor. I do know he's been smuggling raw diamonds."

I told Alana how I'd discovered that Koa had approached a local jeweler with the raw stones and asked him to make the rings that ultimately became gifts for both his wife and his lover.

"It's still just a theory. All we have is photographs of Asian goods that he can easily pass off as products for his company. I still can't believe Koa would do this. How could he have killed his sister?" she asked.

"It may not just be him. I doubt this is a one-man operation. We don't know who made the decision to kill Nalani and Gabriel. Maybe Koa didn't know anything about it until it was too late. What's he going to do then? He can't go to the police without implicating himself in the smuggling operation," I said.

"So he just sits there and let's someone get away with murdering his sister?"

"Not to mention attacking you."

Alana was about to respond when she looked past me toward the door.

"What the hell are you doing here?" she asked.

I turned and saw Liam Hayes in the doorway. He looked right at me.

"I'm sorry. I tried calling you earlier, but you didn't answer. I thought you might be here," he said.

I checked my phone and saw two missed calls from him. That was one of the drawbacks to driving in a convertible with the top down. You often didn't hear the phone ring. Apparently, the captain wasn't just bluffing when he threatened to release Liam.

"When did you get out?" I asked.

"A couple of hours ago. I didn't want to go back to the hotel. They know I was staying there."

"What do you want, Liam?" Alana asked.

"I didn't do this to you. I hope you know that."

I thought his reply to her was a good representation of how he saw the world. The only thing that mattered in his little universe was how it affected him. It was true that we're all often guilty of that crime, but Liam took it to a new level. He could have asked Alana how she was feeling or expressed sympathy for the attack. Instead, he wanted the first thing out of his mouth to be that he wasn't the one responsible. I felt like opening the window in Alana's room and tossing him headfirst to the parking lot below.

"Why are you here?" I repeated Alana's original question.

"I need help. They're going to find me. I know it."

"Shut the door," I said.

Liam stepped inside and shut the door behind him.

"No more games, Liam. I'm sick of your act. What do you know about U'i Décor? I know your wife told you something," I said.

"It started a couple of years ago. Nalani noticed things. Koa and Moani started driving better cars. They started wearing better clothes. They took more trips. At first, she just thought the company was doing better, but she didn't have access to the books. She helped manage the inventory in the warehouse, and she'd work with the few customers that would come to the show gallery. She started going back to the previous inventory reports. Nothing had increased, but they were obviously making more money, a lot more."

"Is that why she wanted to be made an owner in the company?" I asked.

"We were jealous. I'll admit it. We wanted what they had, but Koa refused. It created a rift in the family. Nalani started resenting them. I did, too."

"When did she start suspecting things weren't on the up and up?" Alana asked.

"She overheard Moani bragging that she had just paid off their mortgage. Nalani asked Koa to sign over his half of the house where we lived. He refused. He said we'd have to pay him. She came to me several months ago and said she thought there was something illegal going on. She didn't know what it was, though."

"Did she eventually tell you what it was?" Alana asked.

"No, and then she left me for Gabriel. We pretty much stopped talking until the day before she died."

Liam turned to me.

"I already told you and that captain what happened next. Nalani called me from work and asked me to come over the next morning. She said she wanted to give me something that she needed kept safe," Liam said.

"Do you think Koa killed her?" Alana asked.

I could see the pain on Liam's face.

"I don't know. I do know he really loved her. I can't see him doing it, but I don't know who else it would be. Then I got those text messages, and I freaked out even more. Maybe Koa sent them. Maybe it was someone he was working with."

"You can't stay here, Liam. Where are you going to go?" I asked.

"I don't know. The police won't help me, and I already called Mason. He told me you guys came by the house and got the drive. He's furious with me."

"Let me make a phone call. I think I know someone who can hide you for a couple of days," I said.

"Who are you going to call?" Alana asked.

"An artist friend. You know him," I said.

I called our friend, Ray London. Perhaps you will remember him from chapter one. He's the talented artist who I ran into in the lobby of the hotel on the way to meet Ms. Portendorfer. I knew Ray and his partner, Stephanie, had a small hut in the back of their property where their caretaker once lived. They'd told me that the caretaker had recently moved out, so I thought the place might still be available.

I explained to Ray what the situation was. I didn't think anyone would be able to find Liam there, but I also wanted Ray and Stephanie to be completely aware of what I was asking them to do.

They didn't hesitate for a moment, proving once again something that didn't need any further evidence: they were great friends.

I drove Liam to their house. Ray escorted us to the back of the property, which reminded me of a small tropical rainforest. The caretaker's hut was surrounded by avocado trees and a small stream that ran off to the side. I could hear some kind of bird squawking as we got closer.

"Think of this as a vacation, Liam," I said.

Liam turned to Ray.

"Thanks again for letting me stay here."

"No problem, anyone who is a friend of Poe's is a friend of ours," Ray said.

I was tempted to inform Ray that in no way did I ever consider Liam a friend, nor was that likely to change. Instead, I kept my mouth shut.

"This is a beautiful little place," I said, as I admired the hut.

"I built it myself. It has electricity and running water, of course, but there's no cable TV or Internet. There's an outdoor shower in the back."

Ray gave Liam a thirty-second tour since the hut was basically one room. There was a single bed pressed against one wall and a tiny desk and chair against the opposite one. There was an accordion-style door in the back corner that led to a toilet and sink. It wasn't a five-star resort like where Ray sold his artwork, but it should have been more than enough for a guy hiding out from a homicidal maniac. What more could Liam ask for?

We left Liam in the hut, and Ray and I walked back to the main house. I spoke with Ray and Stephanie for a couple of hours. Stephanie had a thing for Tarot cards, which I'd grown to be leery of after the last time she read them for me. She asked if I wanted another reading. I declined several times, but she was insistent. I let her do one reading, and I drew the Death card, which was what had happened the last time. Stephanie and I had discovered that the Death card referred to change and not what immediately comes to mind. I hoped the latest reading was referring to my upcoming marriage to Alana. It was a technical change in our relationship status, despite the fact that we were already living together. Of course, the cards could have been predicting something else, but I shuddered to think what the alternatives might be.

I said goodbye to Ray and Stephanie and thanked them again for hiding Liam. I also asked them to call me if they caught him sneaking off the property. The guy was unpredictable and cowardly, and I could see him panicking and running away if something as innocent as that squawking bird got too close to him.

I went back to the hospital to spend more time with Alana. We spoke about the case, of course, and both of us agreed that Koa would have disposed of those statues, or at the very least, dumped the illegal merchandise that had been inside of them. I suspected that they were already long gone. There was no way to know when Koa's next shipment would be. He could have easily made the decision to stop for the time being since the police were potentially breathing down his neck. I doubted Koa and Moani knew that I was on to them, unless they figured that Liam spilled the proverbial beans to me and/or the police.

It was dark by the time I left the hospital and made my way back toward Kaanapali. There is a long coastal road called Honoapiilani Highway that you drive down to get to that part of the island. There are a few sections of the road that twist and turn like a snake slithering across a hot sidewalk. These sections cut through the rock. There are large cage-like fences that are drilled into the rock walls to keep any falling rock from coming down onto the road and wrecking cars. I'd driven through these parts a thousand times in the last couple of years, and I'd gotten to the point that I could pretty much navigate them with my eyes closed. The key was not to take them too fast and you'd be fine, even in the pitch black of the night.

I had the radio turned up pretty loud. I was listening to some old eighties song by The Cure. I don't remember which one at this point. The blasting music, as well as the fact that I was completely lost in thought contemplating the various angles of the case, might explain why I didn't hear the advancing vehicle behind me. It wasn't until I entered one of those sharp hairpin turns that I heard the engine roar. I took a quick look in the rearview mirror and saw the metal grill of a cargo van about to smash into my back bumper.

You know I drive a tiny two-seater, so I immediately knew the van would crush my vehicle and most likely end up running me over in the process. I think the initial instinct when you're about to have a car accident is to hit the brakes. Fortunately, my brain didn't tell my foot to do that. Instead, I slammed the gas pedal down, and the car jumped forward. The little BMW has pretty good pickup. I turned the wheel hard to the right to avoid the oncoming rock wall and make the tight maneuver around the curve.

The cargo van wasn't nearly as maneuverable as my car, so it had to slow down considerably to avoid running off the road. I came out of the curve and entered a long stretch of fairly straight road. I looked in my rearview mirror again and saw the van behind me. I started to slow down since the rational side of me assumed that the driver of the van had just been distracted and hadn't meant to get so close to me. Then the van sped up and came right for me again. I hit the accelerator and sped off.

That's when I saw it in the distance. A second cargo van, also white, was coming toward me in the opposite direction. Could it be a coincidence? I didn't think so. I couldn't turn around since the other van was still coming on strong. There was also no room to turn around on the narrow road. As I made my way down the road, the van in front of me maneuvered to the center line. He clearly intended to ram me. I slowed down, which only allowed the van behind me to get closer. I knew I was about to be sandwiched between these two vans if I didn't figure something out. I guessed I had about four or five seconds to come up with a plan. I looked down at the speedometer and saw I was going about seventy miles per hour.

As I mentioned earlier, I knew this road pretty well. There was a long stretch of beach coming up on my left side. The bad part of that is that the beach was heavily populated with trees, as well as people who liked to pitch a tent and camp out there for the night. It wasn't an official campground, but that didn't stop people from doing it.

Unfortunately, I didn't have much of a choice. The van in front of me was only a couple of seconds from hitting me. We were playing a deadly game of chicken, and I had no idea if he or she intended to back off. I jerked the wheel to the left at the last second, and my BMW hit the sand. The car jumped a few feet in the air when it struck an elevated section of the beach. I hit the brakes, but the car was moving so fast I knew it wasn't stopping anytime soon.

I'd managed to avoid the oncoming van. Now I was facing oncoming trees. I jerked the wheel to the right and then to the left. I managed to avoid a head-on collision with both trees, but the sides of the car were swiped by the low branches.

I saw a campfire on the beach that was surrounded by several people. There wasn't anywhere to go but the water. I turned to the left again and hit the ocean at full force. The car came to a complete stop, and I would have been thrown a hundred yards without the seatbelt. I looked back to the road and saw that one of the vans had stopped. It was too dark to make out the person's face, but he was clearly looking toward me. I think the people around the campfire were the only thing that stopped the driver from climbing out of the van, walking down to the beach, and putting a bullet into my skull. Instead, he turned away from me and drove off.

I looked down when I felt my shoes getting wet. Saltwater had made it under the door and was streaming into the car. It wasn't like I was in any danger of drowning since I was only in a few feet of water, but my car was probably ruined.

One of the guys from the campfire ran over to me and asked if I was all right. I didn't reply because I thought the answer was obvious. I wasn't all right. Not by a long shot.

26

THE CHOICE

I<small>T TOOK ABOUT TWO HOURS FOR THE TOW TRUCK TO PULL MY CAR OUT</small>
of the ocean. I was pretty sure the car was totaled. Both sides were
torn to hell from sideswiping the trees, and the engine had gotten salt
water all over it. I loved the little car, and as pissed as I was by the two
maniac drivers trying to kill me, I think I was more upset about the
damage to the convertible. I know that sounds crazy, but it's how I
was feeling at that moment

I watched them drag the car onto the beach. The incident, if that's
the best word to describe it, had drawn quite a crowd. All of the
campers had made their way over to see what kind of drunk idiot
could have driven his car off the road and into the water. I did my best
to ignore everyone, but I still got pretty tired of people asking me,
"How in the hell did you manage to do that?"

I called Captain Price and told him about the attempt on my life.
He personally drove out to the scene, as did two police officers who
filed a report. I told them I hadn't gotten a good look at either driver,
nor had I managed to get the license plate numbers for either van. All
I really knew was that both vehicles had been white cargo vans, and
there were only about a thousand of those on the island.

I also phoned Foxx and asked him to pick me up. He took one

look at the car and was probably even more upset than I was. It had belonged to his girlfriend, Lauren. He didn't fit in the convertible, so it didn't make sense for him to keep it after she was killed. Still, the car had sentimental value, which is why he'd sold it to me and not some random guy on the island.

We drove back to Harry's after the tow truck left with my BMW. I had a Manhattan to calm my nerves. I thought about phoning Alana, but it was pretty late by then, and I didn't want to wake her. Plus, she needed her rest, and I didn't think she'd be able to get back to sleep after hearing someone had just tried to put me six feet under.

I needed to come up with a plan to end this mess. It wasn't like it was going to stop anytime soon. The truth is, I'd gotten extremely lucky when I'd literally dodged that van attack. There was no guarantee I'd be that fortunate on the next attempt at silencing me. There was certainly going to be another one, too. Unfortunately, we still didn't have solid proof that U'i Décor had committed any crimes. All we had was a bunch of poorly shot photographs that showed statues from Asia. That's when I realized I actually had another photograph that did prove guilt. It just wasn't the same crime.

I went to see Alana at the hospital the next morning. I'd asked her to call Captain Price and request that he meet us in her room. I arrived before he did, so I took the opportunity to tell her about the previous night's events. I even showed her cell phone photos of the BMW. She didn't say much in response, but I could see the fury building behind her eyes. I told her all of this would be done with before the week was over, if my plan worked, that was.

Captain Price finally arrived, and I told him and Alana my scheme to put U'i Décor out of business. They agreed the plan had a better than average chance at succeeding. I asked the captain to lend me the services of two plain clothes police officers. One would be employed to follow Koa. I suspected it was only a matter of time before he hooked up with Brooklyn. You don't give a ring that valuable to someone and not expect something in return. The other officer would assist me in setting up the recording device I'd hide on my body.

The plan actually came together much faster than I'd anticipated. The first officer called to say that Koa had already gone to see Brooklyn at her little apartment. He probably needed to blow off steam after the failed attack on my life.

The second officer drove me to Koa and Moani's house. I guessed I had a couple of hours at the very least before Koa was due back. The truth is, I was a little nervous about talking to Moani. I knew it was my only way to take them down, but I'd wanted more time to write and rehearse my speech before approaching her. I'd have to wing it, though.

The officer stopped his car several houses down and hooked up the recording device. I exited the car and walked to Moani's house. I rang the doorbell, and she answered within seconds. She looked shocked to see me, as I'm sure you could have imagined, but I wasn't sure if she was shocked to see that I was still alive or that I was standing on her front porch.

"Koa's not here," she said after she opened the door.

I thought it was a little odd that she'd made that the first comment out of her mouth. A simple and polite "Hello" would have been much more preferable. Furthermore, I hadn't even asked to speak with him.

"That's okay. I'm actually here to speak with you. Do you mind if I come inside?" I asked.

She looked past me. I'm not sure what she was looking for. She hesitated another moment and then nodded and said, "Okay."

I followed her inside, and she led me to a room in the back of the house. It was a nice place, not too large but also not too small. They'd done an okay job of hiding their newly found wealth in terms of where they'd chosen to live. I suspected they might have gotten away with it all if they hadn't had Nalani working for them. She knew them too well, so she'd been much more finely attuned to the changes in their lifestyles. Of course, there was the flashy jewelry that people like Ms. Hu also noticed, and Moani hadn't been very smart when she bragged that they'd paid off the mortgage so early.

I looked around the room and noticed they'd chosen not to decorate their house with the objects they sold at U'i Décor. Maybe they were sick of looking at the stuff after being in the sales gallery all day, or maybe they just secretly knew their merchandise was junk.

"How is Alana? I've meant to go over there again, but work has been so busy."

I'm sure it is, I thought.

"She's had complications. They're going to have to operate again," I said.

It was a blatant lie on my part, but I wanted to increase her guilt level as much as possible.

"Oh, my God, is she going to be all right?" she asked.

"I don't know."

The conversation went silent for a few moments.

Then she asked me, "Why are you here?"

"I thought you knew," I said.

"No. I have no idea."

"Sure you do. What else could it be?" I asked.

She said nothing. I let it sink in for several long seconds. Then I looked at her left hand. She had the ring on it. My plan could still go into action even if she hadn't been wearing it, but this worked out so much better.

"That's a beautiful ring. Is it custom-made?" I asked.

She looked down at her hand and then back to me.

"Yes, it is. Koa had it done for me."

"He's such a loving husband. You know what, though? I think I've seen the ring before. I actually have a picture of it."

I reached into my pocket and removed the printout I'd shown Mr. Banks in his jewelry store. I handed it to her and waited for a response as she unfolded the page. She studied the image for a few seconds.

"I don't understand," she said.

"That's not your hand?" I asked.

She turned the printout toward me.

"This is supposed to be a one-of-a-kind ring," she said.

"You're right. That isn't your hand. It belongs to this woman."

I reached back into my pocket and removed a second printout. This one showed the entire photograph of Brooklyn holding the camera on the beach. I handed it to Moani.

"Koa gave a duplicate ring to her. I'm sure you know who that is. Koa's at her house right now. I'm guessing they're having sex. Of course, I could be wrong, and they could just be going over her next photo assignment."

I waited for the words of Koa's betrayal to sink in. I'll give this compliment to the lady. She did a remarkable job of holding it all together.

"I'm assuming you didn't know about the affair. I don't know how long it's been happening. Maybe it started around the same time that Nalani started seeing Gabriel."

"You doctored this photo," she said.

"Believe what you want to believe, but how did I get a photo of your ring?"

"Maybe the jeweler gave it to you."

"Okay, call Koa right now. Ask him where he is. Did he tell you he was going back to work? Did he have some extra paperwork to take care of?"

She balled up the photograph of Brooklyn and tossed it on the floor. Had I accidentally nailed the exact same excuse that Koa had given her for leaving the house?

"The police know Koa is smuggling diamonds into the country. I suspect it's more than that. They also think you're a big part of this. I don't necessarily agree, though. I'm convinced you know about it, but I don't think it was your idea. Am I right?" I asked.

"If the police think they know something, then why aren't they here?"

"It's one of the advantages I have of being engaged to a police detective. I convinced them to let me talk to you first. It's deal-making time, Moani. Turn on your husband, a guy who has already turned on you, I might add, and cut a deal with the police. Option two, pretend you have no idea what I'm talking about and go to prison for the rest of your life. It's not just smuggling. There are two people dead, and a decorated police officer is in the hospital. How do you think a jury is going to see you, especially when the prosecutor tells them that you had your own sister-in-law murdered?"

"I had nothing to do with that," she said.

"Can you prove that?"

"I don't have to. The police have to put me there, and I wasn't."

"Okay. No problem."

I stood and looked down at the crumpled-up photograph of Brooklyn.

"You can keep the picture, by the way. I appreciate your time. I'm going over to Brooklyn's apartment now to make the same offer to Koa. What do you think will be his decision, especially after I tell him you now know about the affair?" I asked.

I didn't wait for her to answer. Instead, I turned and walked toward the front door. I didn't even make it out of the den before she called out.

"He had a choice to make."

I stopped and turned back to her.

"What choice?"

"This wasn't Koa's idea. He got approached about a year ago by this man. I never met him, myself. He would set it all up, and Koa would make the trips back and forth. I didn't want to do it, but Koa insisted we'd be on the streets if we didn't. We'd sunk everything into this business, and it wasn't doing well. I didn't say yes, but I didn't say no, either."

"What is this man's name?" I asked.

"I don't know. I still haven't met him. I've never even heard his voice."

"Why kill Nalani? Did she threaten to go to the police?"

"No. It was the choice. Koa got greedy and started skimming some of the diamonds for himself. The man found out and told Koa he had to pay a price for his betrayal. He had a choice to make: my life or his sister's."

"And Gabriel?" I asked.

"We didn't know Nalani had told him anything. Then he sent Koa those photographs."

"So Koa killed him, too."

"No. Koa didn't commit either of the murders. It was some other person. We don't know him. He works for the same man that Koa works for."

"You don't know his name, either?" I asked.

"Koa might, but I don't think so," she said.

I found that impossible to believe, but maybe it was just another lie that Koa had told his wife to ease her guilt.

"When is the next shipment?"

"I don't know, but I can find out. What will happen to me?" she asked.

"Call Alana when you know about the shipment. I'm sure you'll spend some time in jail, but there's a big difference between a maximum security prison and one of those country club-style places where you get plenty of sunshine."

I turned and walked out of the room.

"Tell her I'm sorry. I had no idea they were going after her," she called out.

I didn't stop this time. I just left the house and walked back toward the unmarked police car. We'd captured everything on audio. It was just a matter of time before it was all over.

27

MAN'S BEST FRIEND

MOANI CALLED ALANA A COUPLE OF DAYS LATER. SHE'D FOUND OUT about the shipment at the last minute. Koa had been the one to make most of the trips to Asia, but his boss, whoever that was, had decided to send one of his own people on this latest run. Koa hadn't told Moani that, but he'd made a comment at the sales gallery about the incoming shipment that night. It was a mad scramble to pull the police resources together in just a few hours, but Captain Price told us that he'd be ready. I tried to convince him to let me tag along. I insisted that I'd stay far in the background. He said no, of course, and Alana just shook her head at my request. Hey, you have to ask some-times. The worst they can say is no.

Alana was due to be released from the hospital the next morning, so I left her room to go home and rest. I was beyond exhausted. I got home and Maui the dog raced up to me. He flopped on his back for his typical belly rub. Afterward, he ran to the front door, and it was obvious he needed to go to the bathroom.

I got his leash and took him for a long walk. The night air was cool, and the walk gave me the time to reflect on the investigation. Moani said that her husband had been given a choice: her or his sister. I thought he actually had a third option, which was to go to the police and turn himself in. He would have saved both women by doing that, but he made the decision to save his own hide. It was more than that, though. He'd also made a choice to kill. I couldn't comprehend that. He'd spent a lifetime with his sister, yet he'd picked wealth over her.

I looked down at my phone and saw that it was after eight o'clock. I'd brought my phone with me since I hoped I would be receiving a call from Alana at any point, informing me that Koa was arrested and the entire smuggling operation had been shut down. She didn't call, though, at least not on that long walk.

I got back to the house, and Maui the dog collapsed in the front foyer from exhaustion. He liked to cool his body down on the tiled floor. I walked to the kitchen and drank a bottle of water. I looked at my cell phone again. I hadn't missed a call. Maybe something had been delayed, though, and the raid hadn't even started yet. I walked into the den to watch some television. I normally kept the remote control on the table in front of the sofa, but it wasn't there. The next logical place was to check the sofa since I often fell asleep while watching TV. I didn't see it on top, though, so maybe it had fallen between the cushions as it often did. I pulled two of the cushions apart, and that's when I heard it. The unmistakable sound of someone chambering a round of ammunition.

I turned and saw Koa standing on the other side of the table. The sliding glass door to the backyard was open behind him. One of two things had obviously happened. Koa had either escaped the police during the raid, or Moani had a change of heart and had tipped him off. I suspected it was the latter. It was a good plan on her part, especially since Koa's mysterious boss had sent another man on the latest trip to Asia. Perhaps, Moani thought they could pin the entire operation on someone else and claim they were the unwilling pawns in the smuggling operation. I cursed myself for not anticipating that move.

"Moani told you," I said.

I didn't know why I said it. I guessed it was just my insatiable curiosity that made me want to know. It didn't really matter, though. I was about to get several rounds in the head and chest. Several things went through my mind in those few seconds. I thought back to the beach and my car getting pulled out of the water. I'd known then that they would come back for a second attempt on my life, but I'd mistakenly believed I'd dodged that bullet when Moani agreed to work with us.

I also thought about Alana lying in the front room. I'd thought she was dead. We'd gotten lucky, though, and she'd survived. Now she was going to come home in the morning and be the one to find a loved one dead in the house. It was weird how life worked out like that, or maybe I should say death. It comes for us all, and no one knows when it's due to arrive.

Then something happened that I hadn't anticipated. I heard Maui the dog charging. The dog let out a growl that he only used in those rare times when he was truly upset. Koa turned at the sound just as Maui lunged for him and sank his teeth into the flesh of Koa's exposed lower legs.

I used the brief distraction to make my move. I climbed onto the wooden table in front of the sofa and dove for Koa. He turned and fired the gun at me a half-second before my body collided with his. His aim was way off, but I still heard the bullet pass by my left ear. Koa was a much bigger man than me, but I had somewhat of an advantage now since I'd come at him from the added height of the table. My body impacted with his upper chest, and we both fell to the floor. I landed square on top of him, and I could feel the air escape his lungs. Maui continued to growl and bite at Koa's legs.

Koa reached for the gun that had fallen out of his hand. It was only a few inches from his fingertips. My natural instinct was to try to grab the gun before he did. Instead, I head-butted him in the nose. He yelled, and I grabbed his ears and slammed the back of his head repeatedly against the tiled floor. I could see his eyes start to glaze over. I sat up on his chest and struck him in the throat. I aimed for his Adam's apple as I punched him again and again. I wasn't sure if I'd crushed his windpipe or not. That hadn't been my intention, but I heard him wheeze and gasp for breath.

I climbed off of him and snatched the gun off the floor. I aimed it at him as I backed away and walked over to the kitchen to grab my phone. The dog continued to attack him.

"Maui, no!" I yelled.

He stopped and backed away.

I called 911 and told them I had an intruder. I then called Alana and told her to call Captain Price. I couldn't remember his cell phone number, and I didn't want to be distracted by searching through my call logs. Koa never made a move to get away. He just lay there on the floor. Blood flowed from his nose and the back of his head. He kept coughing, too.

I walked back over to him.

"Did you attack Alana?" I asked.

He looked up at me. I couldn't tell if he intended to answer or not, but he went into another coughing fit.

It took the police almost half an hour to get there. Captain Price wasn't one of them. I guessed he'd allocated most of his officers to the raid at U'i Décor. I placed Koa's gun on the kitchen counter as I heard the cops running up the stairs of the garage. I didn't want them to overreact and shoot me if they saw the gun in my hand. I pointed to Koa and informed them that his gun was in the kitchen. One officer placed Koa in handcuffs, while the other took possession of the gun.

"Does Captain Price know about this?" I asked.

"He's on his way here. I don't know how close he is," the officer nearest to me said.

It was another thirty minutes before the captain arrived. Both officers were still at my house, although they'd shoved a handcuffed Koa into the back of their squad car. Captain Price entered my house and looked at the blood on my living room floor.

"Did you do that?" he asked.

"Me and the dog."

He looked down at Maui, who was calmly sitting at my feet.

"That little guy?" he asked.

"Don't underestimate his heart. He saved my life."

"Man's best friend," he said, and he let out a laugh.

"What happened with the raid?" I asked.

"We caught a couple of Koa's guys who worked in the warehouse. They were moving the statues that had the diamonds."

"Just two people?" I asked.

"Yeah, and the guy who is really pulling the strings was nowhere to be found. Maybe we can get Koa to give him up."

"I doubt it. He's probably scared to death of him," I said.

"You're probably right, but at least we'll get Koa for the two murders and the attack on Alana, not to mention the smuggling. He'll never see sunlight again."

Captain Price looked back to the blood on the floor. Then he turned to me again.

"Glad you're safe. Alana was right. You're not to be underestimated. I guess you and the dog make a determined team."

He kneeled to the floor and patted the dog on the head.

"Good boy," he said.

He stood and pointed to my cell phone which was on the counter right beside me.

"You should call Alana. I'm sure she's..."

He stopped talking when he heard my cell phone ring.

"I'm not going to even look at the display. We both know who it is," he said.

He smiled and walked toward the door that would lead him to the garage and outside.

I looked at the phone display and confirmed that the captain was right. It was Alana.

"Well, this has been an exciting night," I said.

I walked outside to see if the police cars had left, so I could shut the garage door. Captain Price had driven away, but the original squad car was still parked on the street in front of the house. That's when I noticed a small crowd of neighbors had appeared and were anxiously looking toward my house.

"I think Koa and I woke up the neighborhood," I continued.

"This is no time to make a joke. Are you all right? What the hell happened?"

I was about to answer her when one of the officers approached me on the driveway.

"One second, Alana. One of your co-workers wants to say something."

I put the phone at my side.

"Thank you for your assistance, officer," I said.

"No problem. That guy wanted me to tell you something before we left. He said he didn't hurt her. Know what he's talking about?" he asked.

"No idea," I said.

The officer shrugged his shoulders and walked back to his car. He climbed inside and drove off with Koa in the backseat.

I put the phone back to my ear.

"Sorry about that," I said.

"What did he want?" she asked.

"Nothing much. He just wished me a good night. So, let me tell you what a hero our dog was tonight. I'm thinking of calling that news reporter from the other day and offering to let her run a story on Maui the dog."

We spoke for a while, and I eventually told Alana I needed to get off the phone so I could clean the house before her arrival the next morning. She made me promise that I would get there early since she didn't want to spend an extra minute in that hospital.

I grabbed a bucket and rubber gloves from the garage, so I could clean up the blood on the floor in the den. I kneeled on the floor and dunked the sponge into the soapy water. I stopped for a moment and thought of the police officer's words to me: "He said he didn't hurt her."

If Koa hadn't been the one to attack Alana, and I had suspected he hadn't, then who did?

28

I KNOW IT WAS YOU

I GOT TO THE HOSPITAL EARLY IN THE MORNING AS I PROMISED I WOULD. Alana was already dressed and ready to go. We thanked the doctor and all of the nurses and told them we would forever be in their debt. We walked out to the parking lot, and Alana was surprised to see the rental car.

"I forgot all about the BMW. What did the insurance company say?" she asked.

"I looked up the Blue Book value on the car. There's no question they'd total it. Foxx knows a guy who knows a guy with a garage. I had him take a look at it. It's going to cost a small fortune, but I told him to go ahead and fix it. I've gotten attached to the little car, and I didn't have the heart to send it to the junkyard."

"When will it be ready?" she asked.

"He said six to eight weeks, but I suspect it will be even longer than that."

I took Alana back to the house, and Maui the dog spent several minutes jumping and dancing around her. You'd have thought she'd been gone for years.

"I was worried he'd forget about me," she said.

"Are you kidding me? You're his favorite person."

We both spent the remainder of the day watching television and resting. She found a World War II documentary marathon on one of the cable channels, and she ended up watching several back-to-back episodes. It's strange to be admitting this to you, but I found the whole day comforting, despite the rather grisly subject matter she chose to watch.

We had dinner out by the pool and listened to the sounds of the waves as we ate. Hani and her mother came over at some point in the early evening. They brought Alana flowers, and we spent about an hour talking about the wedding, as well as Hani's plans for the baby's nursery. She still hadn't changed her mind about not knowing the baby's sex, so she was trying to figure out the best neutral color to paint the room. They settled on yellow with white trim on the baseboard. I didn't think it really mattered since I assumed the child's crib would be filled with toys, and he or she would spend most of their time staring into the eyes of a teddy bear or stuffed puppy dog.

Foxx came by after Hani and her mother left. I suspected he'd been keeping an eye out for their car. He did live just down the street, after all. He sat outside with us, and we talked about the night he picked me up from the beach. I tried to signal him to cut it out since I didn't want to upset Alana. I hadn't told her just how dramatic the night had been, but she knew now thanks to Foxx's descriptions of the two vans that tried to crush me and how I'd hit the water at seventy miles per hour. It was ultimately my fault since I'd been the one to tell Foxx. I knew he couldn't keep a secret, especially one that involved me. Fortunately, she knew Koa was already behind bars, so she seemed to take it all in stride.

We didn't do much of anything for the rest of the week. Alana got occasional reports from Captain Price. Moani had admitted that she'd been the one to tip off Koa about the raid. The prosecutor's office rescinded the deal they'd offered her, and the district attorney told Moani that she intended to throw everything at both her and Koa.

Mr. Banks called me to let me know he'd received three tennis bracelets, and he was convinced Alana would certainly love them. I asked him to bring them to the house since she was still weak, and I didn't want her to have to come to the store, even though it wasn't very far from the house. He jumped at the chance. Imagine that.

Alana was surprised when she opened the front door and saw him there. We walked into the living room, and he laid the jewelry on the table. She liked them all, as he had predicted, but one jumped out more than the others. She tried it on and didn't want to take it off. I told her she didn't have to. I wrote Mr. Banks a check since he didn't want to pay the service fee for my credit card. He smiled and wished us both a good day.

Alana commented that life was finally getting back to normal, if you can call it that. I was still bothered, though, because I knew things weren't back to the way they had been before the case of Nalani Hayes. Our house had been violated, and Alana's health was never going to be the same. There was something else that bothered me. Her attacker was still out there, and I thought I was one of just three people who knew that: Myself, the killer, and the one who helped him, who was still walking around the island a free person.

I told Alana I needed to go to Harry's to meet with Foxx about the business. I did drive to Harry's, but I didn't go inside. Instead, I walked toward Gabriel's gallery. I'd called Brooklyn earlier and asked her to meet me there. She said the gallery had closed, and the landlord had indeed taken possession of all of the photographs to pay the back rent. She didn't mention the pro photography gear, and I assumed that's because she'd decided to take it herself, as I had expected her to.

We met outside the gallery door and walked to a bench in a small park area down the street. I had misled Brooklyn about the nature of my call. I'd implied that it had something to do with my upcoming wedding and my search for a top-notch wedding photographer. We sat on the bench, and I looked at Brooklyn's finger to see if the diamond ring was still there. It was.

"I didn't think they'd take the ring. They don't know about you," I said.

She looked down at her hand and then back to me.

"You didn't call me about a wedding, did you?" she asked.

As I'd said in an earlier chapter, she was a smart girl.

"I know it was you," I said.

She didn't say anything in response.

"No one else has picked up on this but me. You had his login information for his email account. I'm sure you knew his phone passcode, too. Hell, I figured it out in sixty seconds. You were bound to know it."

"I've done nothing illegal," she said.

"Sure you have. You went into his email and his text messages and deleted the incriminating messages."

"You can't prove that."

"That's debatable. Here's what's not: You were the one who helped kill your boss," I said.

"That's crazy."

"Is it? You knew what Koa was up to. He gave you that ring. You sometimes wore it on your left hand, which was stupid by the way. You thought he was going to marry you. I'm sure he told you he'd leave his wife for you. They always say that, and they never mean it."

"He gave me the ring, but that doesn't mean I knew what he was up to. I do now, thanks to all the media coverage."

"He asked for your help in getting rid of Gabriel. You lured Gabriel to his gallery. Maybe you didn't need to. Maybe you already knew he was going there, but you waited for him to arrive, and then you let the killer in the back door."

"That's not true," she said.

"There's a security camera that shows the front of the gallery. All it shows is Gabriel coming to the store in the morning. No one else, including you, went inside, but we know someone did because Gabriel got his neck snapped in half."

"Then how do you know it was me?" she asked.

"Because the cops got lazy. There's a camera on a store that shows the entrance to the back parking lot."

I reached into my pocket and removed a DVD in a clear plastic case.

"You didn't drive there that morning because you didn't want anyone to notice your car, but you did walk through the parking lot. I'm guessing you parked down the street and then walked over. Maybe you even did what I do and park at my bar, Harry's. I saw you on the security footage, and it's time-stamped."

Was any of this true? Not one bit, at least not the part about the second security camera. She didn't know that, though. So why had I felt confident enough to gamble with that detailed story? Because I knew she had to get into the store somehow, and the back door was the only way. The DVD was also garbage. It was blank, and I'd taken it from my home office before I left for our meeting.

"You don't have any response?" I asked.

"What do you want?"

"I want the name of the guy who killed Gabriel. I'm pretty sure he's the one who attacked my fiancée. Give me his name, and I'll toss this DVD in the recycling bin. Don't give it to me, and I'll leave here and go straight to the police station. I've become friends with Captain Price. I'm sure he wouldn't mind locking up another person for the murder of Gabriel Reed. The guy loves the media attention. It would give him another excuse to do a television interview."

That part wasn't really true, either. The captain hated the media, and he did everything he could to avoid them.

"How do I know he won't figure out who told you? He'll kill me if the police don't catch him."

"Right now the entire department is looking for him. What are the odds that he'll think you were the one to point them in his direction?" I asked.

"I only know his first name."

"What is it?"

"Bryan. That's all I know. I don't know where he lives, where he works, I don't know anything else."

The name instantly registered with me. Why? Because I had spent the last week going over my notes from all of the interviews I'd conducted. The name Bryan had come up. There was just one reference to him, and it almost seemed unimportant, but I have a habit of writing everything down.

"Thank you," I said, and I stood.

"Can I have the DVD?" she asked.

"No, but I won't give it to the police, unless I find out this Bryan guy is bullshit."

I left her there sitting on that park bench. I walked back to my rental car, which I'd left at Harry's. I grabbed my little notebook and looked up the number for Kaylee King.

"Hello," she said.

"Kaylee. This is Poe. You mentioned the name of a guy when I first met with you. You said his name was Bryan, and Nalani had an affair with him. You said he scared her and you. Do you know his last name or where he lives?"

"I know both. Are you ready to write it down?" she asked.

"Yes, and not a word of this to anyone. Agreed?"

"Agreed," she said.

29

RAGE

I SPENT PARTS OF THE NEXT FEW DAYS TAILING BRYAN SANDERS. I'D told Alana each time that I was going to Harry's. She didn't suspect a thing, at least I don't think she did. I wasn't sure if she'd figured out that Koa wasn't the one who attacked her. I don't even know if it was even a vague question in her mind. I certainly didn't bring it up.

I did find her early one morning standing in the front room of our house. She was staring at the spot on the carpet where I'd found her. I'd hired a professional carpet company to remove the blood stains, but she was still looking exactly where they had been. She made a remark that she wanted to replace the carpet. I said yes without hesitation.

There had been just one other small mention of the attack. I'd walked into the master bedroom and found her standing in front of a full-body mirror that she had in the corner of the room. She was holding her shirt up so that her stomach was revealed in the mirror. She remarked that the scar from her surgery was going to be an ugly one, and she asked my opinion as to whether or not I thought a plastic surgeon could remove most of it. I said I thought that could be done, and I recommended that she contact one when she was ready.

All in all, I thought Alana had done a remarkable job of getting over the attack. She seemed comfortable in our home, even though it had been the place of the assault, and I didn't find her waking violently from some sort of nightmare. It seemed like I was the one having a harder time putting it behind me. Maybe that was because I knew the one responsible was still a free man.

It took all of my energy not to attack Bryan Sanders during my surveillance. The guy was huge, maybe even bigger than Foxx, but I didn't care. He'd almost taken Alana's life. There was one moment when I'd spotted him walking from his truck toward a hardware store. I was tempted to run him over with my rental car, but there would have been too many witnesses. He needed to pay, but it had to be handled correctly. The law couldn't be involved. Sure, they would put him in jail eventually, but he wouldn't suffer the way Alana had, not by a long shot.

Bryan lived in one of those Airstream trailers. He had it parked near a secluded beach. I thought this remote location had its advantages and disadvantages. On the one hand, an attack could easily be concealed. I doubted there would be anyone around who might hear or see it while it occurred. However, it would be difficult to get inside that trailer without him hearing me. It wasn't a big trailer, and I was certain he'd hear me picking the lock.

I'd visited the trailer once when he was gone. It took me less than a minute to get past the lock. It took me about twenty minutes to go through the inside of the trailer. I found several of the raw diamonds that had been smuggled inside the U'i Décor statues. I assumed he'd either stolen them from Koa, who had stolen them from his boss, or they'd been payment for the murders of Nalani and Gabriel, as well as the attack on Alana. I also found Alana's engagement ring. I thought briefly about taking it, but I knew that would tip him off to my presence. It was also the only thing I knew of that tied him to the assault on Alana.

I made the decision to time my assault for three in the morning. I assumed he'd be asleep at that hour, and I thought I'd read somewhere that the human body is least awake or alert at that time. I would need every break I could think of to get to him.

I told Alana once again that I was going to Harry's. I mentioned that I might stay late to help Foxx close the bar. She said that she'd probably be asleep when I got back, and I told her that I'd try not to wake her. I did go to Harry's since I needed somewhere to be before the trip to Bryan's Airstream. I burned the hours away by playing on the computer in the back room and sitting at the bar watching the giant television. Foxx walked up to me just a few minutes before I was about to leave. He and I and one of our bartenders were the only people left in the bar at that hour.

"You okay, buddy?" Foxx asked.

"Yeah, why?"

"I don't know. You just seem a little distracted. Also, you've been up here for four hours. You're almost never here that long. Did you and Alana have a fight or something?"

"No. We're good. She and Hani are going over the wedding plans tonight, and I didn't want to be there."

"Okay," he said, and he walked away to leave me alone at the bar.

I left the bar around two-thirty in the morning and walked out to the parking lot to my rental car. I opened the driver's door and was about to climb inside when I saw Foxx exit the bar.

"Can I ask you something?" he said, and he walked over to the car.

"Sure, what is it?"

"What the hell are you about to get yourself into?"

"Nothing. I'm going home."

"We both know that's bullshit. Are you seeing some other chick?" he asked.

"No. I would never do that to Alana."

"I didn't think so, but I know you lied to me back there."

"How did I lie to you?" I asked.

"You really expect me to believe that Hani and Alana are going over floral patterns and place settings at this time of the night."

"I'm just a little overwhelmed from all that's happened. I didn't want Alana to see me in a mood like this," I said.

"Okay. I can buy that. You've been acting weird all night."

"I'm fine. I'm going home. That's all."

Foxx looked past my shoulder at a small gym bag that was on the front passenger seat. In hindsight, I should have put it in the trunk.

"What's in the bag?" he asked.

"Nothing."

"You heading to the gym at three in the morning?"

Foxx walked around the car and opened the passenger door. He then unzipped the bag.

"What the hell?" he asked.

Foxx looked around the parking lot to see if anyone was in earshot.

"Why do you have a Taser and a hammer?" he asked.

"I'm leaving Foxx. Please shut the door."

Foxx tossed the bag into the backseat and climbed into the car. He then shut the door.

"What are you doing, Foxx? Get out," I said.

"I know what you're up to."

"What am I up to?"

"You found the guy who beat Alana half to death. I'm going with you," Foxx said.

"No, you're not."

"The hell I'm not. You have two choices. You either physically throw me out of this car, or you let me come along. But I'm not letting you go by yourself."

I climbed into the driver's seat and shut the door.

"Do you know what will happen if we're caught? Plus, this guy's a killer. I don't even know if we can get him."

"You're forgetting I was there with you in your house. I saw what he did to her. He's not getting away with it."

I sat there for a long moment and tried to figure out what to do. The truth is I hadn't thought once to ask Foxx to help me. I didn't want to risk him going back to jail, but the odds of success against Bryan Sanders would go up considerably if Foxx came along.

"All right. Let's do this," I said.

"About damn time," Foxx said.

I drove us out of the Harry's parking lot and made my way over to Bryan's trailer. I gave Foxx the quick rundown on how I'd discovered it was him. I also told Foxx about my previous visit to the trailer and how I'd found Alana's ring inside.

We parked about a mile down the road from the trailer and made the rest of our way on foot. It was actually after three when we arrived. There were no lights on inside the trailer, and we saw Bryan's pickup truck parked in front of it, so I assumed he was home.

Foxx took the Taser and stood beside the door. He pinned himself against the side of the trailer. I took the hammer and walked around to the back. I rolled partially under the body of the trailer. I was also below the window. I didn't think he'd be able to see me in this position, even if he leaned against the back window and looked down toward the ground. I banged hard against the metal skin of the trailer with the hammer. I kept hitting it and didn't pause once.

I barely managed to hear the trailer door swing open on the other side. I stopped banging the hammer, though, just in time to hear the Taser zap Bryan Sanders. I crawled from under the trailer and ran to the front. I saw Foxx standing above Bryan, who was lying on the ground by the door.

"So, this is the guy," Foxx said, and he kicked him hard in the ribs.

Bryan did his best to move away, but he hadn't regained control of his limbs due to the Taser's paralyzing effects. Foxx leaned toward him.

"This is the moment you've dreaded your whole life," Foxx said.

He put the Taser in his back pocket. Then he grabbed one of Bryan's arms and popped it out of the socket. Bryan screamed, and his arm dangled at his side after Foxx released it. It was the most brutal display of raw power I'd ever seen from Foxx.

I looked around the area in front of the trailer and saw a small section off to the side. There were two short tree trunks that looked like they were being used as benches. They were placed around a fire pit. I turned to Foxx.

"Drag him over there," I said.

Foxx grabbed him by his bad arm and dragged him to the fire pit. Bryan screamed the entire way.

"Place his hands on one of those logs," I said.

Foxx grabbed both of Bryan's wrists and forced his hands onto one of the logs. I walked over to Bryan and kneeled on the ground in front of him. We made eye contact for a long moment. I could see the pain in his eyes. Then I smashed the hammer into one of his hands. I kept swinging the hammer over and over again until I'd hit every finger. I then went to work on the backs of the hands.

"Enough!" I heard Foxx yell.

I didn't stop, though, not until he pulled me off of Bryan. I looked down at Bryan. He was slumped over the tree trunk and screaming from the pain we'd inflicted on him.

I went inside the Airstream and found his cell phone. I brought it back outside and walked over to Bryan. He was still moaning in agony. I dialed 911 and placed the phone on the log beside him.

Foxx and I ran back to the rental car and climbed inside. We drove off before we ever heard a siren. I drove straight back to Harry's to drop Foxx off. Neither of us said a word on the way back. I pulled into the parking space beside Foxx's car. His was the only one there when we got back.

"Thank you," I said.

Foxx nodded and climbed out of the car. I looked at the backseat. The gym bag with the Taser and hammer was there. I would clean the hammer in the garage sink when I got home. I would also store the Taser in the garage. I assumed it had left a burn mark on Bryan, but I'd bought the Taser at a popular store on the island, and I'd paid cash. It was the most popular model they had, and it made sense that I'd buy one after Alana's attack, at least that's what I would tell the police when they inevitably showed at my doorstep.

I watched as Foxx backed out of his parking space and drove away. I placed my hand on the gearshift to put the car in reverse. That's when I noticed my hands were shaking. I grabbed the steering wheel hard with both hands and tried to command them to stop shaking. It didn't work.

30

I SAID YES

I GOT BACK TO THE HOUSE AROUND FIVE IN THE MORNING. I STRIPPED off my clothes and took a long shower. I used the bathroom in my office so as not to disturb Alana by using the master bath. It wasn't the first time that I'd done it, so I hoped she wouldn't find it suspicious. When I got out of the shower, I noticed that my clothes were covered in blood. I don't know why I hadn't noticed that before, especially when I'd been cleaning the hammer in the garage.

I balled my clothes up and shoved them into a small trash bag that I had under the sink. I then hid the bag in the office closet. It wasn't a brilliant hiding place, and it would certainly be found if the police conducted a search. I considered leaving the house again and trying to find a place to dispose of the clothes. Instead, I decided to wait until the morning. Alana would notice the garage door opening again, and I didn't know how I would explain that.

I put on a T-shirt and pair of sweat shorts and climbed into bed. I stared at the ceiling for at least an hour. I could hear Alana breathing quietly beside me. I thought of Bryan Sanders. He would probably be in the hospital by now. The police would have been dispatched to his trailer after the 911 operators had heard him screaming into the phone.

They would take one look at his hands and immediately take him to the emergency room. I found it ironic that he would be treated at the exact same place as Alana had. Perhaps he would even be in the same room in the ER and be treated by the same nurses and doctors. Would they know who he was and what he had done? Of course not. It was their job to heal and not to judge.

I hadn't wanted Foxx to come with me. I was more than willing to take the fall if and when the police showed up, but I didn't want to taint him by having him take part in the attack. I felt like a different person now, and I imagined he did as well. I didn't like this new version of me. I hate to admit this, but I think I would have killed Bryan Sanders if Foxx hadn't been there to pull me off of him. There hadn't been any part of me that told myself to stop beating him. I'd wanted him dead, and I suddenly realized that I might not be better than the killers I had investigated and caught. I'd judged them and viewed myself as superior, but that night I had proved that I was anything but better than them. I didn't know if I could continue to work as an investigator now that I had come to this new conclusion on who I really was.

I felt sick to my stomach, and I almost went back into the restroom so I could vomit. Instead, I stayed in bed and pushed the bile back down my throat. I might have slept an hour or two that night. My nightmares were filled with visions of Bryan attacking me with the hammer I had used to hurt him.

I climbed out of bed around seven in the morning when Maui the dog whined at me. He needed to go outside to do his business. Often, I would just let him into the backyard in the morning. I took him on a long walk this time, though. It was normally an activity I enjoyed, but I didn't feel that way on this walk. I felt like I didn't deserve this experience. I was outside in the cool air and bright light, while a man I'd hurt was in the hospital in pain and despair. I supposed I should have felt some sense of revenge. I didn't, but I also didn't feel remorse. I'd done what needed to be done. Does that make any sense? Probably not, but I'd brought a certain amount of darkness into my being, and it had been absolutely necessary to protect the one I loved more than anyone else.

I found Alana in the kitchen when the dog and I got back to the house. She suggested that we have breakfast outside by the pool, so I sliced up a pineapple and some oranges for us to eat. She made a comment as we walked to the patio table that I'd been out far later than she'd anticipated the night before. I told her that Harry's was exceptionally busy, and I'd stayed to help out the bartenders. She seemed to accept the excuse, and we sat down to have our breakfast.

We talked about the wedding while we ate. Alana commented on how pleased she was with the job Hani had done. I admitted that I had my reservations at first, but I agreed that Hani had ultimately been the best person for the job. Alana said that she'd encouraged Hani to potentially take this up as a profession. She said Hani had excellent taste, and she could easily see her making good money doing this for a living. I offered to help Hani set up a company if she decided to move forward. I told Alana I'd done so with my former architecture business, and I knew the basic steps Hani would need to take if she wanted to incorporate. Alana said she'd pass the information to her sister.

"Hello, there," we heard a male voice say.

I turned and saw Captain Price standing outside the back fence gate. He'd arrived much sooner than I ever anticipated, but his facial expression seemed pleasant, which didn't make much sense considering why he was there.

"May I come back?" he asked.

"Of course," Alana said.

He opened the gate and made his way toward us.

"I rang the doorbell a couple of times. Figured you must be back here."

"What brings you by?" she asked.

"I have something for you."

Captain Price reached into his pocket and removed something small, which he handed to Alana.

"My ring! Where did you find this?" she asked.

"We got a 911 call last night. The officers knew they'd walked onto a crime scene as soon as they arrived. They searched the place and found your ring along with several of the raw stones Koa smuggled onto the island."

"Whose house was it?" Alana asked.

"It was one of those Airstream trailers. Owned by a guy named Bryan Sanders. Apparently, he was an enforcer for Koa. We had no idea he even existed. He might have been the one who actually killed Nalani Hayes and Gabriel Reed."

"Was he the one who attacked me?" Alana asked.

"We think so. That's why he had the ring. This doesn't clear Koa by any means. The theory now is that Koa ran the operation and used Bryan Sanders to get rid of anyone who threatened them."

"You said the police got a 911 call?" Alana asked.

"Yes, and we're not sure how he managed to do it."

"Why's that?"

"Because every bone in his hands was broken. Looks like someone used a hammer or rock on him. It was a bloody mess. The person who attacked him must have made the call. That's the only thing we can figure."

"Do you have any leads on who did that to him?" Alana asked.

"We don't know. They worked him over pretty badly. He'll be in the hospital for weeks. I spoke with the doctor this morning. He doesn't know if Mr. Sanders will ever regain the use of his hands. He's scheduled for surgery this afternoon."

Alana slipped the ring back on her finger.

"I didn't think I would ever see this again," she said.

Captain Price turned to me.

"I'm sure your fiancé is surprised, too," he continued.

"Of course. We thought it was gone for good," I said.

Captain Price turned back to Alana.

"I hope your recovery is going well. We can't wait for you to get back to the office."

"Thanks for bringing my ring back."

"Of course."

Captain Price turned back to me once more.

"Mr. Rutherford, would you mind walking with me to my car?"

We left Alana by the poolside and made our way back to the driveway where he'd parked his unmarked police sedan. We stopped beside the driver's door, and I fully expected him to put me in handcuffs.

"You and I need to come to an understanding," he said.

I didn't reply.

"I can't have you going around the island acting like a vigilante. The police are here for a reason."

"Of course they are."

"I know what that man did to Alana. I also know how much you care for her, as well as how much the department cares for her."

He paused a long moment.

Then he asked, "What would you do if you were me?"

"I don't know."

"That's not much of an answer."

"But it's all I can say right now. I know how important the law is to you. I also know what's important to me."

"You've put me in a terrible position."

"I'm sorry."

Captain Price looked toward the gate that led to the backyard. He turned back to me.

"That girl's like a daughter to me. Do you know that?" he asked.

"I didn't, at least not until I started working with you. I know that now."

"It would destroy her if I were to take you into custody."

I said nothing.

"This is your one pass, but I'm not doing this for you. If you ever do something like this again, I will lock you up. Do I make myself clear?" he asked.

"As clear as can be."

"Have a good day, Mr. Rutherford. Take care of our lady."

"Always," I said.

He climbed inside his car and backed out of the driveway. I

walked back to the poolside and sat down. Alana didn't ask me what Captain Price had wanted to talk about, which would have been something anyone else would have asked. We finished our breakfast in silence.

Things were different between us for the rest of the day. I don't mean to imply that we were angry with each other or avoiding each other. We weren't, but things were odd. Of course, it could have just been my imagination, but I didn't think so.

We both went to bed early. I woke up around midnight to use the restroom. Alana was awake when I climbed back into bed. I closed my eyes and tried to go back to sleep.

"Did you do it?" she asked.

I opened my eyes and turned to her.

"Do you really want to know?"

"Yes."

"I did do it," I said.

"Did you hurt him as badly as the captain said?"

"No. I hurt him worse."

"Why did you do it?" she asked.

"Isn't it obvious?"

"Why not call the police? Why not tell me first?"

"He put his hands on you. He'll never do that again. He won't be able to."

I turned away from her and looked at the ceiling.

"Are things different between us now?" I asked.

"Why would they be?"

"Because of what I did. I acted in a way I didn't think possible. Maybe you don't want to be with me anymore."

"If the roles had been reversed, I wouldn't have been able to stop swinging that hammer. I would probably have killed him."

I turned back to her.

"Was Foxx with you?" she asked.

"I'd rather not answer that," I said.

"He visited me every day that I was in the hospital. He's also come by the house every day since I've been back. He didn't come by today."

"Foxx is just like me. He'll do anything to protect his friends."

"I have news for you, Poe. No one is like you. It's why I said yes when you proposed."

"So, you haven't changed your mind about marrying me?"

"No. Not a chance."

31

THE WEDDING

THE NEXT FEW MONTHS WERE A GIANT BLUR. EVERYTHING SEEMED TO happen all at once. Mara Winters called me with a couple more jobs, but I turned them down. I didn't have the time, and I had no desire to throw myself into another investigation.

Alana went back to work a few weeks after returning home from the hospital. She said she'd missed it, but we also had a ridiculous amount of fun exploring the island during her recuperation. I was half-tempted to ask her not to go back, but I knew I couldn't keep her away from something she loved so much. She kept me up to date on the arrests of Koa, Moani, and Bryan Sanders. Their trials were due to start soon. The cases against all three of them were substantial, and it looked like they would spend serious time behind bars. The district attorney doubted Koa and Bryan would ever get out.

The biggest news by far was the birth of Hani and Foxx's baby. It was a girl, and they named her Ava. It was a beautiful name, as I'm sure you'll agree. The baby had Hani's looks. If she'd inherited Foxx's height, then she was destined to be a supermodel. Foxx and I will have our work cut out for ourselves trying to keep the boys away from this girl in the years to come. Foxx still didn't change his mind regarding the potential proposal to Hani. He was firmly against it, but he had made good on his promise to be nice to her. He spent a ton of time at Hani's house so he could see his daughter. It was an amazing sight to see such a large guy cradle such a small baby.

I got my BMW out of the shop. Foxx's friend of a friend did an amazing job. It almost looked better than it had before the accident. I spent the entire day driving it around the island with the top down. I'd never taken the fun little car for granted, but I had a newfound appreciation for it after having driven that piece-of-junk rental car for two months. I made a stop at the place where I'd driven the car off the road and into the ocean. I couldn't believe how lucky I'd been to survive. The car's maneuverability had saved me.

Liam Hayes found a marketing job with a hotel in Lahaina. How do I know this? He stopped by Harry's for lunch. I'd been meeting with Foxx when I saw him walk inside. He told me that he'd been staying at the Londons' house and was about to move out to be closer to his new job. The original plan had been for him to stay at their caretaker's hut for a few days, maybe a week at the most. Apparently, though, they'd hit it off, and the Londons extended the invitation for Liam to stay there until he found new employment. They were quite possibly the nicest people I'd ever met, and it made me wonder if I was being an asshole for having such negative feelings about Liam. On deeper contemplation, I came to the determination that I can be an asshole (just ask Ms. Portendorfer) but that I'd pegged Liam correctly. I just didn't like the guy. He was a person of low character, and I hoped he wasn't going to make Harry's a regular lunch stop.

Speaking of the Londons, Ray and Stephanie gave Alana and I a two-foot-tall ceramic giraffe on roller skates for our wedding gift. Ray said he'd made it especially for our wedding. I placed it by the front door of our house so I could see it every time I took Maui for a walk.

Foxx's wedding gift to us was a painting of Lauren's. I was almost brought to tears when I saw it. As I've mentioned before, Foxx made the decision to keep all of Lauren's paintings that were hanging on the walls of her house, as well as some of the unfinished work in her home studio. The artworks, even the unfinished ones, were worth millions. Still, he couldn't bear to part with any of the pieces. That is until he gave us one as a gift. I recognized the painting at once. It had been on Lauren's easel in her studio. I loved it for many reasons, and I'd often found myself going into her studio just so I could look at it. Foxx had made the decision not to touch anything in there either, so the studio looked the same as the day she died.

The uncompleted painting depicted a woman standing on a beach at sunrise. A whale was breaking the surface of the water in the background. The sky hadn't been completed. Lauren had painted the part of the orange and red sky that touched the water, but the top part remained a white canvas. The woman on the beach looked like Alana, and the uncompleted sky reminded me how so much of our lives has yet to be written. As they say, it's the journey and not the destination that counts.

So, how did our wedding turn out? Well, it was spectacular, and all of its success was due to Hani and her meticulous planning. She really had come through for us. By the way, she asked me for her second-half check on the morning of the wedding. Tacky? You bet, but I gladly paid her.

Alana asked her mother to walk her down the aisle. Her father was a no-show. Hani had let it slip to me that their mother had sent their father an email and told him about Alana's wedding. As far as I know, her mother never got a reply, and Alana never got any kind of acknowledgement either. It was a pretty tasteless thing to do, and I hoped I'd never have the unfortunate opportunity to meet the guy. I still didn't know what caused the break-up of her parents' marriage years ago, nor did I know why he left Maui and returned to Japan. Maybe I would never know. There was a part of me that was curious but not enough to ask such an uncomfortable question.

Speaking of in-laws, Ms. Hu and I continued to have a rather odd and unpredictable relationship. There were days before the wedding where she was genuinely kind to me, but then she would go back to her nasty self. She certainly was that way the day of the wedding. She kept looking at me like I owed her money or had kicked her dog or something. It was a strange way to look, especially on her daughter's wedding day, but I did my best not to let it get to me.

Alana and I did choose that resort in Wailea to have the ceremony and the reception. I found it kind of ironic that this tale started and ended at the same place. Did we owe it all to Ms. Portendorfer and her habit of picking up strange men at hotel bars? I like to think so, and I shall always have a place in my heart for the unfaithful lady.

I also found it quite interesting that I'd spotted our minister at that same bar the morning of the wedding. I thought he'd gone there to have one drink before the ceremony. Maybe he got nervous before a big event like everyone else. Either the guy couldn't handle his liquor, or he'd decided to have more than one drink, but I'm pretty sure he was drunk when he pronounced Alana and I husband and wife. He probably charged the drinks to my bar tab, too.

Alana and I danced the night away at a beautiful outdoor reception space by the water. I couldn't stop thinking about how lucky I was that she was still here with me. Life is so unpredictable, which I suppose can be viewed as both a good thing and a bad thing. But that night, I felt like nothing could possibly go wrong.

We retired to a hotel suite sometime in the middle of the night. I'd booked one so we wouldn't have to make the long drive across the island after the reception. We took a long walk on the beach the next morning. When we got back to the room, Alana said she wanted to take a shower.

My cell phone rang just after she shut the bedroom door. I didn't recognize the number.

"Hello," I said.

"Mr. Rutherford, I believe congratulations are in order."

"Thank you. Who is this?" I asked.

"Oh, we haven't met. Not yet, at least. You worked my man Bryan over pretty good, though."

I didn't respond as I tried to see if I recognized this man's voice. I didn't, though.

"You've really impressed me, so I'd like to extend you an offer. Come work for me. I could use someone with your talents."

"No, thanks," I said.

"Are you sure? It would be quite lucrative," he said.

"I already have enough money."

"That's unfortunate. That was the one and only time I'm going to make that offer. Now I'm going to have to kill you."

He ended the call.

DID YOU LIKE THIS BOOK?

YOU CAN MAKE A DIFFERENCE.

Reviews are the most powerful tools an author can have. As an independent author, I don't have the same financial resources as New York publishers.

Honest reviews of my books help bring them to the attention of other readers, though.

If you've enjoyed this book, I would be grateful if you could write a review.

Thank you.

ACKNOWLEDGMENTS

Thanks to you readers for investing your time in reading my story. I hope you enjoyed it. Poe, Alana, Foxx, and Maui will return.

ABOUT THE AUTHOR

Robert W Stephens is the author of the Murder on Maui series, the Alex Penfield novels, and the standalone thrillers The Drayton Diaries and Nature of Evil.

You can find more about the author at robertwstephens.com.

Visit him on Facebook at facebook.com/robertwaynestephens

ALSO BY ROBERT W. STEPHENS

Murder on Maui Mysteries

Aloha Means Goodbye (Poe Book 1)

A gruesome murder. A friend framed. One detective races to stop another bloody masterpiece.

Edgar Allan "Poe" Rutherford just lost his job, his girl, and his chance at a relaxing island vacation. When the brutal murder of a celebrity artist is pinned on his friend, Poe refuses to lose his best buddy to the Maui penitentiary. As he works his way down the gallery guest list, he navigates through bloated egos, heated rivalries, and more than a few eccentric personalities along the way. But he never expected the hunt for truth to reveal a second chance at love.

Wedding Day Dead (Poe Book 2)

A marital murder. A guest list of suspects. Just another night on Maui. Poe has just started his new life on Maui. He's moved in with his best friend and he's dating the woman of his dreams. But when Detective Alana Hu's ex-boyfriend comes to town, Poe discovers more than a few secrets that rain down on his corner of paradise. It's all he can think about until a member of the wedding party is fatally stabbed.

Blood like the Setting Sun (Poe Book 3)

A death threat. A birthright on reserve. Can Poe stop a wealthy hotel mogul from checking out? When an elderly hotel mogul claims to have received threatening letters, Poe chalks it up to old age. But as the threats continue to escalate, he investigates the real possibility that one of her adult children heirs wants her dead... but which one?

Hot Sun Cold Killer (Poe Book 4)

An old murder. A new threat. Can Poe find the killer before it's too late? When a client asks Poe to look into a decade-old death on the beach, he can't help but be intrigued. The police ruled it a suicide, but it's up to him to prove otherwise. As soon as Poe takes the case, people related to the victim start turning up dead--a sure sign that he's on the right track. But can Poe identify the killer... before he becomes the next victim?

Choice to Kill (Poe Book 5)

A murder close to home. A case that seems open and shut. Will Poe's rush to judgment make his fiancé the next victim? Poe didn't think twice when he took his fiancé's case. After all, Detective Alana Hu had known the victim since childhood. Besides, the evidence is easy to decode: all signs point to the victim's estranged husband. As Poe works to get the killer behind bars, he can't help but be distracted by his fast-approaching wedding. But Maui beaches have a knack for luring people into a false sense of security, and Poe's error could extract the highest cost imaginable. After all, you can't have a wedding... without the bride.

Sunset Dead (Poe Book 6)

A murdered mistress. A wrongful arrest. Can Poe and Alana take down a killer from both sides of the law? Poe can't stand to take another case after his last one nearly killed his wife. When he's accused of murdering his supposed mistress, he's forced back into a familiar role to prove his innocence. But can he do it from behind bars?

Ocean of Guilt (Poe Book 7)

A murdered bride. A suspicious groom. Can Poe catch the killer before the anchor drops? Poe is ready to dive back into his work as Maui's top private investigator. But before he can unpack his suitcase, his sister-in-law begs him to photograph her client's extravagant nautical wedding. Poe is confident he can handle the wedding party from hell, until he finds the bride's dead body on the top deck.

The Tequila Killings (Poe Book 8)

A deadly fall. A dodgy past. Can Poe uncover the truth before a match made in paradise ends in disaster? Poe has the luxury of picking and choosing the cases that spark his curiosity. So when his love-struck mother-in-law demands he trail her latest squeeze, he thinks he's wasting his time. Until a mysterious woman from the boyfriend's past falls off his balcony to her death.

Wave of Deception (Poe Book 9)

A beach execution. A devastating hurricane. Can Maui's best PI solve the case without his family members becoming the prime suspects? Poe is used to weathering difficult cases. And since the victim is his sister-in-law's abusive ex-boyfriend, Poe hopes nobody looks too hard at his own compelling motive. Ignoring the sound advice to keep his nose out, Poe spars with the island's newest police detective who seems to have her own hidden motivations, especially when she asks Poe to help her with another case. Poe has never taken on two murder investigations at once. But as he gets closer to the truth, will he like the answers he finds?

The Last Kill (Poe Book 10)

Lights. Camera. Murder. When lies become reality, can Poe find the truth before a killer strikes again? As Maui's best private investigator, Edgar Allan "Poe" Rutherford understands the importance of keeping a low profile. That becomes impossible when a new reality TV show comes to the island, which features an eccentric handful of divorcees looking for love. But when one of the women is poisoned to death, the show's production comes to a grinding halt. At the same time, a few miles down the beach, a divorce attorney is stabbed multiple times while she sits on a lounge chair and watches the sun set over the Pacific Ocean. The methods of murder, as well as the victims, couldn't be more different, yet Poe has a sneaking suspicion they're somehow related.

Mountain of Lies (Poe Book 11)

A cold body. A warm paradise. A murder with more than one culprit. Private investigator Edgar Allan "Poe" Rutherford is worried. His latest client may have committed homicide, and sharing his suspicions with his detective wife is an argument he'd rather not have. But when she arrests his new employer, catching the true perpetrator means keeping it in the family. Never one to let loose ends go untied, Poe's off-the-record investigation uncovers another suspect connected to foul play from years before. And now he's not sure if he's solving one lethal crime or two.

Rich and Dead (Poe Book 12)

Texas Hold 'em in paradise. A table full of suspects. The minimum bet could cost him his life. PI Edgar Allan "Poe" Rutherford is tired of taking down murderers. So, when a detective comes to him with a suspicious case of a millionaire who drove off a Maui cliff, he declines her request for help. But when the victim's scorned lover demands money in exchange for information, Poe is pulled back into the game. Demanding answers from the selfish vulture, the relentless private eye uncovers a connection to a high-seas, high-stakes illicit poker ring. And after he discovers the vicious men involved, he's convinced the death was no accident. But to find the murderer, the charming PI needs to get on the yacht and take a seat at the table. Can the sharp-witted investigator flush out a sinister cabal before he's dealt a dead man's hand?

Alex Penfield Novels

Ruckman Road (Penfield Book 1)

To solve an eerie murder, one detective must break a cardinal rule: never let the case get personal. Alex Penfield's gunshot wounds have healed, but the shock remains raw. Working the beat could be just what the detective needs to clear his head. But when a corpse washes up on the Chesapeake Bay, Penfield's first case back could send him spiraling. As Penfield and his partner examine the dead man's fortress of a house, an army of surveillance cameras takes the mystery to another level. When the detective sees gruesome visions that the cameras fail to capture, he begins to wonder if his past has caught up with him. To solve the murder, Penfield makes a call on a psychic who may or may not be out to kill him. His desperate attempt to catch a killer may solve the case, but will he lose his sanity in the process?

Dead Rise (Penfield Book 2)

Detective Alex Penfield has to solve a murder case before it happens. His own. Retirement never suited Penfield, but there's nothing like a death omen to get you back in the saddle. A psychic colleague warns the detective that his own murder is coming. When a local death bears an eerie resemblance to the psychic's vision, he can't help but get involved. As the body count rises, the case only gets more unfathomable. Witnesses report ghastly encounters with a man sporting half a face. And the only living survivor from a deadly boat ride claims he knows who's to blame. There's only one problem: the suspect's been dead for 20 years.

The Eternal (Penfield Book 3)

Detective Alex Penfield has put away plenty of serial killers. He never expected to protect one.

Detective Alex Penfield is no stranger to crime scenes. But when he tracks down a killer, he discovers she's in a whole different league. And this assassin is far from alone. It turns out that Penfield's detective skills have uncovered a secret government program that's better left buried. And the men and women of that program have put a target on his back. To survive the day, Penfield's only chance is to trust a ruthless killer. He hopes his risky choice won't be the last one he ever makes.

Standalone Dark Thrillers

Nature of Evil

Rome, 1948. Italy reels in the aftermath of World War II. Twenty women are brutally murdered, their throats slit and their faces removed with surgical precision. Then the murders stop as abruptly as they started, and the horrifying crimes and their victims are lost to history. Now over sixty years later, the killings have begun again. This time in America. It's up to homicide detectives Marcus Carter and Angela Darden to stop the crimes, but how can they catch a serial killer who leaves no traces of evidence and no apparent motive other than the unquenchable thirst for murder?

The Drayton Diaries

He can heal people with the touch of his hand, so why does a mysterious group want Jon Drayton dead? A voice from the past sends Drayton on a desperate journey to the ruins of King's Shadow, a 17th century plantation house in Virginia that was once the home of Henry King, the wealthiest and most powerful man in North America and who has now been lost to time. There, Drayton meets the beautiful archaeologist Laura Girard, who has discovered a 400-year-old manuscript in the ruins. For Drayton, this partial journal written by a slave may somehow hold the answers to his life's mysteries.